Book o' the Dead

CREDITS

Written and Designed by: Lester Smith

Developed by: Shane Lacy Hensley, John Hopler, Hal Mangold, Nate Perkins, & Matt Forbeck

Editing & Layout: Matt Forbeck

Cover Art: Brom   **Logo:** Ron Spencer

Interior Art: Paul Daly, John Knowles, Andy Park & Loston Wallace

Maps: Jeff Lahren

Cover Design: Hal Mangold

Special Thanks To: John "the only good hero is a dead hero" Goff

Playtesting and Advice: Roger Arnett, John & Joyce Goff, Michelle & Caden Hensley, Christy Hopler, Jay & Amy Kyle, Ann Kolinsky, and Ashe Marler

Pinnacle Entertainment Group, Inc.
P.O. Box 10908
Blacksburg, VA 24062-0908
www.peginc.com or deadlands@aol.com
(800) 214-5645 (orders only)

Dedicated To:
Ashe, who let me skin his Ranger
— Lester Smith

 PINNACLE ENTERTAINMENT GROUP, Inc.

Table O' Contents

Posse Territory

-LOSTON-
'97

Chapter One: Army of the Damned

I imagine you're all wondering why I called you here tonight.

Heh, heh. I've always wanted to say that.

No need to sit there starin' at me all solemn like. A little funnin' never hurt nobody, an' y'all are way past hurtin' anyhow.

Shoot. The dead ain't got no sense o' humor.

All right, then. If that's the way you want it, let's get right down to business.

Y'all know me. The name's Coot Jenkins, though most o' you stiffs just call me the Prospector. See, I'm always diggin' for treasure, though not the sort most people think of. My treasures are corpses. Least, the ones that have Harrowed souls in 'em, like all you damned souls sittin' here tonight.

Most of you been dug up by me before. I keep an eye on the papers, an' when I read one of you got shot up, cut down, or beat to a pulp enough to seem done for, I go hopin' whoever planted you didn't know your dirty little secret.

The rest of you I dug up right after your first time. Right after you "shuffled off this mortal coil," as the preachers say, only to find yourself wakin' up again in the grave, thinkin' there musta been some mistake. Well, there was a mistake all right, but it wasn't the undertaker's. It was a manitou's.

You all know how it works by now. You died, but a manitou—that's what the Injuns call these evil spirits—decided your mind and body were tough enough and cussed enough to make a mighty fine host for its own self. The manitou took up residence with your damned soul in the hopes of usin' your body to wreak a little havoc on God's green Earth. But that ain't how things worked out in the end.

The fact you're sitting here with me tonight says something special about you. You ain't out hauntin' folks and causing the devil's own mischief, as the manitou would have it. Nor are you rottin' in some shameful grave like others of your kind who I put down for good. They let the manitou have control, and I had to waste 'em for it.

Even a manitou can't survive in a body with its head blown apart by a scattergun. Just keep that in mind.

What's important is that you ain't like those others. Nope, you're all somethin' special. You wasn't content to let some filthy spirit run around in your body causing trouble. You wrestled with the fiend for control, and somehow, you won!

Some of you done it all on your own. Others got a little extra help from my special elixir. But whichever way, it was you and you alone that bested the manitou, and now you're callin' the shots. That makes you a tough bunch o' hombres.

I know you still have to wrestle the fiend every day, keepin' it caged up inside where it can't do no harm. I know it ain't easy, and I know your battles tear your souls apart.

don't stay in its grave. There are things to be fought out there—dark things a mortal soul shouldn't have to face, shouldn't even have to know about. My pappy used to say fight fire with fire, and there's no one better to fight these things than you.

You've got the motive.

You're the restless dead! You can't enjoy life no more, but you can't give up the ghost, neither. You got to keep up the fight with the demon every day, 'less you want to become just another monster the rest of us gotta put down.

You've got the ability.

In life, you were something special, else the manitou would've never given you a second glance. Even dyin' couldn't keep you down. That ornery streak is a powerful weapon. But on top of that skill and cussedness, you've now got control of the manitou's powers, something you're gettin' better at every day.

Now, you've got the mission.

You are the Army of the Damned if there ever was one. And I'm appointing myself your General. Most all of you here tonight owe me—bigger than you might even know—and now I'm callin' in those markers.

For the moment, your orders are just to patrol the Earth, watching for evil and battling it. Now and again, I'll get in touch and ask you for special help, but mostly you just need to seek out the things that hadn't oughta be traipsin' across my frontier. When you find 'em, send 'em packin' back to Hell.

Someday, when the time is right, I'll be calling you all together. Then we'll have our own little "Reckoning." It won't be easy, and it sure as Hell won't be pretty, so you'd best spend the meantime developin' your powers and learning everything you can.

And remember, I'll be watching you. Let that surly critter inside you take control and I'll be puttin' you *in* the earth 'steada draggin' you out of it.

That's all I got to say to you for now, but it sure ain't the last you're gonna here from this grizzled soul.

I want you to leave this conversation with one thing in your mind. I'm askin' you for your help because I need it, and you darn well owe it to me.

But if you decide otherwise, I'm gonna know. I got me one little policy in my scrap with the Reckoners: If you ain't with me, then you're against me.

Take me at my word. Dead or not, you don't want to be against me.

I also know some of you got sins to atone for, evil things the manitou did with your body in the time before you got up the gumption to take control. Some of you got years of such evil to make up for.

So, are you ready to pay the manitou back for what it's done to you? Do you want to make it sorry it ever decided to take up residence in your carcass?

Then it's time to be a hero. 'Cuz every time you help someone out, or defeat some evil, you make the devil inside you suffer—and maybe the Reckoners as well.

The fact of the matter is, that demon burrowing about inside your soul's just as trapped as you are. You're stuck with each other permanent-like, and as much as you hate the evils it's done with your body, it hates any good you do with its power twice as much.

Some of you've got some tricks up your tattered sleeves. Powers you've learned by tapping into your manitou. Some of you've even "counted coup" on strange critters and walked off with something of their power to show for it.

That's why I've sought you all out. See, there's something wrong with a world where a body

WELCOME TO HELL!

In the dangerous world of *Deadlands,* death isn't necessarily the end. There are evil creatures plaguing this Earth from beyond the veil—ghosts, haunts, zombies, and all sorts of other critters too horrible to name in polite company.

But there are also a few heroes too ornery to stay down once they've been killed. In *Deadlands,* they're called the Harrowed. Energized by evil spirits that plan to use these corpses as their own, the Harrowed battle daily for Dominion over their own bodies and mastery of their souls.

The *Book o' the Dead* is dedicated to those Harrowed heroes. It expands upon the information presented in the *Deadlands* rulebook, fleshing out the concepts presented there, answering questions it raised, and helping you develop your Harrowed characters even further.

If you're currently playing a Harrowed—or hoping to begin playing one sometime soon—the information here is invaluable. Don't let your hero leave the grave without it.

LAYOUT OF THE BOOK

Like the *Deadlands* rulebook, the *Book o' the Dead* is divided into three bits: Posse Territory, No Man's Land, and the Marshal's Handbook.

Posse Territory contains information anyone playing a Harrowed character might know, though other players wouldn't. It's assumed if you're reading this book you already know something about the Harrowed and your Marshal has cleared you to learn more.

If you're not planning to play a Harrowed yet, it's best not to read any farther than this paragraph. Save the rest for when you have a character who just won't lay down and die.

So stop already. Geez.

No Man's Land has material that might become available to experienced Harrowed. There are secrets revealed there that come only to those with some "time on the job." If you're playing a Harrowed, hold off reading this material until your Marshal directs you there.

The Marshal's Handbook provides information only that esteemed individual should see. Among other things, it explains more about the nightmare scenario that begins a Harrowed's descent into madness. It also details many of the problems that plague a Harrowed's existence after he's popped up out of the bone orchard. There's even a detailed adventure for the Marshal to run when the time is right.

MAKING A HARROWED HERO

There are two main ways to create a Harrowed hero.

The first is to start a normal character with the rules in the *Deadlands* rulebook, get him killed during play, and hope he's "lucky" enough to come back from the dead.

Your Marshal has the details for how that might take place, but it's an awful rare happenstance, so don't count on it taking place too often. Otherwise, the world would be chock full of Harrowed (which it's not, despite what Lacy O'Malley of the *Tombstone Epitaph* might have you believe).

The second way to cheat death (at least for a while) is to plan on running a Harrowed character from the get-go and build that character from scratch using the rules in the next few chapters of this book. You'll miss out on the fun of playing the character back when he was alive, but the end result won't be quite so iffy.

Keep in mind, though, that while Harrowed characters are tougher than normal folks, they also have bigger problems. For one thing, of course, they're in a constant struggle for control of their own bodies—and quite often, they lose.

They also tend to draw trouble like flies to carrion. The more powerful they become, the worse the problems they attract. And the longer they survive, the tougher it is for them to amble around with normal humans.

This all means that Harrowed characters can wreak total havoc with a campaign if you're not careful. Not every Marshal wants to have a dead man walking about with the other player characters, causing dogs to slink away, spooking townsfolk, and ruining dinner with their God-awful stench.

Be sure, then, to get a nod from the Marshal before you wake the dead by creating a Harrowed.

A GOOD DAY TO DIE...

With all that said, it's time to turn to the business of living (so to speak) as an undead hero. It's time to turn away from the light and ignore the voices of loved ones calling you to paradise. It's time to return to your cold flesh, scrape the grave dirt from your eyes, and start learning the forbidden secrets in this book o' the dead.

And never forget: *You* are the bogeyman.

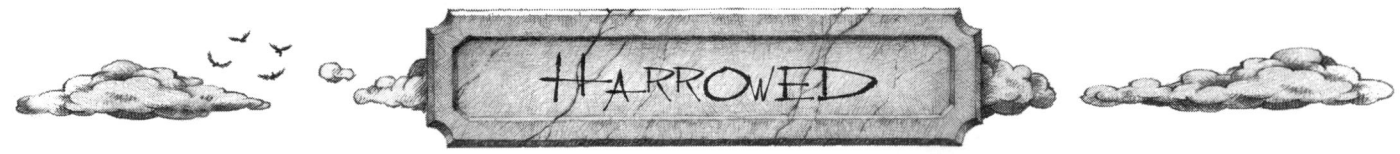

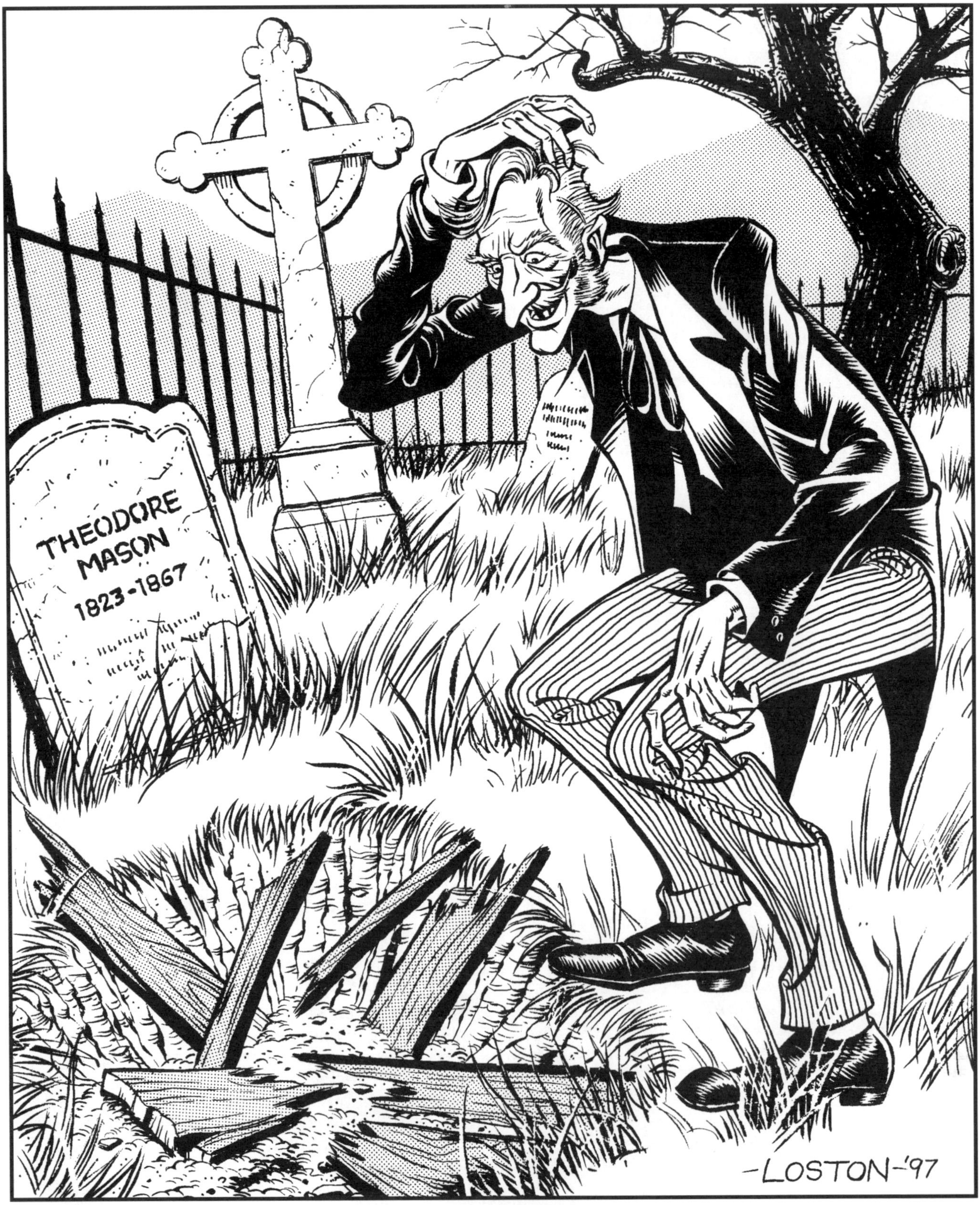
THEODORE
MASON
1823-1867
-LOSTON-'97

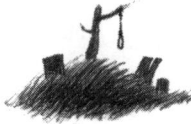

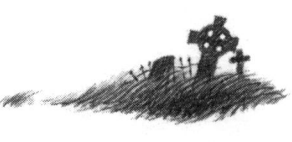

CHAPTER TWO: WHAT HARROWED ARE MADE OF

This chapter contains all the nifty rules for building a Harrowed character from scratch. Of course, that means it also contains all sorts of powers and information for heroes who are already undead. So even if you're already running a Harrowed character in your *Deadlands* campaign, you should browse through this chapter, paying special attention to the new powers your hero may be able to pick up, and the new problems that will plague him as a result.

There are four (well, five) steps on the road to Perdition once you've got your living hero in place.

We'll lead you through them one at a time.

STEP ZERO: GETTIN' THE OKAY

Not every Marshal wants to start right off with the walking dead in her campaign. Some Marshals might like to begin with a fairly normal set of Wild West adventures, then slowly start slipping in bits of horror to begin spinning the plot toward the supernatural. That's the way we intended the game.

HARROWED TEMPLATES

Here's a special note for those of you who might be in a hurry or just like doing things the easy way. Some folks just don't care to go to all the trouble of coming up with a whole new character—dead or alive. That's just fine.

If you like, you can use any of the character archetypes in the *Deadlands* rulebook or *The Quick & the Dead* for step one of making an undead hero. Then all you have to do is go through the rest of the procedure on the following pages.

Of course, if you're really in a hurry, there are three Harrowed archetypes on pages 15-17, all ready to go. You don't even have to bother with killing them, because they're already dead and raring to go. You can hop right in their sagging skins and start playing right away.

Needless to say, this can be difficult if one of the heroes is a zombie. If your group is already at this point, it shouldn't be a problem, but you should definitely talk it over with your Marshal first.

You should also make sure *you're* ready to play a walking corpse. Harrowed characters are powerful varmints, but they're also a heap of trouble, as well. Even in a world of legends, a fellow who can turn to mist and walk through walls tends to draw attention. If the locals see you, they're going to panic and form a lynch mob.

Besides which, when you play a Harrowed, you're not always going to be in control of your character. Sometimes that manitou that's keeping your hero mobile is going to step up and take a turn. If you're the kind that doesn't likely having others play with his toys, you might dislike this too much for it to be any fun.

So the moral is, be sure both you and your campaign are ready for you to play a Harrowed character. Otherwise, you'll kill more than just your hero. You'll kill your chance to walk slowly into the Weird West and learn its dark secrets the way they were meant to be learned—one terror-filled step at a time.

STEP ONE: MAKE A HERO!

Making a Harrowed hero from scratch starts just like creating any other hombre. The first thing you do is make a regular hero just like you normally would.

Don't think about your character's impending demise yet, especially when it comes to picking Hindrances—you'll be able to take extra Hindrances that reflect his more recent past in Step Four.

So go to it. Pick up your trusty *Deadlands* rule book, make your character as usual, then come back here for the rest of the show.

STEP TWO: NOW KILL THE BASTARD

Once you've made your hero, you're going to have to put him down. Sorry, but the sad truth is a cowpoke actually has to *die* to come back from the dead.

It's up to you to figure out how he died. Your hero probably shouldn't have died from something too mundane—your hombre will be a little red-faced if he croaked while cleaning his pistol.

Try to come up with an open-ended death, some bit of unfinished business that drives your weary gunslinger on in the face of incredible horror. The first order of business for many Harrowed is to avenge themselves on their killers—assuming that they were murdered, of course.

There are lots of ways to die. Try to come up with one for your hero that you haven't seen before. After all, if he's tough enough to be Harrowed, he deserves to leave the stage in a dramatic fashion. You owe him at least that much.

PICKLED OR DRY AS A BONE

We're talking about time here, compadre. How long has your grim avenger been back from the grave? A few days? A few years?

It's up to you, but remember, no Harrowed can be more than 13 years old, since the Reckoning came about in 1863. There are other types of undead that have been around forever, but not the Harrowed. They might even appear to be Harrowed, but they're another animal of an entirely different stripe.

Step Three: Whose Mind Is It Anyway?

Okay, so you killed the poor slob. You already know he's coming back. But just how susceptible is he to the manitou inside him?

Let your friends wonder, but you need to know. Remember that a Harrowed has as many Dominion points as his *Spirit*. These measure just how much influence the manitou has over you (see Chapter Four to see how we've changed the Dominion rules).

To find out your hero's current state, you have to engage the manitou in a *Spirit* contest. The Marshal already knows the manitou's *Spirit*.

Unless you go bust, the hero and the manitou start with half the total number of Dominion points. Every success and raise on the contest steals 1 point away from the loser.

If you go bust, the manitou has total Dominion. Bad luck, amigo!

Step Four: The Cool Stuff

All of the Harrowed have a couple of things in common, as the *Deadlands* book explains. That information is repeated in the next chapter along with some new tidbits just to keep everything in one place.

But you want to know how many other keen powers you get, don't you? Thought so.

Choosing Powers

Your Harrowed gets 10 points with which to buy powers. There's a complete list of these awesome new abilities in Chapter Three.

These powers should fit your character's background, but other than that, there's no restriction.

Each power level costs double its value. A level 1 power costs 2 points, a level 5 power costs 10, and so on.

If your character is a *veteran of the Weird West* (see *Quick & the Dead*), he can have another 5 points worth of powers. You can take that Edge *now* if you wish, but it means your hero has been Harrowed for at least a few years.

Now the bad news. Five of those 10 power points are freebies, but the last 5 must be compensated for with new Hindrances.

These Hindrances should come from bad things that happened to your character after returning from the grave. *Enemy, outlaw, ugly as sin,* and the like are good Hindrances of this kind, particularly if your hombre was up to no good in the past.

If these aren't enough, we've got a list of brand new Harrowed Hindrances that only undead types can take. We're done here, so we'll tell you all about them right away.

Harrowed Hindrances

Besides all the Hindrances we've given you before, the undead have a special pool of bad tidings they can draw from their sordid pasts. Needless to say, only walking worm-food can take these Hindrances. Breathing folks couldn't handle them anyway.

Angst   1–5

It's time to get a little heavy. Think about coming back from the dead from your character's point of view.

It can be a depressing experience. Sure, you've cheated death, But now you have a whole new set of troubles.

First, there are your friends and family. Maybe they know your coffin is empty, and they're looking for grave robbers. That's sure to cause them grief, which can make you feel guilty.

On the other hand, do you dare contact those loved ones? Having attended your funeral, they're liable to react poorly if you show up on their doorstep holding in your slimy innards. Perhaps they'll think you're a cruel impostor. Or maybe you'll just scare the Hell out of them.

Then there's the problem of how to deal with this whole undead thing. Once, you thought you'd live till you died, and then things would be over. You'd spend the rest of eternity playing harp on a cloud somewhere.

But now you're back on Earth with no idea of what the new "rules" are. How long do you have this time? Will you stay this way forever? What about your soul? Learning that your body is energized by an evil spirit can't make you feel too confident about reaching Heaven any more.

For that matter, the whole issue of the manitou inside you is a thorny one. You have to stay in control, or who knows what evil it might do with your sorry carcass. It's sort of like being joined by leg irons to an ax murderer. As a Harrowed, you're trapped with no hope for parole and no end in sight. Ever.

It isn't any wonder, then, that many Harrowed live under a permanent shadow of anxiety and depression. For many of them, angst is a constant companion. It greets them every morning with a sardonic smile and taunts them in their restless sleep every night, day in and day out. (The dead *do* sleep, by the way, as you'll see later on.)

A character with the *angst* Hindrance has a difficult time rising out of apathy, depression, and guilt to get started on any major course of action. This means that whenever a new game session begins, he suffers a penalty to all his dice rolls equal to the level of the Hindrance. For instance, if he's got 3 points of *angst*, he takes –3 to every roll.

Once the action is well underway, however, the character finds it easier to stay motivated. One way to escape depression and uncertainty is to just get up and do something.

In game terms, each time the character spends a Fate Chip, besides getting its normal effect, he also loses some of the *angst* penalty for the remainder of the current session. A white chip negates 1 point of angst, a red chip negates 2, and a blue chip negates 3. These chips must be spent during play—they can't just be tossed away at the beginning of the night.

Of course, once the action is over (between your regular gaming sessions), the Harrowed has time to mull things over and sink into that same old "slough of despair" again. At least until he buys off his angst in the next session.

AURA O' DEATH   1–5

Some Harrowed characters wear their undeath like a shroud. People around them instinctively know there's something disturbing about these folks, though they can't quite put their finger on exactly what it is. Still, just as animals tend to slink away from the Harrowed, people avoid those with an *undead aura*. This doesn't keep them from whispering about the "creepy strangers" behind their backs, however.

This uneasiness means that whenever such a Harrowed makes a roll for Mien or any Aptitude falling under that Trait, she suffers a penalty equal to her level of *undead aura*. The one exception is the *overawe* Aptitude, which actually receives a bonus equal to that level, instead of a penalty.

Besides these modifiers, the Marshal should roleplay the Harrowed's general effect on people. It's much harder for him to form relationships, get information, and ask for help.

DEGENERATION   1–5

When a manitou enters a corpse and creates a Harrowed, its supernatural energy does more than simply bring that body back to life. Its animating power also makes the body resistant to damage, and it quickly regenerates the flesh when wounds are suffered. Still, undead flesh can't help but stink a little.

For whatever reason, some manitous either don't care to keep the flesh pickled or just can't manage it. The Harrowed still heals with supernatural quickness, but his body resumes the process of decay, though perhaps very slowly.

The *degeneration* Hindrance represents that situation. The level of the Hindrance determines what state of decay the Harrowed has reached, as shown in the table below.

Players who choose this Hindrance for their Harrowed should keep in mind that living creatures (human or animal) react very poorly to the sight of a decaying corpse up and moving about. They're especially particular about obvious cadavers. To disguise his condition, the rotten apple needs some heavy clothing and a load of perfume or whiskey to mask his mortuary stench.

DEGENERATION

Level	State of Decay
0	**Normal Harrowed:** Animals avoid the character, and he bears a slight odor of decay, noticeable on a Fair (5) Cognition roll by anyone right next to him. Any *horse ridin'*, *animal wranglin'*, and *teamster* rolls he makes are at –2.
1	**Pallid:** At this stage, the Harrowed has an unhealthy grayness to his complexion. His eyes are dull, and the odor of decay is stronger, noticeable on a Foolproof (3) *Cognition* roll by anyone next to him, or on a Hard (9) roll by anyone in the same room.
2	**Slimy:** The flesh of the Harrowed has a slick film, and his eyes are milky. His odor is noticeable on an Onerous (7) *Cognition* roll by anyone nearby. Those who get a long look at him should make a *guts* check against a Terror score of 5. His various animal-handling aptitudes suffer a penalty of –4.

3 **Bloated:** Decay has distended the Harrowed's abdomen with gas and pestilent fluids. The character has watery eyes, and his various orifices leak a bit. The smell of decay is automatically noticeable, and animal-handling skills are at –6. It can be as embarrassing as you probably think. The undead's Terror score is 7.

4 **Tattered:** The Harrowed is losing flesh right off the bone. His skin is tattered, showing the stringy remains of his muscles beneath. In some places, bare bone peeks through. His eyes are sunken. Even if they don't notice these obvious physical clues, anyone nearby smells the odor of decay on an Onerous (7) *Cognition* roll. Animals won't have anything to with him, and his Terror score is 9.

5 **Desiccated:** All that remains of the Harrowed's body is parchment skin over stringy ligaments and bleached bones. The character's eyes look like little dry raisins. They're so stiff, in fact, that the Harrowed must subtract –4 from any *Cognition* rolls made to notice things by sight. There is little odor, if any, but the Harrowed creaks slightly when he moves. His animal handling aptitudes go back down to a –4, but the near-mummy takes double damage from fire. His Terror score is 9.

HAUNTED   1–5

The manitous have a good time when they subject mortals to the terrors of the Hunting Grounds. Sometimes, the manitou inside a Harrowed can use these memories to keep the host off-guard.

The souls of *haunted* undead are dragged kicking and screaming into the Hunting Grounds every time they go dormant (see Sleep on page 22). There they are subjected to horrible nightmares by the cruel parasites inside them.

This Hindrance does not function like *night terrors*—the Harrowed do not suffer fatigue and incur no penalties from restless nights. Instead, the effect is to erode the hero's will and give the manitou a greater chance the next time it tries to gain control of its host.

Every level of this Hindrance subtracts a like amount from the hero's *Spirit* roll when checking for Dominion.

Mark o' the Devil   1–5

Certain folks can see right through the taut skin of the undead to the rotten, worm-riddled core. That's when they can get a glimpse of the manitou sitting there and stare straight into the eyes of Hell.

On the other hand, some Harrowed seem to wear their damnation like a shiny tin star—at least to people who know what they're looking for.

This Hindrance means anyone with the *arcane background* Edge—or at least 3 levels in *academia: occult*—has a chance to see the evil demon wriggling around inside your hero, no matter how good he looks or what kind of disguise he might be using. There's just no way of properly hiding from prying eyes with the right sort of education.

Mad scientists are an exception. They *have* to have *academia: occult* at level 3 or more to see the *mark o' the Devil*, despite their *arcane background*. Scientific types just don't tend to see these things unless they've researched them on their own.

Whenever a person with one of the above qualifications gets within a few feet of your hero, she can make a *scrutinize* roll versus the manitou's *Spirit*. The viewer can add the level of your Hindrance to her roll.

If successful, the viewer sees some sign of the manitou in your hero—perhaps the Harrowed's eyes glow red or the watcher can see the manitou's hideous face peeking out at her. Needless to say, such folks won't trust your character until he's burning on a stake.

Rage   1–5

Wine gets better with age. The Harrowed just get meaner.

The perpetual struggle with the manitou within, the temptation of greater power, and the frustration of being undead all push these characters toward bestiality.

Get your hands off your horse. That's not what we're talking about.

Whenever a Harrowed with this Hindrance is wounded by an opponent or gets particularly upset, she must make a *Smarts* check. The base difficulty of the check is Fair (5), and the undead must subtract her level in *rage* from her *Smarts* roll.

If failed, the hero goes into a blood frenzy and attacks. She refuses to go into cover or seek to protect herself—she just runs straight at the foe and rampages all over his unfortunate kiester. She can fire a gun along the way, but if the enemy's still alive when she gets to him, she drops her pistols and gets up close and personal with her bare hands (or *claws* if she's got them).

Once the foe's dead (and we mean *really*, messily dead), the Harrowed can make another *Smarts* roll. If she makes it, her blood lust is sated and she can act like a normal walking corpse again—whatever that means. If she fails, she starts raging on her former enemy's companions.

She won't attack her own comrades, but she probably won't be reading them any bedtime stories either.

Unnatural Appetite   1–5

Here's a delightful habit. For some inexplicable reason, a rare few Harrowed develop a craving for one thing or another that, while technically edible, thoroughly disgusts most people.

Your character must eat the item of his craving at least once a day. For each day that he goes without that item, he loses 2 Wind. This damage cannot be recovered except by gorging on the item he craves. For each day he spends eating that item again, he avoids suffering any more damage and regains 1d6 points of lost Wind.

The level of the Hindrance depends on just how disgusting your appetite is. Once you eat someone's tongue, your companions are likely to think that snacking on scorpions is a step up.

Some examples of disgusting vittles are listed below.

Unnatural Appetite

Level	Vittles
1	Rotten food, mold
2	Grave dirt, raw meat
3	Bugs, living raw meat, animal blood
4	Human blood
5	Raw human organs, such as the heart, liver, lung, brain, or eyeball

Buying off Harrowed Hindrances

Well, at least it's a short section. You can't. As the Prospector says, "You pays your money, you takes your chances. What manitou has joined, let no one put asunder."

Fresh-Dead Soldier

Traits and Aptitudes

Deftness 4d10
  Shootin': Pistol 3
Nimbleness 2d12
  Climbin' 1
  Dodge 2
  Fightin': Brawlin' 3
  Horse Ridin' 3
  Sneak 2
Strength 3d6
Quickness 2d10
Vigor 1d8
Cognition 2d6
  Scrutinize 2
  Search 1
Knowledge 2d6
  Area knowledge 2
  Native tongue 2
Mien 3d8
  Leadership 2
Smarts 4d6
  Scroungin' 2
Spirit 1d6
Wind: 14
Grit: 1
Dead: 2 months
Dominion: Harrowed 5; manitou 1
Harrowed Powers:
  Animate 2
  Ghost 1
Edges:
  Big Ears 1
  Light Sleeper 1
Hindrances:
  Angst –2
  Loyal –3
  Rage –1
Gear: Army .44 pistol, 50 rounds of ammunition, horse, $85.

Personality

So you want to know my story, do you? All right, listen. I ain't told this to no one else, but you and me is friends, right?

Truth is, near as I can figure, you're talking to a dead man. It happened like this:

I came west with the Army, same as many others done, to help fight outlaws and Indians. Thought I'd be a hero and protect white settlers out here.

Just this last winter, my unit set out after a band of Apache raiders, followed 'em into a pass way up in the mountains. Next thing I knew, there were Apache with carbines both in front and in back of us, and boulders fallin' on us from above.

Nobody got away. I thought we all died.

Then, a few days later, I woke up in the abandoned Apache camp. Don't know how I got there or where the Indians went, but you can be sure I high-tailed it out before they came back.

I didn't go reporting back to the Army. I figure I already done my duty. Sure, my enlistment's supposed to last another four years, but you can't expect a dead man to show up for reveille, now can you?

Quote: "Look. I really don't want a fight today, so how's about you just put down that shootin' iron and we have a drink together nice and peaceable like.

"Otherwise, one of us is gonna die, and believe me, you wouldn't enjoy it."

—LOSTON—

Harrowed Head Hunter

Traits and Aptitudes

Deftness 4d10
  Shootin': Pistol 3
  Shootin': Rifle 1
  Shootin': Shotgun 2
Nimbleness 2d6
  Climbin' 1
  Dodge 2
  Fightin': Brawling 2
  Horse Ridin' 2
  Sneak 1
Strength 4d6
Quickness 3d8
Vigor 1d8
Cognition 2d12
  Search 2
  Trackin' 4
Knowledge 1d6
  Area knowledge 2
  Native tongue 2
Mien 2d10
  Overawe 2
Smarts 2d6
  Bluff 1
  Streetwise 1
Spirit 3d6
  Guts 3
Wind: 14
Grit: 1
Dead: 13 years
Dominion: Harrowed 4, manitou 2
Harrowed Powers:
  Jinx 2
  Ghost 1
  Death mask 1
  Possession 1
  Reconstruction 2
  Spook 3
  Stitchin' 3
Coup Powers:
  Chill o' the grave 3
  Hell wind 1
Edges:
  Thick-skinned 3
  Sand 1
Hindrances:
  Greedy -2
  Grim servant o' death -5

Degeneration -4
Aura o' death -3
Gear: Peacemaker, 30 rounds of ammo, Buffalo gun, 50 rounds of ammo, double-barreled shotgun, 20 shells, Bowie knife, horse, handcuffs, rope, 2 pounds coffee, $7 cash.

Personality

Don't move. This shotgun's got a hair trigger. For that matter, so do I. And your poster does say "Dead or Alive."

Nice camp fire. Mind if I help myself to some of your coffee? Course not.

I have to say, you led me a merry chase. Caused me a lot of trouble. That one ambush you tried was pretty clever. Too bad the avalanche had to spoil things for you. I thought maybe you got crushed in it. I know I nearly did.

Okay, put your hands behind your back and slip on these here handcuffs. Then I'm going to tie you across your horse and lead you back to town. You're not going to give me any trouble. Know how I know that? Wait a second. Okay, here, look at my face again real good now.

Hah! Scart ya, did it? I think you done wet yourself. Oh, stop gibberin'. See, the stories you heard about a zombie manhunter were true. Too bad nobody's ever gonna believe you.

Quote: "Why hunt outlaws? It ain't the money. Let's just say I'm salvin' my guilty conscience."

Undead Muckraker

Traits and Aptitudes

Deftness 2d6
- Lockpickin' 1
- Shootin': Shotgun 1

Nimbleness 3d6
- Climbin' 1
- Dodge 2
- Fightin': Wrasslin' 1
- Fightin': Knife 1
- Sneak 2
- Teamster 1

Strength 2d6

Quickness 1d8

Vigor 1d6

Cognition 4d10
- Arts 1
- Scrutinize 3
- Search 1

Knowledge 3d8
- Academia: occult 1
- Area knowledge:
  - Northwest 2
  - Home county 2
- Language: Sign
  - language (Indian) 1
  - Native tongue 2
- Professional:
  - Journalism 3

Mien 2d10
- Persuasion 2
- Tale Tellin' 1

Smarts 2d12
- Bluff 2
- Scroungin' 1
- Streetwise 3

Spirit 4d6
- Guts 1

Wind: 12

Grit: 1

Dead: 8 years

Dominion: Harrowed 8, manitou 4

Harrowed Powers:
- Cat eyes 1
- Claws 1
- Soul flight 3
- Spider 1

Edges:
- Keen 3
- Purty 1
- "The voice" 1

Hindrances:
- Hankerin' -3: Alcohol (likes to smell fresh)
- Scrawny -5
- Undead aura -1
- Unnatural appetite -1: Spiders
- Unnatural feature -1: Unnaturally long limbs.

Gear: Pad and paper, camera, 10 photographic plates, single-barrel shotgun, 20 shells, knife, mule, buckboard, $83 cash.

Personality

Yes, I do know what I'm asking. Yes, I know the rail companies are dangerous. Believe me, I know better than you think. I've tangled with them before, and they think I'm not a threat anymore.

Look, if it makes you feel any better, I swear I won't reveal where I got my information. You know a reporter has to protect her sources.

Oh, for cryin' in the milk, will you quit your whinin'. I'm just a little thing, and I ain't half as scared of them as you are. I've seen their worst, and I'm still up and walking around.

Okay, have it your way. But I'll be back tomorrow, and the day after, and the day after, until you decide to tell me what I need to know. One way or another, I'm going to expose them for the monsters they really are.

—LOSTON—

Quote: "Come on, honey. Do I look like the kind of gal who would kiss and tell?
"I do?
"Well, why not trust me anyway?"

POWERS

Chapter Three: Powers of the Harrowed

Now it's time to find out why you'd want to play a walking corpse. The manitou inside your hombre is a powerful critter. When your hero can control it, he can access the phenomenal powers of the Hunting Grounds.

It's a wild ride on an angry bronco, but an experienced Harrowed can usually hang on just long enough to have the ride of his unlife.

Common Powers

As you already know, all Harrowed are born back into the world in a similar state of undeath. This gives them a slew of common powers they share with the rest of their grisly kinsmen.

There's some new information besides what we gave you in *Deadlands,* so make sure you don't skip this part.

Undeath

Harrowed can ignore bleeding and Wind caused by physical damage, drowning, or other indirect damage to their organs.

Undead can take Wind from magical sources, and they're still affected by Wind from mental stress such as failed *guts* checks.

Killing an undead forever means destroying the head (maiming the noggin). "Maiming" the guts area means the Harrowed is down until it regenerates its damage to "critical."

Needless to say, fire, acid, and anything else that totally destroys the body destroys the head as well.

Pain

The undead feel pain, but not the way mortals do. It's more like a ringing alarm clock than crippling agony. For this reason, they can ignore 2 levels of wound modifiers in each area they're wounded.

If the undead's wound penalties are great enough to affect them anyway, the penalties aren't due to pain—they're because their opponents have severed vital muscles or simply blown off most of their sorry carcasses.

Decay

The parasites we call the manitous keep the Harrowed's flesh fresh—mostly. The undead don't rot, but their skin looks pale and sunken.

What little decay the Harrowed suffered occurred while it was battling for Dominion with the manitou—usually back in its grave. For this reason, anyone who gets a good close whiff of a Harrowed can smell a faint trace of spoiling meat on a Fair (5) *Cognition* roll.

Animals are a little craftier. They always know the difference. The various animal handling skills; *horse ridin', animal wranglin',* and *teamster* rolls are made at -2.

REGENERATION

Besides keeping the Harrowed's skin soft and smooth (relative to the average cadaver, of course), the manitous also rebuild their hosts' flesh from damage—as long as they have some other meat to replace the undead flesh—see "Food" below.

Unlike the kind of hero that breathes, who can only make a natural healing roll only every a week, the Harrowed may roll to heal from damage once day. This can come in really handy after facing down an hombre that wants to put the undead character straight back into his grave.

If the Harrowed can't get the food, then she can't make the healing roll. A Harrowed that's been dismembered and can't find any one to feed it any food is still alive; it's just not real mobile. This can be a unique kind of personal Hell if the Harrowed is trapped in this way for any length of time. Remember, the only thing that can kill a Harrowed is for its brains to be destroyed. They can even survive a beheading (although it sure puts them in a rough position).

Note that the brains are the motivator of the Harrowed's body. A body part that's amputated and loses a path to the brain doesn't work any more (with the exception of the *dead man's hand*

power described later in this chapter). If the Harrowed was somehow decapitated, the head would still work fine, but its control over the rest of its body would cease. Someone would have to sew the head back onto the body and feed the head some meat so that it could heal the head back to the body. Then the Harrowed would be as good as new.

If the Harrowed's digestive tract is destroyed, that's okay. She's just got to put the meat in her innards by hand and her body absorbs it.

A body part that is totally removed or destroyed cannot be regenerated (unless the hero has the *reconstruction* power). A Harrowed can sew cosmetic body parts back on (such as an ear or a chunk of flesh), but hands, eyes, and the like won't start working again right away just because they've been stitched back on. (A removed hand that's sewn on can start moving by means of *dead man's hand*, but the hand isn't really healed.)

It takes time to heal severed body parts, but this can be done normally (roll once per day for each wound). Once the wound is healed from maimed to critical, the damaged limb can be used again normally, and the stitches (or whatever) that were holding the limb on can be safely removed.

Finally, the undead can never benefit from any form of healing that regenerates *living* flesh. This includes *medicine* as well as hexes, rituals, or black magic. It is rumored some hucksters have found ways of healing *dead* flesh (see *Hucksters & Hexes*), but such individuals are rare indeed.

OLD WOUNDS

A cowpoke that was missing an arm before he embarked for the great trail ride in the sky is still looking for it when he scratches his way out of the dirt. If he can somehow find it and reattach it (however unlikely this might be), then he can heal it onto himself normally. Until then, though, he's plumb out of luck.

Similarly, Harrowed still bear any scars or marks on them that they had when they passed on. If your undead gunslinger's got "Rosie" tattooed in a heart on on his arm, he'd better be serious about that girl, because he's going to be wearing that little picture for the rest of his unnatural existence, which could be a mighty long time. He can try to remove it if he likes, but when it heals, it's still there, ink and all.

Harrowed don't have to bother cutting their nails or trimming their hair either. Those things aren't growing on them any more. Sure, they

might keep on for a day or two after the guy hauls his carcass into the sunlight, but they soon cease. If they're ever cut or trimmed, they "heal" right back to where they were beforehand.

DEATH WOUNDS

There's one kind of wound that most people can't heal: their last one. Even the Harrowed have a hard time getting around this limitation. After all, they weren't Harrowed when they took their mortal injury, and so they weren't protected by their manitou at that final point in their lives.

However, the first thing the manitou does when entering the Harrowed is heal the wounds that caused its host's departure from the land of the living.

Since these particular injuries were sustained before the manitou took hold of the body, they don't heal entirely perfectly. Gunslingers that lost their last duel usually have large pockmarks where the bullets entered and exited their bodies. Folks that were hanged might have rope burns permanently on their throats, and their necks are likely a tad longer than they used to be.

No one's likely to notice these details unless they're looking for them, but they can be a dead giveaway to someone who's wise to the ways of the walking dead.

Most Harrowed go out of their way to cover up as much of their wounded flesh as they can get away with. In the dusty Weird West, they just blend in with the crowd, since most other people are well-clothed too. Some Harrowed stick to the northerly parts of the world so they have an excuse to cover up. The fact that the frigid air helps control the stench of death doesn't hurt any either. There's nothing more embarrassing than being followed around by a horde of flies in the dead of summer.

Of course, some means of death leave scars that can't be covered up. Someone who died after sustaining third-degree burns over most of his body is going to have a mottled texture over the better part of his skin and may even appear to be partially melted. He might be able to explain this away as if he had actually survived the kind of event that did him in, but it's not going to make him stick out any less in a crowd.

Harrowed can solve some of these problems by taking the *death mask* power (see later), but that actually requires some amount of concentration, so it's not a permanent solution. However, they should take some level of the *degeneration* or *ugly as sin* Hindrances to represent their scarring.

When you're thinking about how your character died, try to take all of this into account. Also remember that there are certain wounds that even a manitou can't heal, even partially. If the brains are gone, there's no chance in Hell.

GRIT

Anyone who crawls out of a grave after a journey through the maddening Hunting Grounds is one tough hombre. All undead gain a point of *grit* when they emerge Harrowed.

FOOD

Strangely, the undead do need to eat—at least if they want to repair any damage their carcasses have taken. Theirs is a diet of meat; fresh or long-dead, it doesn't matter. The manitous draw energy from the meat and use it to rebuild the flesh of their hosts.

A Harrowed who hasn't eaten at least a pound of meat in the last 24 hours can't make a healing roll. This is why Harrowed are sometimes mistaken for ghouls by those with just enough knowledge of the occult world to be dangerous.

DRINK

The undead don't need to drink, but a full bottle of whiskey a day can keep the body "pickled" so it doesn't stink so much. Of course, the cadaver might smell like liquor, but at least the booze obscures the stench of rotting meat for a while.

Whenever an undead drinks a quart or so of alcohol, the difficulty of detecting his undead state by smell (by critters or common folk) goes up by +6 for the next 24 hours. By that time, the rotgut seeps out the rotten innards and any other holes he might have in his carcass. In the meantime, he just smells good and liquored up, which can cause its own problems of course, should he happen to run into someone who takes offense at his apparent drunkenness.

The undead can never get drunk, by the way. Some of them think they get drunk and act accordingly, but it's all in their rotten noggins.

SLEEP

A manitou needs a few hours of "downtime" every night. It's hard for the manitou inside to regenerate flesh, build conduits to the Hunting Grounds, and keep the host from rotting away, all while watching the world through the

Harrowed's eyes to look for something it can use the next time it gains Dominion. That's a lot to ask, even of a fairly powerful spirit servant of the Reckoners.

For this reason, a Harrowed must "sleep" for 1d6 hours out of every 24. During this period, the manitou channels energy from the Hunting Grounds into the body to keep it "alive."

In fact, if the Harrowed doesn't voluntarily crawl under a rock for a few hours of shut-eye, the manitou may well shut everything down for him. This is one of the few ways the manitou can affect its host when it doesn't have Dominion. The manitou won't zonk his host out in the middle of a firefight, but it may well do it while he's supposed to be on watch. Who cares about the rest of the posse anyway?

When the demon decides it's time for some maintenance (usually at the same time normal folks sleep), and the Harrowed decides he isn't ready for the Land of Nod, he can resist by making an opposed *Spirit* roll every hour to stay awake.

Fighting the manitou like this is exhausting work. The undead subtracts 1d4 Wind for every 24-hour period he doesn't go dormant. When he finally does shut down and let the manitou do its work, he regains 1 of these lost Wind for every hour spent dormant.

A Harrowed who drops to 0 Wind in this way falls to the earth like—well, like a corpse. Once the body returns to at least 1 Wind while dormant, then the manitou puts him to sleep for 1d6 hours as usual.

Dormant Harrowed aren't entirely unaware of their surroundings, by the way. The manitou always keeps one eye half-open for trouble. Should someone sneak up on the hero, allow her a *Cognition* roll versus the opponent's *sneak*. The dormant stiff can add +2 to her roll as if she's a *light sleeper*, or +4 if she's a *light sleeper* already.

SEX

It just can't happen. Without getting into any gritty details, undead males can't even get their shootin' irons out of their holsters, if you catch our drift. And even if they do somehow manage to find some way to draw, they'll be shooting blanks.

This doesn't mean they might not try—they are still men after all. They're just doomed to failure.

Female Harrowed can fake it a little better than males, given some preparation. Undead saloon gals (who cover themselves in perfume) might actually improve in their chosen profession.

FAITH

When the manitou takes over, it can use any of its hosts' Aptitudes or other abilities except *faith* and *faith*-based magic. A manitou cannot use shamanic rituals or blessed miracles, and if the creature must make a *faith* total, it uses its own score.

The blessed and shaman Harrowed who wish to use their *faith*-based magic can do so. The blessed perform their miracles normally. Shamans must deal with nature spirits, who worry that the petitioner might lose control to the hated manitou inside after receiving their favors. This means they must gather 1 extra Appeasement Point before they are granted favors.

SACRIFICE

Shamans often have to make some sort of sacrifice to the nature spirits as part of the rituals they perform to petition for favors. However, some things that might be a real sacrifice for the living don't mean anything to a Harrowed at all.

For a ritual to have any effect, the sacrifice must mean something to the person who's making the sacrifice. For instance, it usually doesn't matter if a Harrowed *fasts*, since she normally doesn't need food. However, if she's in a situation in which she desperately needs food (say she's wounded or has an *unnatural appetite*), then *fasting* would be meaningful, and the spirits might favor her request.

It's also pretty pointless for a Harrowed to *maim* herself, unless the body part is discarded and can't be *reconstructed*. A Harrowed cannot *scar* or *tattoo* herself normally either, as she can usually heal over such wounds (and doesn't really have a choice about it).

The nature spirits have long memories, and while they might be fooled once or twice, they're sure to catch a cheating shaman eventually. When they do, the shaman can be sure such tactics are never going to work again, maybe even when the sacrifice is for real.

Magic

Undead hucksters function no differently than normal. When the manitou is in charge, however, it can use its host's hexes, and it *never* risks suffering backlash. To a manitou-controlled hexslinger, Jokers are just wild cards.

Harrowed with access to black magic (usually extras instead of player characters, see *The Quick & the Dead*) use their own *faith* score or the manitou's, whichever's higher. Should such a Harrowed fail with a spell, it suffers the backlash just like any other servant of the unholy Reckoners.

Gaining New Powers

Now it's time to get to the good stuff. These are the powers that set your undead bag of bones apart from the few others stalking the Weird West.

When it's time to gain a new power, whether you're just creating your character or you're picking up a new one, there are three ways to figure out which powers he can learn.

The first is to pick a power you feel is appropriate and then get your Marshal's approval for it.

The second is to let the Marshal choose for you. Then she can slowly hint at the power your hero develops before you actually get to use it.

The last way is to roll on the table below. Use this if your hero's dispositions don't easily fall into those listed by the various powers.

HARROWED POWERS

d100 Roll	Power
1–2	Arcane Protection
3–4	Bad Mojo
5–6	Berserker
7–8	Burrow
9–10	Cat Eyes
11–12	Charnel Breath
13	Chill o' the Grave
14–15	Claws
16–17	Dark Vision
18–19	Dead Man's Hand
20–21	Dead Reckonin'
22–23	Death Bond
24–25	Death Mask
26	Devil's Touch
27–28	Etchin'
29–30	Eulogy
31–32	Evil Eye
33–34	Fast as Death
35–36	Ferryman's Fee
37–38	Ghost
39–40	Hell Beast
41–42	Hell Fire
43–44	Hell Wind
45–46	Infest
47–48	Jinx
49	Luck o' the Draw*
50	Mad Insight*
51–52	Marked for Death
53–54	Mimic
55–56	Nightmare
57–58	Possession
59–60	Reconstruction
61–62	Relic
63–64	Rigor Mortis
65–66	Sicken
67–68	Silent as a Corpse
69–70	Skull Chucker
71–72	Sleep o' the Dead
73–74	Soul Eater
75–76	Soul Flight
77–78	Speakin' with the Dead
79–80	Spider
81–82	Spook
83–84	Stitchin'
85–86	Supernatural Trait
87–88	Trackin' Teeth
89–90	Undead Contortion
91–92	Unholy Host
93–94	Unholy Reflexes
95–96	Voice o' the Damned
97–98	Varmint Control
99–100	Wither

* These powers are only useful for characters with a certain kind of *arcane background*. Reroll if the power isn't appropriate.

POWERS

The powers below have the same elements as those in the *Deadlands* rulebook. We've repeated the original powers here as well to make things easy on you. This way, you don't have to go flipping from book to book, looking for the power description you want.

Anyhow, the power descriptions all work like this:

Speed is the number of actions it takes to activate the power. A few powers are "always on" and don't require any kind of activation.

Duration is how long the power lasts. Concentration means the Harrowed must maintain her concentration on the power and can take no complex actions without interrupting it. Some powers might also require Wind, or might give you the option to spend Wind *instead* of concentrating.

Dispositions are Edges, Hindrances, and backgrounds that tend to lead to these powers.

ARCANE PROTECTION

Speed: Instant
Duration: Instant
Dispositions: High *academia: occult* Aptitude, *arcane background, doubting Thomas*

Manitous being the masters of the Hunting Grounds, they can sometimes shirk the effects of other supernatural creatures on earth.

Sometimes.

A Harrowed with *arcane protection* can force his manitou to negate spells, hexes, and other supernatural attacks. The manitou isn't always successful, but it usually tries its best, since protecting its host from eldritch attacks usually goes hand-in-hand with keeping its own self alive.

Whenever the hero is a direct target of a spell or other supernatural attack, the hero can attempt to simply ignore it. To do so, the character must first vamoose, discarding his highest card and moving in some direction to dodge the attack.

If the Harrowed has no card, he cannot vamoose and doesn't have time to stop the enemy spell. It sure seems like he really should have kept that card up his sleeve.

Once the Harrowed vamooses, he can make a *Spirit* test versus the opponent, adding his power level to the final total.

If the Harrowed is successful, the enemy attack is cast but does not actually harm him.

A spell that affects an area may still affect the character as long as he wasn't directly targeted. It cannot be negated with this power.

BAD MOJO

Speed: 1
Duration: 1 casting
Dispositions: *Bad luck, doubting Thomas, intolerance*

Through their manitous' connection with the Hunting Grounds, some Harrowed are able to interfere with a huckster's hex-casting ability. The Harrowed's manitou talks with the manitous hovering about the Huckster, and the poor hex-caster finds himself wrestling a little harder for his magical powers.

In game terms, the Harrowed spends an action to initiate an opposed *Spirit* versus *Spirit* roll with the huckster. If the huckster wins, nothing happens at all.

If the Harrowed succeeds, the huckster might be in for a double helping of trouble. For each level of power the Harrowed possesses, the huckster has to draw one extra card whenever he slings his next hex. These extra cards do not count toward the huckster building a hand for the hex, but they do give extra chances for the huckster to draw a Joker and suffer backlash as a result.

Needless to say, this power doesn't much endear Harrowed to hucksters. More than one huckster has been killed by the effects of this power.

However, the Harrowed can only affect a huckster that he can see. The range is effectively limited only to any huckster in sight.

The Harrowed can affect only one huckster at a time with this power. Also, no matter how many Harrowed in the area might have this power, a huckster can only be affected by one *bad mojo* at a time.

Smart Harrowed keep a card up their sleeve so they can hit the huckster with *bad mojo* at the start of a combat round.

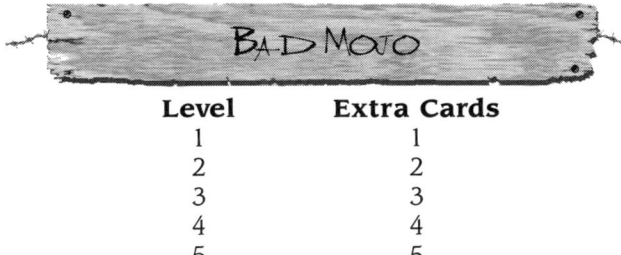

BAD MOJO

Level	Extra Cards
1	1
2	2
3	3
4	4
5	5

BERSERKER

Speed: 1
Duration: Special
Dispositions: *Bloodthirsty, loco, mean as a rattler, rage*

Harrowed characters tend to grow more savage and dangerous as time goes on. That's just a fact of their torturous existence. Still, at their worst, they're nowhere near as fierce as the manitou inside them can be.

The manitou has nothing of the decency of humanity to it, only cruel, bestial cunning. With the *berserker* power, a Harrowed can learn to tap into that manitou's nature just a bit, becoming a little more brutal and a little less human. This can be useful when a fight turns nasty and the Harrowed feels the need to draw upon the soul of a cold-hearted killer.

When the power is initiated, all of the Harrowed's Corporeal Traits are all temporarily boosted by one die type, while all Mental Traits (and their related aptitudes) are decreased by one step. A Trait cannot be decreased below 1d4 this way.

The altered Traits affect any Aptitude checks as well. This physical boost and mental decline make the Harrowed quite a killing machine for the duration of the power, though not much of a conversationalist.

The length the *berserker* power can be maintained depends upon the Harrowed's level with the power, as shown on the table below. Once that duration is over, the undead's Traits

revert to their normal rankings. The undead suffers 1d6 Wind from the exertion and cannot use the power again until this Wind is recovered.

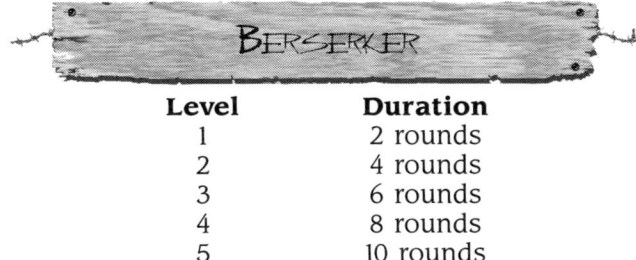

BERSERKER

Level	Duration
1	2 rounds
2	4 rounds
3	6 rounds
4	8 rounds
5	10 rounds

BURROW

Speed: 1
Duration: As desired
Dispositions: *Aura o' death, bad eyes, death wish, degeneration, sand, thick-skinned, unnatural appetite.*

Taking a dirt nap can do a lot for a fellow's affinity for Mother Earth. After all, there's not many people that actually get to see sunlight again after spending a few days buried six feet under.

A Harrowed with this power can tunnel through the earth with unbelievable speed. She doesn't dig her way through the muck so much as it moves out of her way by means of professional courtesy. The dirt recognizes a kindred soul trapped in the undead (although whether it's the Harrowed or its manitou is impossible to say), and it moves aside at the Harrowed's will.

Many Harrowed with this power first figure it out when they try clawing their way out of a not-so-shallow grave that they just happen to have found themselves buried in. Instead of having to scratch and dig toward the surface, the dirt just skirts aside for them like an old friend met on the street.

As ways to start your second chance on this old Earth go, it's not a bad one—given the alternative. Some Harrowed without this power have found themselves trapped in a grave that was made a bit better than the manitou inside them had realized. Needless to say, this makes for some awfully angry manitous. They get out eventually, and they're ready for blood then.

This isn't to say that the dirt doesn't touch the Harrowed. In fact, it clings to them like a long-lost lover. A Harrowed that *burrows* to the surface is sure to be encrusted with soil and covered with all sorts of tiny creatures that dwell within it: worms, millipedes, insects, and such.

The more powerful a Harrowed is, the faster it can move through the soil and the tougher the kind of earth it can move through. Strangely, however, a Harrowed can never burrow deeper than six feet down (although it can burrow directly up if it happens to be lower than that).

A Harrowed can run (double her Pace) when *burrowing* through the Earth, but if she does so, she runs the risk of getting lost. Just because she can move through the earth doesn't mean she can see through it. Every round the Harrowed *burrows* faster than her Pace, she must make a Fair (5) *Smarts* roll or get lost.

If a Harrowed is lost under the earth, it's up to the Marshal where she ends up. A *burrower's* inner ear tells her which direction is up, but otherwise she's just lost.

If the Harrowed goes bust on her *Smarts* roll, then she doesn't even know she's lost. She definitely going to be in for a big surprise when she resurfaces.

It's impossible to pick up the Pace while *burrowing*. In fact, simply "running" while *burrowing* costs 1d4 Wind per round.

No matter what the Harrowed's power level, it's impossible to *burrow* through anything solid, be it a large boulder, a steel plate, or a wooden wall. Basically, if it ain't dirt, it ain't moving.

The basic Pace while *burrowing* is 2 per level. A level-5 *burrower*, for instance, can move through the dirt at Pace 10—Pace 20 if running.

CAT EYES

Speed: 2
Duration: Concentration
Dispositions: *Bad eyes, curious, eagle eyes, keen, mark o' the devil, "the stare"*

Cat eyes grants an undead character the ability to see things others cannot, even stare directly into the murky depths of a man's soul (to a certain extent). When used, the Harrowed's eyes glow slightly, as an animal's do when they catch the moonlight just right.

The undead actually has to concentrate to use the ability. It is not considered "always on." This is fine, since otherwise the constant eerie glow in the Harrowed's eyes would be enough to get the witch-hunters preparing themselves a mighty big bonfire.

Harrowed characters with this power should be careful how and when they decide to use it. Sometimes the glowing side-effect can actually show an enemy just where to put his bullet if a Harrowed with *cat eyes* is trying to sneak up on him in the middle of a dark night.

The ability gained at each level is shown on the table. The Harrowed has the abilities of his level and any levels below that too.

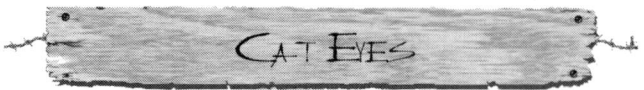

Level Power

1 **Distance:** The character can see twice as far as anyone else. Add +4 to Cognition checks made to spot distant sights.

2 **Heat:** The Harrowed can detect heat sources at least as warm as a normal human at 50 yards. Note that background heat might obscure lesser sources.

3 **Night:** As long as there is any light source at all, the character can see in otherwise total darkness as if it were daylight

4 **Darkness:** The character can see in complete darkness as if it were daylight.

5 **Soul Sight:** The final stage of cat eyes allows the Harrowed to look directly into another's soul. When activated, he can tell a person's general inclination, if he's lying, or if he's an abomination or Harrowed by making a Hard (9) *scrutinize* roll. He can also add +4 to his *scrutinize* rolls.

CHARNEL BREATH

Speed: 1
Duration: Instant
Dispositions: *Big mouth, degeneration, grim servant o' death, habit, heavy sleeper, mean as a rattler, unnatural appetite*

Most folks don't believe in supernatural things like the walking dead. Those who do expect that even if the dead do walk, they surely don't breathe (and they don't have to if they don't want to, although it sure comes in handy when trying to talk to someone). Anyone who's met a Harrowed with this power definitely wishes they didn't.

Charnel breath is the ability to dredge up all the worst stench of decay in a Harrowed's body, supernaturally fester it even further in a bare moment, and blow it out all over an unsuspecting target within arm's reach. The

victim suffers damage to his Wind as a result, partly from the corrosive effect of the gas on eyes, nasal passages, and windpipe, and partly from the violent retching that it produces. The stench is enough to make even those in the room wrinkle their noses and hold their breaths until a breeze can clear the place of the noxious fumes.

This power can only be used on a victim within an arm's length of the breather (about 3 feet). Beyond that reach, *charnel breath* does little more than offend.

The Harrowed's level with this power determines the type of dice used in an opposed roll against the victim's *Vigor*, as shown on the table below. The Harrowed's *fightin': brawlin'* skill determines the number of dice rolled. The difference between the opposed rolls is how much damage the victim suffers to his Wind.

Note that nonliving beings are immune to this particular power, though they still won't likely appreciate a ghastly belch in the face.

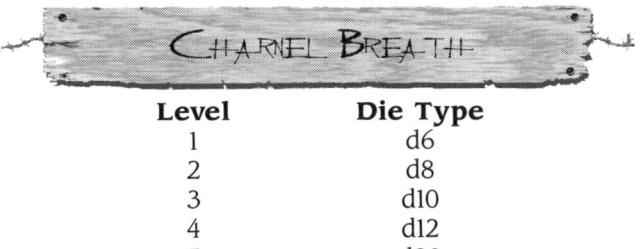

Charnel Breath

Level	Die Type
1	d6
2	d8
3	d10
4	d12
5	d20

Chill o' the Grave

Speed: Special
Duration: Concentration
Dispositions: *Geezer, miser, nerves o' steel, scrawny, thin-skinned*

They say the grave is damp and cold. By the use of this power, a Harrowed can radiate that chill from the Hunting Ground through his body, lowering the temperature and increasing the humidity in his general vicinity. The level of the power determines just how large that "vicinity" can be, as shown in detail on the table on the next page.

For each level of power the user possesses, he can lower the local temperature by 5° Fahrenheit. This change occurs at a rate of 5° per minute. At the same time, he can raise the local humidity by 5% per level of power possessed, at a rate of 5% per minute. When control is released, the local temperature and humidity return to normal at the same speed at which they originally changed.

Manipulating the local temperature and humidity with this power allows for some pretty dramatic changes in the weather. When the Harrowed uses the power at lower levels, living creatures in the area feel a disturbing chill and dankness. At higher levels, the user can actually summon up mists and ground fogs. Of course, the Marshal has the final say as to what effects are possible under the current weather circumstances.

There are two basic purposes for which the Harrowed might use this power.

One is to simply spook other people in the area. A Harrowed trying to impress listeners with a frightening tale might generate a subtle chill to help give them goose bumps. Or a more dramatic Harrowed might be more blatant about creating eerie mists as a sign of his power. This might add a bonus to an *overawe* attempt or tack a penalty onto an initial *guts* check.

The other main use of *chill o' the grave* is as cover for sneaking about. Again, a mist that builds slowly is not likely to signal itself as a supernatural power, but it can grow thick enough to hide an undead within it (the visibility is about two yards). There's nothing like using a strange mist to sneak into town—or out.

Additionally, a fog that springs up in bare minutes can provide for a pretty impressive entrance when the Harrowed steps out of it abruptly to confront the object of his visit. If

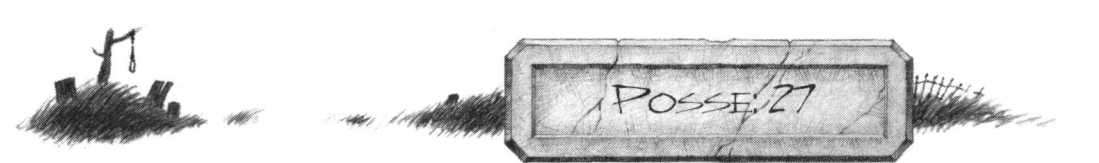

—LOSTON—97

he's careful with his use of the power, the Harrowed can make the fog fade rather quickly too, making his control over it obvious to even the most skeptical observer.

Using the *chill o' the grave* power can be exhausting. It's not easy to radiate dank. For each minute that the power is maintained, the undead suffers 1 point of Wind damage. This includes the time that must be spent to cause the effect in the first place.

In general, the humidity must be near 100% to generate a fog. Also, the temperature must be at least 15° colder than the air outside the Harrowed's radius of effect. In other words, the conditions must be right for the Harrowed to be able to pull this off. It's impossible to generate a rolling bank of fog in the middle of the day in Death Valley, but it would be extremely easy to do so in the City of Lost Angels on a mild spring evening.

The Harrowed cannot usually cause rain with this power, since the clouds are too far away to affect. Atop the Rockies, though, this could be possible. In fact, if it's cold enough, it might even snow.

CHILL O' THE GRAVE

Level	Maximum Temperature Change	Maximum Humidity Change	Effect Radius
1	5° F	5%	10 yards
1	10° F	10%	20 yards
1	15° F	15%	30 yards
1	20° F	20%	40 yards
1	25° F	25%	50 yards

CLAWS

Speed: 1
Duration: As desired
Dispositions: *Two-fisted, all thumbs, bloodthirsty, grim servant o' death, nasty disposition, one-armed bandit, rage, ugly as sin, vengeful*

Saloon gals can leave vicious scratches down a fellow's back, but that's nothing compared to what a Harrowed can do. These claws can go right through a spine like a razor-sharp Bowie knife.

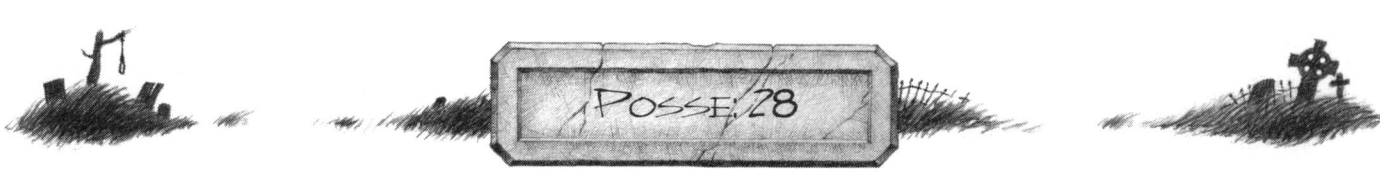

The character's hands turn into cruel claws at will. The higher the level, the bigger the claws. The damage of the claws is added to the character's *Strength* roll whenever she hits using *fightin': brawlin'*, just like the claws were a hand-held blade.

The Harrowed can extend or retract the claws by simply thinking about it, and this simple act can pierce even leather gloves (if worn). Keeping them out or in requires absolutely no concentration on the Harrowed's part.

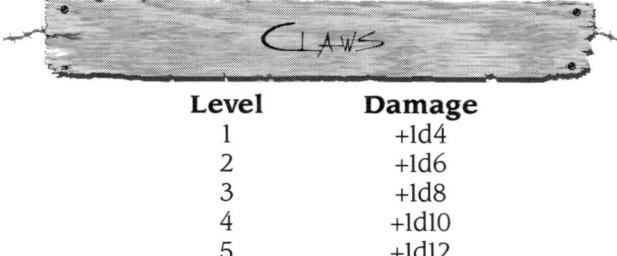

CLAWS

Level	Damage
1	+1d4
2	+1d6
3	+1d8
4	+1d10
5	+1d12

DARK VISION

Speed: Varies
Duration: Varies
Dispositions: *Bad eyes, curious, eagle eyes, keen, mark o' the devil, "the stare"*

A Harrowed's manitou exists sort of halfway between this world and the next, able to view both the Hunting Grounds and this Earth. This kind of double vision might drive a living soul insane, but Harrowed are usually made of tougher stuff.

By stealing a glimpse of the manitou's sight, an undead can glance into the Hunting Grounds to gain some sort of idea as to how tainted his current locale is.

In order to initiate the power, the Harrowed must sit quietly and enter into a deep trance, entirely oblivious to events in the natural world. Only a wound can rouse the Harrowed from the trance before its duration comes to an end. At the end of this time, the Harrowed may catch a vision of the Hunting Grounds.

Stealing this glimpse is tiring work. Every round spent staring into the maddening Hunting Grounds causes the Harrowed incredible mental strain. This is reflected in the amount of Wind taken per round, and depends on the Harrowed's power level.

The distance of the Harrowed's power is not sight as any sane person would assume. Instead, due to the strange nature of the Hunting Grounds, the vision's effective distance is based on the Harrowed's power level. Objects in the real world, such as walls, do block these visions. Harrowed must actually be able to gaze into a person's dark soul or study an object's presence before he can see its spirit-self.

What can be seen by the vision are basically things like manitous swirling around a powerful huckster, how dark a general location is (representing its fear level), any magical effects on people or objects, or even whether or not a manitou is wriggling around inside of someone. In the latter case, the manitou's demeanor might even indicate whether or not it is currently controlling its Harrowed host.

Finally, any creature with a Terror Score leaves a dark trail through the spirit world. Up to one hour after an abomination has moved through an area, it leaves a trail of pure taint. A Harrowed with *dark vision* can follow such trails as long as he maintains his ability.

DARK VISION

Level	Speed	Wind
1	1 hour	5
2	10 minutes	4
3	1 minute	3
4	2 rounds	2
5	1 action	1

DEAD MAN'S HAND

Speed: 2
Duration: Concentration (variable)
Dispositions: *Aura o' death, curious, mark o' the devil, one-armed bandit, sneak*

Harrowed with this power can continue to control their own severed limbs for short periods of time. The Harrowed could cut off his hand and let it run around a room on its own, or give an eyeball to a compadre so the Harrowed can spy on what's going on when he doesn't happen to be around.

If a Harrowed attempts to attack with an animated severed limb, he uses his own statistics but he must subtract -4 from the *fightin': brawlin'* roll. The damage from an animated hand, by the way, is half the character's normal *Strength* total read as brawling damage. These limbs are much better at opening jail cells and causing distractions than beating the Hell out of someone.

The undead typically only remove their hands or eyes for use with this power. It just doesn't make much sense, to slice off your foot and send it after someone.

The duration that the body part can be controlled while separated from the owner's body depends on the user's power level. After that, the parts rot like normal dead flesh unless reattached. Only one of the character's body parts can be manipulated at a time.

DEAD MAN'S HAND

Level	Duration
1	1 Wind/Round
2	Concentration
3	Concentration or 1 Wind/Round
4	10 minutes
5	1 hour

DEAD RECKONING

Speed: 3
Duration: Concentration
Dispositions: *Death wish, grim servant o' death, sense of direction, veteran o' the weird west*

Several of the Harroweds' powers center upon corpses and graveyards. But what's a fellow to do when he wants to raise an undead posse, but there just isn't any sign pointing to the local boot hill? Well, that's when the *dead reckoning* power is useful.

Dead reckoning is the ability to sense the direction to the nearest human corpse. It may lead you to the undertaker's shop or a cemetery or just the site of a recent bush-whacking, or it might even lead you to a walking corpse, whether that be a zombie or even another Harrowed. It all just depends upon what's closest.

As far as *dead reckoning* is concerned, it doesn't matter how far away that nearest corpse is; the power just points a direction. All that matters is that the body still has at least some flesh on its bones. *Dead reckoning* can't lock onto bare bones.

Fortunately for the Harrowed, once he arrives at the corpse he sensed, the power can be redirected to point the way to the next nearest corpse. This way, if he doesn't find exactly what he's looking for the first time, he can go looking someplace else.

As a Harrowed gains higher levels of ability with this power, he also begins to gain some sense of the distance to the corpse being sensed, and the condition of that corpse.

This power can also come in handy to recognize Harrowed that are posing as living, breathing folks. Assuming the Harrowed is the only corpse nearby, it usually works like a charm. All you've got to do is turn it on. If the nearest corpse is a lot farther away than the fellow you're curious about, then you know he's not walking around when he should be sleeping with the worms.

If you've only got the power at level 1, though, it might take some triangulation to figure out if a cowpoke's Harrowed or not. After all, if there's a boot hill off yonder behind him, your hero might be detecting that instead of the target's well-preserved cadaver.

Picking a Harrowed out of a graveyard, though, is darn near next to impossible. The power is certain to pick up the corpses in the ground rather than the target. Of course, if you're standing close enough to touch the person in question, then the power should work. Your hero had just better pray that, if the target actually is Harrowed, he's friendly too.

Not a lot of people would be willing to lay money on that.

DEAD RECKONING

Level	Power
1	The Harrowed can gauge the corpse's direction only. No indication of distance is given.
2	The Harrowed knows the direction and rough distance of the nearest corpse, within a 50% margin of error. (A corpse 10 miles away might seem to be as little as five miles distant or as much as 15.)

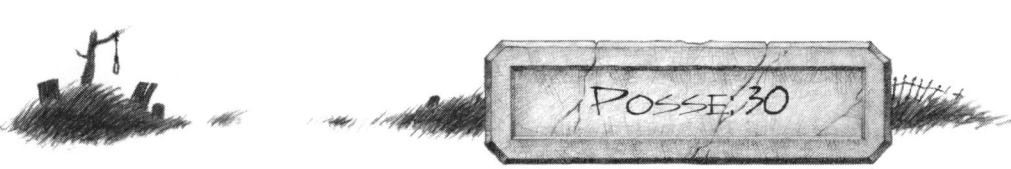

3   The Harrowed knows the direction, rough distance, and basic condition of the corpse (about how many days it has been dead).

4   The Harrowed knows the direction, precise distance (within a 10% margin of error), and rough condition of the corpse).

5   The Harrowed knows the direction, precise distance, and precise condition of the corpse (how long it has been dead, its death wounds, how much it has decayed, and if it has been reanimated somehow).

DEATH BOND

Speed: One minute
Duration: Special
Dispositions: *High falutin', oath, rank, renown, sidekick*

Evil creatures often have servants—grunts to do the dirty work that their masters plan. Lots of times, these masters give a special follower some token of power, a sort of down payment on the rewards he will receive when his lord rules over all.

Some Harrowed can make a similar sort of pact with a living person, lending some of their powers to a friend or colleague for a short period of time.

It isn't a pleasant experience, though. For one thing, Harrowed powers are spooky enough when wielded by a walking corpse. It's even creepier when a normal, living person uses one. For another thing, the process by which powers are loaned is pretty gruesome on its own, and not everyone is willing to endure it.

To lend Harrowed a power to a living person, the recipient has to drink some of the thick, tarry stuff that passes for blood in the Harrowed. This causes the living person to lose 1d6 of Wind from the substance's nauseating nature. If a cowpoke can manage to gag this stuff down—which is at least a Fair (5) *guts* check (at least the first few times that he sucks on the Harrowed's veins—the foul mixture causes the drinker to lose another 1d6 Wind. This lost Wind can't be reclaimed until the power is used and released.

Once the blood is exchanged in this way, the Harrowed relinquishes any one level of one power of her choice, and the living partner receives one level of that power. A Harrowed with 3 levels in *cat's eyes*, for instance, could

grant his minion 1 level of *cat's eyes*, allowing the mortal to see twice as far as normal and add +4 to *Cognition* checks involving seeing distant things. The Harrowed would then only be able to use his own *cat's eye* power at level 2.

The loan lasts until the Harrowed decides to reclaim the power herself again, at which point the living person loses it automatically.

If a Harrowed loses control to her manitou, that lent power may be lost at the most inopportune time—for the borrower. Imagine being two stories up the side of a building when the manitou decides to take back its *spider* power, for instance!

The level at which a Harrowed possesses the *death bond* power determines how many power levels can be loaned out at a time. These power levels can be lent to one person or divided among several, and can come from one power alone, or from various different ones.

For example, an undead with three levels of *death bond* could loan three levels of the same power to one person, or divide those three levels among two or three people, and so on. Keep in mind, though, that each level loaned requires its own ritual of blood transfer. Note that Harrowed can't borrow powers in this way.

Also, when a power level is loaned away, the Harrowed loses the use of that level for herself. This power doesn't allow someone to duplicate another power. The levels are literally taken from the hero and transferred to someone else.

Even the *death bond* power can be transferred to another person. The minion can then loan out the powers that have been loaned to him. Remember, though, that loaning out *death bond* also brings down the number of power levels the Harrowed can loan out herself.

If someone with a loaned power is killed, the power returns to the Harrowed who loaned it. In this way, a Harrowed can keep track of her underlings in a crude way. If a loaned-out power comes flowing back to the Harrowed, then she knows that an ill fate has befallen her friend.

DEATH BOND

Level	Lendable Power Levels
1	1
2	2
3	3
4	4
5	5

DEATH MASK

Speed: 2
Duration: Concentration
Dispositions: *Cautious, gift of gab, lyin' eyes, ugly as sin*

One thing about death, it's usually ugly as sin. And the corpse of a Harrowed comes chock full o' sin, courtesy of the manitou inside. But there's a cure for that—at least for the way it looks, if not the manitou itself.

When it comes to the realm of the supernatural, things are seldom as they seem. With this ability, an undead can use the supernatural power of illusion to disguise his true appearance from normal people. This can come in especially handy for a tattered, rotting Harrowed who needs to go into town for supplies. But undead with more experience can even use this power to help disguise themselves as someone else.

Death mask doesn't physically change the Harrowed's features, though. It just fools other people into seeing what the undead wants them to believe.

The Harrowed has to concentrate to keep up the illusion, so he suffers a penalty of –2 to all dice rolls while using the power. Also, because the illusion isn't real, it doesn't project a reflection, so anyone spotting the undead in a mirror can see him for what he really is.

The undead's concentration may not be broken when he's wounded (this is up to the Marshal, depending on the circumstances). If not, the illusion holds. However, the fact that the Harrowed just took an injury and wasn't too bothered by it should tip most people off to the fact that the Harrowed is not exactly what he might appear to be.

Remember that most Harrowed don't really look too dead. They don't normally need this power to disguise their status as cheaters of death. Most often, a loaded .45 is enough to keep the curious away.

Of course, in the case of Pinkertons, Texas Rangers, and other people who know what they're looking for, this isn't always the case. Against such foes, this power can prove invaluable.

Harrowed with the *degeneration* Hindrance are those most in need of this power. It's awful hard to stroll into the local saloon if you've got a skeletal face and raisins where your eyes once happened to be. It tends to clear a room real fast.

DEATH MASK

Level	Extent of Disguise
1	**Face:** The undead can disguise his face to appear living. Other parts of the body—including the rest of the head—must be kept covered if they aren't to be seen in their (un)natural state.
2	**Head and Hands:** The undead can disguise both head and hands to look as they did in life. Hair color can be anything the Harrowed desires, and facial hair can be changed at will.
3	**Entire Body:** The undead could be naked, and no one would know from sight that he wasn't alive. Still, he can only appear as himself.
4	**Changed Appearance:** As above, but the Harrowed can look like someone other than himself, though the height and body size must be roughly the same.
5	**Impersonation:** The undead can appear to be anyone else, so long as he knows what the person looks like. He looks so much like this other person, that even that person's closest friends and family cannot tell the difference from looks alone. Voice and mannerisms are another matter entirely. This ability basically adds +5 to any *disguise* rolls the Harrowed has to make versus a *scrutinize* roll. The Marshal can modify this bonus as she sees fit. Against people who have only briefly met the person being mimicked, the Harrowed might get a +9. When dealing with family members, the Harrowed might not get any bonus at all.

DEVIL'S TOUCH

Speed: 1
Duration: Concentration
Dispositions: *All thumbs, doubting Thomas, mechanically inclined, superstitious*

Here's another trick for wanton destructiveness from the repertoire of the Harrowed. As if it isn't enough that they can spread decay and disease, some can also make

mechanical devices prone to break down or malfunction in their vicinity. This power is called *devil's touch*.

Devil's touch modifies the reliability rolls of a single device used in the Harrowed's presence, making it more likely to fail. The Harrowed's power level serves as a die roll modifier, added to the number rolled.

Naturally, this makes mad scientists' devices more prone to malfunctioning. But the power can also affects any other single device with moving parts in the vicinity—from the spurs on a cowboy's boots to the revolver in his hand—giving it a temporary Reliability number of 20. Don't forget to add the bonuses to the Reliability to these rolls too.

The power's level also determines exactly what the term "vicinity" means in relation to the Harrowed using *devil's touch*. When the power is activated, the Harrowed can choose any range up to and including that listed for his power level.

It doesn't take much imagination to realize that an undead tinkerer never need worry about running out of work.

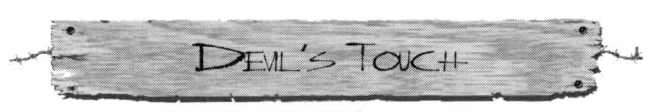

Devil's Touch

Level	Die Modifier	Range
1	+1	5 yards
2	+2	10 yards
3	+3	15 yards
4	+4	20 yards
5	+5	25 yards

Etchin'

Speed: 1
Duration: Permanent
Dispositions: *Big mouth, dinero, sense of direction*

Even after meeting with the Grim Reaper, some folks got plenty to say to the world. Sometimes what's written on their tombstone just ain't enough.

Telegraphs being what they are in the Weird West, most folks would prefer to rely on alternate means of communication. Harrowed with this power can send a message from beyond death. This may not sound so impressive, considering they're already up and wandering around, but they can also send it a long ways from where they're standing.

Basically, the Harrowed can etch a hand-lettered message in any surface that he's seen and knows the current location of. Since this makes working with mobile things like the side of a train difficult, most times the Harrowed goes for things like walls, floors, and even headstones.

The maximum distance from the Harrowed to the surface the message can be etched upon is determined by the Harrowed's level with the power. This is all shown on the table later.

Of course, the Harrowed can only write messages in languages that she can read and write. If the Harrowed is illiterate, this is a pretty useless power, although it could be used to draw rough pictograms instead.

The real trick here is that there's no way to make sure that the intended recipient gets the message. The Harrowed has just got to put the words where she thinks they're likely to be seen and hope.

The message usually looks like someone scratched it with a knife into the material on which it appears. This can change depending on the material and the effect desired. If used on a wall, it might look like fresh blood. If the message is supposed to show up on glass, it would appear etched. If it materialized on a bit of stone, it would seem carved.

Once sent, the message is permanent, just as if it had been written by the Harrowed's own hand. It doesn't disappear unless someone actually makes a successful attempt to obliterate it.

The message can be of any length, but the Harrowed player must actually write the note out on paper by hand. The note is then given to the Marshal (or to another player if that's the intended recipient and the message gets to him) who can interpret it as she wishes.

ETCHIN'

Level	Distance
1	100 yards
2	1 mile
3	10 miles
4	100 miles
5	1000 miles

EULOGY

Speed: 1 minute
Duration: Permanent
Dispositions: High *tale-tellin'* Aptitude, *big mouth, vengeful, "the voice"*

When this cowpoke wants to say a few final words, they're meant for someone else. And they are *final*.

The Harrowed player delivers a short speech, talking about the intended victim as if he had just passed away. It can be sweet or vicious, but its purpose must be clear.

The target must be able to hear and understand the Harrowed's words for the power to work. If it's not spoken in a language the target understands, it just doesn't work.

It only works on humans beings too. As much as you might swear that mare could understand you, she's just not going to really get it.

Once the speech is over, the Harrowed makes a *tale-tellin'* roll against the target's *Spirit*. The Harrowed adds +1 to this roll for every level he has with the power.

If the Harrowed gets a success, the target has a heart attack. He must make a Hard (9) *Vigor* roll. If he makes it, he loses 3d6 Wind.

If he fails it, he loses 3d6 Wind and one step of his *Vigor*. He also has to make a second Hard (9) *Vigor* roll. If he fails this, he dies unless saved by an Incredible (11) *medicine* roll within 2d6 rounds. If his *Vigor* falls below d4, he dies either way.

This power can only be used against once against any particular victim. Even if it entirely fails, it can never be used against that person again.

EVIL EYE

Speed: 1
Duration: Special
Dispositions: *Bad eyes, curious, eagle eyes, keen, mark o' the devil, "the stare"*

Having a Harrowed set its eyes on you is bad enough. Getting vexed by one with the *evil eye* will likely seal your fate.

This simple curse makes a mortal clumsy, stupid, slow, and usually, dead. Every action roll the target takes suffers a penalty equal to the level of the Harrowed's power.

Evil eye works only on living humans. Animals, abominations, and other critters can't be cursed.

The Harrowed may only vex one person at a time. He cannot vex another with his *evil eye* until he lifts the first curse (which he may do at any time), or the target kicks the bucket.

The target must be able to look into the Harrowed's *evil eye* to be vexed. This makes its effective range about 25 yards.

FAST AS DEATH

Speed: 1
Duration: 1 round
Dispositions: *Fleet footed, yeller*

Normally, of course, dead bodies don't move very fast. They just sort of lie there. The Harrowed break that rule just by being up and moving around. But some can even move with supernatural speed when the need arises. They call it *fast as death*.

Harrowed with this power can add extra distance to their movement for the round. Any time they decide to take a movement action during the round, they can declare that they are moving as *fast as death*.

The Harrowed can then add the entire roll of a pickup die to that action (see the Gitalong Table in the *Deadlands* rulebook), rather than splitting that die roll over all the actions for the turn like you would normally. By doing this on multiple actions of a turn, they can cover a considerable distance in less time than it takes to whistle "Dixie" in Dodge.

Using this power costs a Harrowed Wind. The amount is determined by a die roll based upon the Harrowed's level with the power. The higher the power level, the less Wind it costs.

A Harrowed can use this power as many times during a round as she likes. The only limitation is how much Wind the Harrowed has left.

And yes, a Harrowed can actually knock the Wind out of herself by using this power too liberally. If this should happen, the Harrowed manages to complete her move before collapsing in a heap.

Of course, the Harrowed is free to push her movement normally in addition to using this power. Those that do can move along at quite a clip.

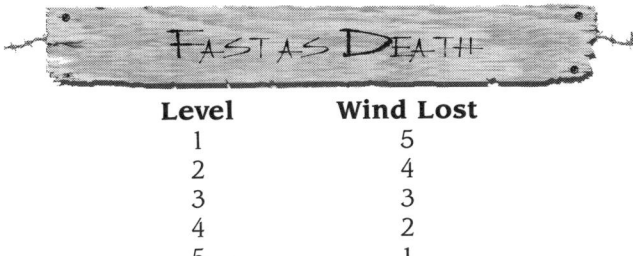

Fast as Death

Level	Wind Lost
1	5
2	4
3	3
4	2
5	1

Ferryman's Fee

Speed: Varies
Duration: Concentration or 1 Wind/round
Dispositions: *Arcane background, fleet footed, high falutin', sand, self-righteous, stubborn*

Some Harrowed smell like they haven't touched water for years. With this power, they can make sure they don't.

The reason they put coins on dead folks' eyes is so they've got something to pay Charon with when they're bargaining for a ride over the river Styx. The ferryman always does a fine job, but you've got to pay his fee.

A Harrowed with this power can put a down payment on his final fare. To activate the power, he lays two coins across each of his eyes. Any coins will do, but copper ones like pennies are traditional—the ferryman works cheap. After all, the dead may not have much on them when they reach the river, but there's lots of them.

Once this is done, the Harrowed must wait for the coins to be absorbed into her eyes. The amount of time this takes varies with the level of the power as shown on the table below. If the Harrowed is interrupted at any time while absorbing the coins, they fall from her eyes, and she must start all over again.

After the coins are fully absorbed, they disappear, melting into the Hunting Grounds. Then the Harrowed can get up, and for as long as she can maintain her concentration, walk across water.

The power level also determines how rough the water can be for the Harrowed to maintain herself above its surface. In any case, really turbulent seas—like the kind you would see during a hurricane—cannot be walked over. The Harrowed's concentration would surely be shattered by the rolling surfaces on which she was trying to stand.

The Harrowed can even carry things or people across the water. For all practical purposes, the water is solid to the Harrowed (don't turn this power on if being dropped into a lake from a height!). This means the Harrowed can even carry as much over water as she normally could on land.

The Harrowed also gets as much traction on the water as she would on dirt. If necessary, she could even tow a boat behind her, although she wouldn't likely be able to move it very fast.

Ferryman's Fee

Level	Activation Time	Maximum Water Roughness
1	15 minutes	Still pond
2	5 minutes	Running water
3	1 minute	Lapping waves
4	1 round	Choppy seas
5	1 action	Rough seas

Ghost

Speed: 2
Duration: Concentration (Variable)
Dispositions: *Ailin', aura o' death, bad eyes, curious, haunted, lyin' eyes, night terrors, pacifist, thin-skinned*

The character and any objects he wears or carries can become insubstantial at will. He can walk through walls and ignore physical attacks. Of course, he cannot affect the physical world without materializing, at least temporarily.

A "ghosted" undead is not invisible, however. He appears just as a solid as ever, right up until somebody tries to grab his shoulder and winds up sticking her hand straight through his intangible form.

The amount of Wind required to remain immaterial is shown below.

GHOST

Level	Wind per Round
1	5
2	4
3	3
4	2
5	1

HELL BEAST

Speed: 15 minutes
Duration: Permanent
Dispositions: *Belongings, kemosabe, slowpoke, "the voice"*

You already know that animals don't take kindly to the presence of the Harrowed. Horses shy and buck, rolling their eyes; dogs slink away, growling or howling; cats spit and hiss, their backs arched high; cows get spooked and stampede or just tremble. They all sense instinctively what humans, with all their intelligence, just seem blind to, namely that there's a big slab of dead meat up walking around and pretending it's alive.

With all this animal aversion, it can be a might difficult for a Harrowed to get a ride. Some undead take care of that with special powers that let them command animals. (See the *varmint control* power.) Others just skip the problem altogether by reanimating an animal corpse when they have some need of a critter.

Usually, the *Hell beast* power is used to make an undead mount so a Harrowed doesn't have to walk everywhere he goes. But some Harrowed reanimate themselves some Hellish hounds or hawks or pretty much any other sort of critter they might find use for.

Rumor is that one undead bandit even has a Hell ferret he uses to slip in the windows of houses to steal things for him. The animated creatures must be natural animals, however; supernatural critters are far beyond any Harrowed's ability to raise as undead servants, even at the highest levels of this power.

Animal corpses reanimated with the *Hell beast* power are basically just critter zombies. No matter what they used to eat when alive, they crave meat now, just like their undead master. And their "life" is closely tied to that of their creator. If the Harrowed who raised them is ever destroyed, they revert to nothing more than corpses themselves. These critters can't heal any damage they take as zombies, either. Once your Hell horse has been shot all to pieces, it's time to put it down permanent-like and raise yourself a new one.

The Harrowed can command their Hell beasts with a mere thought, and the creatures hasten to obey—though they do tend to err on the side of destructiveness when there is any leeway in that command. Like other undead, they seem to have an innate hatred of life, and their meat craving drives them to kill whenever they can get away with it.

This isn't to say that it's always obvious that any particular Hell beast is undead. If the master can keep the thing's grisly diet a secret and the critter in some semblance of decent shape, the only other thing that really matters is just how long the critter lay dead before it was "resurrected."

A dog that was pecked at by vultures before being raised will certainly look horrendous. But if it was brought back only hours after death, most humans couldn't tell it from a living hound with a really nasty disposition. The only sure-fire sign is that Hell beasts always have glazed eyes and dry noses.

To keep from giving things away, many Harrowed with this power kill an animal themselves then bring it back immediately. It isn't all that difficult to hide a Hell horse's craving for fresh meat if the animal itself still looks healthy. But riding a mount into town with its rib bones peeking through its skin and maggots spilling from its dangling entrails is a dead give-away.

Of course, the animal's strange diet means the Harrowed ought to be careful in his choice of trail companions. After all, it can be difficult to explain to a wagon train of settlers why there's a cloud of flies centered around your horse's feedbag.

To bring a critter's corpse back to life this way, the Harrowed has to breathe into its nostrils, then stroke the critter until it begins breathing on its own. The process takes about a quarter of an hour.

A Harrowed with the *Hell beast* power can only animate one critter at a time, but it can be of any size or shape that he likes, as long as it's not supernatural in any way.

The Hell beast's diet isn't just for show. If a Hell beast doesn't get at least a good amount of meat to ingest each day (from about a pound for a dog to around five pounds for a horse), the thing starts to rot. Each day that it rots, it takes a wound to every one of its body parts. While the progression of the rotting can be halted in its tracks by feeding the creature what it craves, the damage from the rotting cannot be healed.

A Hell beast can't wander too far from a Harrowed before the Harrowed loses control over it. The actual distance the beast can stray from its master depends on the Harrowed's level with the power and what kind of orders the creature has.

If a Hell beast somehow finds itself outside the Harrowed's realm of influence, it's on its own. The Harrowed can no longer give orders to the beast and has no means to stop it from attacking someone to satisfy its craving for fresh meat.

If the Hell beast returns within the Harrowed's range, it can be controlled again normally. In the meantime, it's up to the Harrowed as to whether or not to continue to grant the creature-corpse the means to move around.

Hell beasts like to sneak outside their master's range, and they take the opportunity to do so at any time they can. Crafty Hell beasts like to leave the Harrowed's range, commit some acts of mayhem, and then return before the Harrowed is any the wiser.

Hell beasts are not animated by manitous, but they have some semblance of intelligence. This is limited to whatever kind of smarts could have been expected from the creature before death.

The Harrowed can retract the gift of undeath at any time that he likes, no matter if the Hell beast is within range or not. When this happens, the beast instantly goes from being undead to just plain dead.

HELL BEAST

Level	Range
1	100 feet
2	100 yards
3	1 mile
4	10 miles
5	40 miles

HELL FIRE

Speed: 1

Duration: Always on

Dispositions: *Loco, self-righteous, veteran o' the Weird West*

From Man's earliest days, fire has been both a source of comfort and an object of fear; it's a means of both purification and destruction. There's a reason why flames figure prominently in the Hells of pretty much every religion. Many supernatural beings have a love affair with the destructive power of fire. That can be as true of the Harrowed as of any abomination.

A Harrowed with this power has gained an affinity for fire and perhaps even some level of supernatural control over it. At its lowest levels, the *Hell fire* power lends its possessor some immunity from damage caused by normal flame. For each level of this power he possesses, he can subtract one wound level from any fire damage he suffers. This protective power is always in effect, even while the undead sleeps or is unconscious.

At higher levels of power, the undead can cause existing flames to ebb or flare at his command. He can even draw heat from the Hunting Grounds and hurl it at hapless (and likely flammable) victims.

Unfortunately, the power also has its negative side effects. For one thing, the possessor develops an unconscious fascination with flames of any kind.

A Harrowed who gains this power is fidgety unless there is a fire somewhere nearby, and he tends to stare blankly into the flame when nothing else holds his attention. He may even forget himself and reach into the fire as if caressing it. At times, firelight seems to flicker deep within his eyes.

By the same token, fire is affected by the moods of the owner of this power. Camp fires, candle flames, and such tend to burn dimmer and slower when he is depressed or weary. When he is energetic—whether angry, happy, or just agitated—they tend to burn brighter and faster, flickering with his agitation. The result is not so obvious as to be immediately apparent to onlookers, but after a while they may begin to notice the changes in flame when the character is around.

HELL FIRE

Level Effect

1 **Flame Retardant:** The Harrowed subtracts 1 wound level from flame damage affecting him.

2 **Excite Flame:** The user can cause an existing flame (up to the size of a normal camp fire) to flare to twice its normal height (and twice its normal heat). This usually won't cause any actual damage to anyone nearby, but it can sure startle the heck out of them. Also, the Harrowed subtracts 2 wound levels from any flame damage affecting him.

3 **Calm Flame:** The user can cause an existing flame (up to the size of a normal camp fire) to dwindle to mere embers in a bare instant. Also, the Harrowed subtracts 34 wound levels from any flame damage affecting him.

4 **Summon Flame:** By touching an easily flammable material (kindling, paper, gauzy cloth, tobacco), the user can

cause it to spontaneously ignite into flame. Anyone viewing any of this must make a Fair (5) *guts* check unless there appears to be an obvious reason for the Harrowed's ability (say he's posing as a stage magician). Also, the Harrowed subtracts 4 wound levels from any flame damage.

5   **Fire Blast.** With any source of fire at hand (which he can generate himself if he likes), the Harrowed can spit a gout of flame up to 20 yards. It costs Wind to do this, but for every point of Wind used (up to 6 at a time), the fire does 1d10 damage. Also, the Harrowed subtracts 5 wound levels from any flame damage affecting him.

HELL WIND

Speed: 5
Duration: Concentration
Dispositions: *Big 'un, death wish, slowpoke, thick-skinned*

Among some cultures, the phrase, "It'll be a cold day in Hell," doesn't make much sense. That's because their version of Hell features freezing cold and bitter winds instead of fire and brimstone.

The *Hell wind* power reflects that chill sort of Hell, rather than a hot one. The power opens a small portal to the Hunting Grounds, high up in the air, through which a whirlwind of deadly cold air invades the world that we like to think of as our own.

Not only does this whirlwind stir up every bit of dust and grit in the local vicinity, it also leaches the heat out of the area, dropping the temperature to just a bit under freezing (assuming it's not already there). As a result, the air fills with clouds of dirt and stinging ice particles, and living things may suffer Wind damage from the unexpected cold. Characters who pass out in these conditions can freeze to death if the Harrowed maintains the power for long enough (see *The Quick & the Dead*).

At higher levels, the undead who summons the *Hell wind* can ride it around, at least to some extent. See the table below for all the gory details.

While the whirlwind itself is only a few yards in diameter at the base, the other effects of a *Hell wind* cover an area with a radius of 10 yards per level of this power that the Harrowed possesses.

HELL WIND

Level   Power

1   **Icy Wind:** Everyone within the local vicinity loses 1 point of Wind per combat round within the *Hell wind's* radius and suffers a penalty of –2 to all actions.

2   **Bitter Wind:** As above, and any attacks that hit inside the wind inflict 1d8 points of Wind per wound level (rather than the normal 1d6), due to the stinging cold, while range modifiers occur at half the listed distance.

3   **Blinding Wind:** As above, except everyone within the wind's area of effect suffers –4 to all actions, and visibility is limited to 2 yards.

4   **Lifting Wind:** As above, and the Harrowed can ride the twister like an elevator, up or down at a speed of 5 yards per combat round, but he cannot take any other actions while concentrating on this. It can also safely catch someone in midair.

5   **Ride the Whirlwind:** As above, and the Harrowed can travel cross-country on the back of the twister, at Pace 20, but he cannot take any other actions while concentrating on this. The Pace cannot be picked up by any means, nor can the Harrowed "run" with the whirlwind. Keep in mind that with the visibility so low, the Harrowed often has a hard time seeing exactly where he's going while riding atop the wild whirlwind.

INFEST

Speed: 1
Duration: Concentration
Dispositions: *Ailin', mean as a rattler, randy, unnatural appetite*

Rattlesnakes, scorpions, and spiders aren't the only creepy-crawlies a feller has to keep on the lookout for in the rough-and-tumble west. Get enough mosquitoes, horseflies, or ants fired up and they'll pick you to death just as sure as a rattler's bite.

Like animals, insects have spirits in the Hunting Grounds as well. The manitous have learned a few tricks to control these creatures as well.

A Harrowed with this power can control swarms of small biting, stinging, insects. The insects aren't summoned from thin air, so they must be available in the current locale.

To use the power, the Harrowed chooses a target in sight and begins to concentrate. At first a few insects will flock to the target. Within seconds, a few more will come, and then more, until the prey is eventually surrounded by a milling crowd of buzzing insects and lines of biting ants and beetles crawling up his trousers.

Each round (even if the target leaves the Harrowed's sight), the insects continue gathering until the Harrowed stops concentrating (in fact, they'll keep attacking the prey even once it's dead—a good way to dispose of bodies!)

The first round a target is infected has no effect. In the second, he suffers a -1 to all his actions. In the third, he suffers a further -1, and so on, up until the total penalty is -5 in the 6th round of concentration.

At this point, enough insects are swarming over the poor sod to cause damage. Starting in the 7th round, the victim must make a *Vigor* roll (don't forget the -5 modifier) versus the swarm's collective Strength, as determined by the Harrowed's power level.

The difference is the amount of Wind the victim suffers that round.

The only way for the victim to stop the infestation is to jump in water or kill the Harrowed who's tormenting him.

It's a slow death, but it's a sure one.

One more thing. Being undead, some clever Harrowed with this power actually gather insects and store them in their bellies. That way they always have a supply of creepy-crawlies on hand should they wish to use their power.

INFEST

Level	Swarm Strength
1	1d6
2	2d6
3	3d6
4	4d6
5	5d6

JINX

Speed: 1
Duration: Special
Dispositions: *All thumbs, bad luck, death wish, grim servant o' death, loco, night terrors*

Some Harrowed court Lady Luck as a mistress. They figure that since they've cheated death once, they must be charmed somehow. Of course, most folks would consider that a danged foolish notion. Their situation doesn't seem all that lucky considering just how ugly and disgusting undeath can be.

Still, even if the little lady doesn't exactly smile on the Harrowed, she can sometimes be coaxed to frown upon their enemies. Those who cross the undead often find themselves at her less-than-tender mercies.

That's what the *jinx* power is all about. *Jinx* allows a Harrowed to cause his enemies bad luck, straight and simple. The greater the Harrowed's power level, the worse the luck the hero's foes suffer.

All uses of the *jinx* power require an opposed *Spirit* roll against the target of the jinx. If the Harrowed is unsuccessful, his power has no effect on his target and the Harrowed loses 1d6 Wind (Fate really doesn't care to have itself trifled with).

The actual effect of the power is up to the Marshal, who must make the call depending on the situation and just how powerful the *jinx* happens to be.

The effects of a *jinx* don't just materialize out of thin air, of course. It's up to the Marshal to come up with what the *jinx* does, as well as some kind of rationale for it, however much she might have to stretch to make it realistic. It doesn't have to be a likely set of circumstances, but it does have to encompass something that's possible.

JINX

Level	Power
1	**Minor Inconvenience:** The opponent suffers a distraction of some sort that causes him a -1 penalty to any rolls made for one entire combat round (about 5 seconds if not in combat rounds.)
2	**Real Inconvenience:** As above, but the penalty is -2.
3	**Major Inconvenience:** As above, but the penalty is -3.
4	**Bad Luck:** The target suffers some minor mishap. Perhaps a round in his weapon is a dud or he trips and falls. Whatever the circumstance, the target loses one action recovering. The results of this are never directly fatal (although they may result in some real problems for the victim).
5	**Calamity:** The target loses his next 1d4 actions due to some troubling if not downright embarrassing setback. Maybe a gunman's weapon jams, a critter knocks itself silly after an attack, or a mounted foe's horse rears unexpectedly. The results are rarely fatal unless the circumstances demand it.

LUCK O' THE DRAW

Speed: 1
Duration: 1 casting
Dispositions: *Arcane background, friends in high places, luck o' the Irish*

The flip side of *bad mojo* is *luck o' the draw*. This power is used by those rare Harrowed hucksters to aid their own hex-casting attempts. Again, the Harrowed's manitou talks to the manitous hovering about, but this time both belong to the same person. The host forces his own demon to convince the other manitous to

POSSE 41

cooperate. Only a manitou could ever convince another manitou to be more generous than normal with the powers it grants a huckster.

Using the power couldn't be simpler. The huckster merely casts a hex and draws as many extra cards as he has power levels.

These cards all count toward building a hand for the hex. Sometimes the manitous hanging about can fool even one of their own, however, so a Joker drawn in these extra cards is just as dangerous.

MAD INSIGHT

Speed: Instantaneous
Duration: 1 invention roll
Dispositions: *Arcane background, friends in high places, loco*

If your Harrowed's a mad scientist, her manitou can make her entirely looney.

Just as *luck o' the draw* can help a Harrowed huckster with his hex-casting, so can the *mad insight* power help a Harrowed mad scientist with her inventing. The manitou for the Harrowed side of the character gets together with the manitous hanging around her mad scientist side, to help convey a mad inventive vision more clearly into her mind.

The result can be either inventive genius or sheer insanity, depending upon the mood of the manitou at the moment. There's simply no predicting how they're going to react when presented with the latest attempt at a blueprint for a new device.

In game terms, whenever drawing cards for an invention, the mad scientist gains one extra card for each level of this power that she possesses. Note that she *must* draw these extra cards; once the power has been gained, there is no choice in the matter.

The extra cards make it easier to gain success with the invention, of course, but they also increase the character's chance of drawing a Joker and gaining a dementia. But what else would you expect from a Harrowed mad scientist?

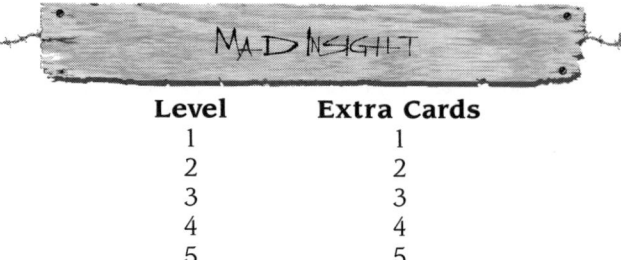

Level	Extra Cards
1	1
2	2
3	3
4	4
5	5

MARKED FOR DEATH

Speed: 1
Duration: Variable
Dispositions: *Arcane background, grim servant o' death, vengeful*

The dead are a merciless bunch of bastards. Get one riled up enough and he'll sacrifice his own flesh to make sure yours gets cooked.

Marked for death works very simply. The Harrowed nominates a target within sight, makes some sort of gesture that the victim can see.

If the Harrowed wins a contested *Spirit* roll (to which he can add his power level), the victim is marked for death. This prevents the target from spending Fate Chips to negate damage. Dirty, eh?

The drawback is that Fate lies outside even a manitou's domain. To manipulate it, the creature and its host must each make a sacrifice. In this case, Fate Chips can't be spend to save the Harrowed's kiester either.

On the plus side, the Harrowed can drop the mark whenever he chooses, although not once an attack hits him.

MIMIC

Speed: Instantaneous
Duration: Special
Dispositions: High *disguise* Aptitude, *kemosabe, loco, lyin' eyes*

Why just be yourself when you can actually be yourself and so much more?

Since much supernatural power springs from the Hunting Grounds in some form or another, a Harrowed with *mimic* can force his manitou to duplicate a power he has just witnessed and recast it himself. This includes huckster hexes, other Harrowed powers, coup powers, and even black magic, but not miracles or favors.

To mimic a supernatural ability, the Harrowed must simply beat the original user (whom he has just seen employ the power) in a straight-up contest of *Spirits*.

Once that is accomplished, the Harrowed can use his new ability exactly as the being he stole it from. Even his "skill" level in using the power (if there is one) is the same as that of the person with the original power. If a cultist cast a *bolt o' doom* with a *faith* value of 3d6 and a power level of 2, the Harrowed uses the same.

Of course, if the ability has a chance of backfiring, such as a huckster's spell, the Harrowed's stolen ability may backfire on the Harrowed as well.

In other words, treat the Harrowed character as if he had exactly whatever ability it is that he steals.

Stolen abilities can be held up to a number of hours equal to the Harrowed's level in the power. When the character wishes to release it, the power is cast out with a speed of 1.

Certain powers that come directly from the Reckoners (usually only granted to particular kinds of abominations) cannot be *mimicked*. The Marshal can use this convenient excuse to outlaw stealing certain powers she doesn't want stolen. Sorry, partner.

Stealing someone else's thunder is difficult for the manitou inside the Harrowed. Whenever the manitou is forced to pull this particular trick, the spiritual backlash from the Hunting Grounds causes the Harrowed damage. Exactly how much damage is inflicted depends on the host's *mimic* power level This damage is a spiritual blast straight to the guts, so it can harm or even kill a Harrowed.

The damage is suffered when the power is used, not when it is stolen. If the power isn't used before the time limit expires, it slips through the Harrowed's fingers. In this case, the Harrowed suffers no damage at all, since the net effect is nil.

When a Harrowed *mimics* a power, he can only use it once. If he wants to steal it again, the power has to be used in his presence again. He can't *mimic* it again from memory.

Powers that friendly characters (like fellow members of the Harrowed's posse) use can also be *mimicked*. However, the Harrowed still has to win at a contested *Spirit* roll. The friendly character can't just grant the Harrowed permission to copy the power. It's always a struggle.

MIMIC

Level	Damage per Use
1	2d10
2	2d8
3	2d6
4	1d6 Wind
5	1 Wind

NIGHTMARE

Speed: 1 minute
Duration: Special
Dispositions: *Heavy sleeper, night terrors, squeamish, ugly as sin*

Dreams take place in the "Happy" Hunting Grounds. Nightmares take place in the Hunting Grounds, and there isn't anything "happy" about them.

One of the manitous' duties in the spirit world is to torment dreamers. A Harrowed who forces his demon to give him this power can use these dark dreams to trouble a living mind. With enough practice, he can even deliver specific images to a victim.

For the power to work, the undead has to lock eyes with the intended victim for a bare instant, just long enough to make an opposed *Spirit* test. If the Harrowed succeeds, the *nightmare* works. Otherwise, the Harrowed cannot attempt to use his power on this victim again until he has slept. The target is none the wiser nor worse for wear, however.

When the power works, the victim doesn't actually realize what has happened. There is just a moment of meeting a stranger's stare, an instant of strange uneasiness, and then things return to normal—until the nightmares start, that is.

At lower levels of the power, the undead simply inflicts a case of *night terrors* on the chosen target (see the *Deadlands* rulebook for more in this Hindrance). As his power level increases, the nightmares become worse and worse until they can actually be inflicted in the middle of the day on wide-awake victims.

In such cases, the message is transmitted immediately, consuming the target's complete attention for a single action or longer if not in a combat situation. Of course, the corresponding nightmares don't take place until the victim beds down for the night.

The Harrowed can also appear in the sent nightmare or vision and deliver a message. The undead doesn't really join in the nightmare, though. Rather, in the moment of eye contact, he plants an image that works its way into the dream or vision on its own at an appropriate moment.

In game terms, the Harrowed player describes to the Marshal how the undead's image appears in the dream, and she explains the intended message. The message can include all sorts of special effects as well, certainly more than just a floating head spitting out some words.

The Marshal decides how the victim reacts, based upon the individual's personality and the image and message described.

Naturally, an undead can't just go around planting nightmares in everyone he meets. For one thing, people are bound to start talking, and once they begin comparing notes and find that the same hombre is appearing in all their dreams, that Harrowed is liable to find a lynch mob looking for him. For another, the power can be used only once per day.

The Harrowed can use this power to send messages to friendly sorts too, but no matter what the intentions may be, the messages are always accompanied by the nightmare. The Harrowed can inflict lesser nightmares if he likes, but he is then restricted to sending shorter messages.

Level Power
1   **Restless Night:** Inflict a one-time instance of *night terrors* on a victim.

2   **Bad Dreams:** Plague a victim with *night terrors* for 2d6 nights.

3   **Recurring Nightmare:** As above, and visit the victim's nightmare to deliver a message once during that period.

4   **Daymare:** Transmit a waking nightmare by means of a daydream, causing an Onerous (TN 7) *guts* check and loss of sleep for one night. The Harrowed may deliver a message in that vision.

5   **Waking Terror:** Transmit a waking nightmare by means of a daydream, causing a Hard (TN 9) *guts* check. If the roll is failed, the victim suffers from *night terrors* until he complies with any orders given to him in the vision the undead delivers.

POSSESSION

Speed: 3
Duration: Permanent until voluntarily ended
Dispositions: *Curious, greedy, haunted, hankerin', high falutin', loco, mark o' the devil, nerves o' steel, yearnin'*

Some people are so filled with empathy they can't bear to see someone else suffering. Then there are those villainous souls who view other people as mere objects to be used and then discarded like burnt beans. Harrowed of this type are prime candidates for developing the *possession* power.

This power doesn't merely force a course of action upon the victim. It replaces the victim's personality with that of the *possessing* undead. The original personality is repressed, and the new one completely controls the possessed body. Memories and skills of the possessed are not available to the possessor. Also, all dice rolls by a Harrowed *possessing* someone suffer a penalty of -4 due to clumsiness with the foreign body. This penalty is reduced by 1 point each week the Harrowed spends "attuning" himself to a particular body.

When the *possession* is initiated, the Harrowed and his victim make an opposed test of *Spirits*. The Harrowed adds his level with this power to his roll; the victim adds her *faith* to her roll. If the Harrowed wins, the victim is possessed until control is relinquished. If the victim wins, the Harrowed can never again try to *possess* that person.

Before a *possession* can be initiated, the Harrowed must actually enter the victim's body. This must be done by means of the *soul flight* power.

Undead with 3 or more levels of *possession* have a different option for entering the victim's body. They can sever one of their own body parts—a hand or an eye—and force it down the victim's throat. That physical presence is then enough for them to attempt possession of the victim, and they can actually maintain control of their own body and the victim's at the same time, although with a -2 penalty to all actions attempted by either (or any) of the bodies.

Theoretically, an undead could possess up to four bodies this way—one for each eye, and one for each hand—but each possession attempt would suffer the cumulative penalties of the previous possessions. Of course, the mutilated original body won't be a lot of fun at shindigs either.

As a final note, Harrowed with this power should beware the exorcist. An exorcism can drive his spirit out. This doesn't put the Harrowed to rest though, as his spirit can still flee back to its own body.

For a merged possessor (one that rammed a hand or eye down some poor sodbuster's throat), this means the appendage is coughed out of the host where it will likely be burned if caught.

If the possessor used *soul flight* to get into the host, then the spirit is kicked out. When this

happens, the Harrowed's concentration is considered broken, and his spirit returns to his own body right away.

RECONSTRUCTION

Speed: Variable
Duration: Special, permanent
Dispositions: *Bad luck, degeneration, heroic, nerves o' steel, overconfident, stubborn, thick-skinned, tough as nails*

Even for the undead, time heals all wounds. Those Harrowed pressed for time can use the *stitchin'* power to heal more quickly, but sometimes healing just plain isn't enough for the job at hand (so to speak).

Even *stitchin'* won't restore a missing arm or eye. For jobs like that, you need *reconstruction*.

The time it takes to reconstruct a missing body part depends on its size and the undead's level in this power. Each pound of flesh (or portion thereof) to be reconstructed requires one "unit" of time. The unit of time can range from one action to one week, as listed on the table below.

For example, a Harrowed with level 3 in this power could regrow a missing hand (assuming it was roughly one pound) in 3 months. A missing arm could require over three years of that Harrowed's time. An entire body (neck down) would take a lot longer.

This *reconstruction* requires energy, of course. The meat still has to come from somewhere, so the Harrowed must eat a pound of raw meat for every pound he needs to regrow. The Harrowed can absorb this, even if it doesn't have a belly.

Reconstruction

Level	Time Unit
1	1 year
2	6 months
3	3 months
4	1 month
5	1 week

Relic

Speed: Special
Duration: Special
Dispositions: A trademark piece of equipment, *belongin's*

Some folks invest more than money in the equipment they use. Some of them put a little piece of their soul into their favorite belongings as well.

A *relic* is just that—an item charged with supernatural energy. These come into being when they are bound closely to an event of momentous importance. The death of a hero and her subsequent resurrection as a Harrowed is frequently more than enough cause to give rise to a relic.

This isn't really a power so much as a bond with a magical item of some sort. These items are simply part and parcel of the hero they once belonged to. A gunslinger's trademark pistol is just as much a part of his life as a Georgian's distinctive Southern drawl or a huckster's curiosity for the unknown.

Only highly prized items can become relics. If a gunman uses different weapons all the time, it isn't likely one would become a relic. A gunfighter who used nothing but his prized Buntline, however, is due for an upgrade to his favorite shooting iron should he come back from the grave.

The exact power of the relic is always up to the Marshal. There's no way in Hell we could come up with a chart that could cover every possibility, so we're leaving it up to you and your Marshal's imaginations.

As your hero gains levels in this power, his relic becomes more and more powerful, useful, or helpful as well. Again, the Marshal must determine exactly what that means, but here are a few pointers.

First, a relic sometimes merely mimics another power, spell, or ability. If it resembles another Harrowed power, the relic's power level would correspond to the levels of the imitated power. If your gaucho is a master of the whip, for example, she may come back to find her trusted weapon now allows her to use the *soul eater* power.

Gunslingers and their prized weapons are also good targets for this power. Each level might add another die of damage to bullets fired from the favored gun. Or the power might add accuracy in the form of pluses to hit.

Not all relics need be weapons. A Harrowed muckraker with an *Epitaph* camera may simply find that it can now take better, faster pictures. Or perhaps it sees more than the human eye, and when the pictures develop, there is some clue as to the muckraker's future.

For a blessed, maybe her family bible now adds bonuses to any miracles she casts. Or maybe it acts as a permanent *protection* to all those within a few yards.

A mad scientist might find that the old tool box his father gave him is irreplaceable. In fact, it adds bonuses to his *tinkerin'* rolls equal to its power level.

The possibilities really are limitless. If you have a neat idea for your Harrowed's relic, talk it over with your Marshal. Together, the two of you should be able to come up with something that is powerful and useful, but still balanced enough that it doesn't ruin the campaign and, more importantly, overshadow your character.

Check out some of the relics in *The Quick & the Dead* for some more examples.

Relics created with this power don't usually have a taint unless they were used in some decidedly evil way.

The real drawback with relics is that they can be taken away from their owners. If that

POWERS

Harrowed's Buntline is stolen, it's gone, along with the Harrowed's access to its powers.

Worse yet, a Harrowed's relic can be used against him. For some strange reason, a relic can always kill the person it was empowered by. A pistol that shot its own Harrowed maker in the gut, for instance, could kill him again even though it's not a head shot.

Such is the way of the mad Hunting Grounds where these awesome artifacts were reforged.

Also, relics, being supernatural in nature, can hurt any Harrowed normally. The relic doesn't even have to literally make contact with a Harrowed to do damage, though, as long as the relic is closely involved in the attack. For instance, bullets fired from a gun relic would be made supernatural by the nature of the weapon firing them, and they'd hurt a Harrowed just like a regular slug would injure the average cowpoke.

If the relic is ever truly destroyed (not just lost or stolen), then the Marshal can permit the Harrowed to work on recreating that relic. The Harrowed has to have something nearly identical to the destroyed relic to start with. Then he has

to use it whenever the opportunity arises (pretty much constantly) until it starts to absorb powers from the undead's manitou.

This process can take up to a month per level of the power to be instilled in the object. Again, the length of the process is really up to the Marshal. If the Harrowed is involved in all sorts of adventures in which he uses the item, then the time should be cut a great deal shorter.

RIGOR MORTIS

Speed: 1
Duration: 1 hour
Dispositions: *All thumbs, degeneration, geezer, lame, pacifist*

With this cruel power, an undead can inflict terrible pain upon a living victim, possibly resulting even in death. The Harrowed has to grasp bare skin for the power to take effect, which means succeeding at an opposed *fightin': brawlin'* roll, with a called shot modifier appropriate to the area being attacked with the power.

Normally, people keep pretty well covered up in the Weird West, what with gritty winds, baking sun, and all. So most of the time, the undead suffers a penalty of –6 for having to target the intended victim's head or hand. Because the target is being grasped rather than merely struck, the brawling attack itself does no damage to the target. Not that this matters much; the power itself is nasty enough to make up for it.

When the power is used at low levels, the undead's touch merely causes severe muscle cramps to the affected area. The location being grasped spasms and is rendered useless for a short while, as shown on the table below. At higher power levels, this spasming affects the entire body at once. At its highest level, the *rigor mortis* power can even induce a fatal heart attack.

RIGOR MORTIS

Level Power

1 **Spasm:** The victim suffers a momentary muscular spasm in the hit location that the undead is touching. This causes 1d6 of Wind damage, and the affected location is useless for the victim's next action. If a leg was affected, the victim falls. If an arm, any held object is dropped. If the torso, the character cannot breathe. If the head, the victim cannot speak or even think clearly.

2 **Cramp:** As above, but the damage is 1d10 Wind instead, and the affected location is entirely useless for one full combat round.

3 **Paralysis:** The affected location suffers such a severe contraction that muscles are torn, causing a heavy wound and 2d6 Wind damage. Legs and arms affected in this way cannot be used again until at least one wound level has been healed in the affected area. Head or torso paralysis results in a penalty of –4 to all dice rolls until at least one wound level in that area has been healed.

4 **Seizure:** At the undead's touch, the victim's entire body suffers cramps as described for level 2 above. The victim suffers 6d10 Wind, and his whole body

is useless for one whole combat round as he flops on the floor like a fish out of water.

5 **Death:** Regardless of what bare flesh the undead touches, the victim undergoes a traumatic heart attack. He must succeed at a fair (TN 5) *Vigor* roll or be maimed in the upper guts. Each success gained on this roll reduces the wound level by one step. Wish the poor sod luck.

SICKEN

Speed: 1
Duration: Concentration
Dispositions: *Ailin', mean as a rattler, randy, unnatural appetite*

One of the best things about being Harrowed is that the Harrowed never has to worry about many niggling things that might have affected her body while she was alive: allergies, colds, viruses, and the like. The only time anyone ever sees a Harrowed sneeze is just for fun, and when one blows his nose, it might even come loose in his hand.

Still, just because a Harrowed can't get sick doesn't mean she can't carry the disease around in her belly or her head. Of course, to become a carrier of an illness, the Harrowed must first find someone or something that's already got the illness and is still contagious. This can be more difficult than it sounds, but determined Harrowed with this power often haunt the local hospitals until they manage to find someone afflicted with some dread disease they'd like to inflict upon someone else.

To pick up a disease, all the Harrowed has to do is touch someone who already has the sickness. Holding on to it and transmitting it are two other things.

Since the Harrowed is already long past being a fertile ground for most kinds of sickness, she can only hold onto an illness for so much time. The higher the Harrowed's power level, the longer she can house the disease.

Harrowed with the *sicken* power can command the disease to attack other people, as long as they're within the Harrowed's reach. To transmit the disease, the undead must touch the target, which normally requires a successful *fightin': brawlin'* roll, at least in combat. In other situations, the Harrowed can be a lot more subtle about touching the target. A simple handshake would suffice.

The effect the disease has on the victim depends upon what it happens to be. This is entirely up to the Marshal as to the illness' symptoms and duration. After all, the Marshal has to present the Harrowed with the disease in the first place, so it shouldn't be much of a surprise to the Marshal exactly how the illness works.

Once contact has been made, the Harrowed must make a *Spirit* roll against the target's *Vigor*. If the Harrowed wins, the target catches the illness. The victim doesn't just instantly fall ill, for sure. The disease first has to incubate and then run its course.

It may be several days before the victim actually begins to feel any symptoms, and when he does he very likely isn't able to determine exactly where he picked up the illness. After all, he probably comes into contact with several people every day—or he might just have picked it up from the very air.

It's possible for the Harrowed to carry more than one disease at a time. She can have up to one illness for every level of *sicken* that she has. However, the Harrowed can only carry one mortal disease at a time, no matter how many levels of this power she may have. Additionally, mortal diseases (being already so much closer to death themselves) expire after only a quarter of the normal time.

SICKEN

Level	Disease Expires After
1	Three days
2	One week
3	Two weeks
4	Three weeks
5	Four weeks

SILENT AS A CORPSE

Speed: 1
Duration: Concentration or 1 Wind/round
Dispositions: *Bad ears, cautious, heavy sleeper, light sleeper, pacifist, scrawny, squeamish*

The dead are awfully quiet folks. When you do hear them, it's often the last sound you'll ever hear.

Moving silently over the earth is easy for a Harrowed with this power. As long as his feet are in contact with dirt, he can move without making a sound. This even works while he's wearing normal footwear like boots and the like. If he's got a couple of tin buckets on his stompers, though, he's plumb out of luck.

In game terms, the Harrowed gets a bonus to his *sneak* roll while using this power. The bonus to the undead's *sneak* roll is equal to twice his power level.

Silent as a corpse won't work on floors, wood, or even stone—only dirt. Fortunately, in the Weird West, most everything that's not actually inside of a building is covered in the stuff.

SKULL CHUCKER

Speed: 1
Duration: Instant
Dispositions: *Death wish, degeneration, grim servant o' death*

There's more than one way to get "a head" in the land of the dead.

Depending on the level, the undead can cast bones with supernatural force strong enough to kill. The exact effects depend on the Harrowed's power level, as discussed below.

In all cases, thrown bones use the Harrowed's *throwin'* Aptitude, and they have a range increment of 10.

Bones don't appear out of thin air. The Harrowed has to supply them somehow. A few twisted souls with the *reconstruction* power have even hurled their own bones at their foes, knowing they could replace them later (skulls excepted for obvious reasons).

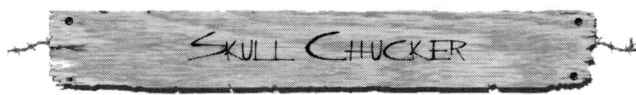

SKULL CHUCKER

Level Effect

1   The Harrowed can hurl bones up to the size of fingers, toes, and teeth with supernatural speed. This shower of shards causes 2d6 Wind to whoever it hits, and it can distract an injured opponent who doesn't make an Onerous (7) *Vigor* roll. This effect works just like the "distracted" result caused by a test of wills (see the *Deadlands* rulebook).

2   The Harrowed can throw a shower of bones up to and including ribs. These cause 3d6 damage if they hit.

3   The shower of bones can include entire skeletons. The damage from the buffeting bones is 4d6.

4   The Harrowed gains the ability to create "explosive" skulls. It takes one action to charge a skull with supernatural energy. Whenever the skull is thrown, it explodes for 2d20 damage with a burst increment of 5. The user may only create and hold one explosive skull at any time.

5   The explosive skull may now be left to explode on its own as a sort of trap. The conditions for triggering the skull must be written in blood on the side of the skull. This takes about one minute. The user may only have one explosive skull at his disposal at any time (this also mean he can't have one each from level 4 and 5).

SLEEP O' THE DEAD

Speed: 1
Duration: 2d12 hours
Dispositions: *Clueless, geezer, heavy sleeper, , pacifist, tuckered*

Manitous, being the demons of dreams, have something of a talent for getting mortals to sleep.

Harrowed with this power can tap into the manitous' abilities to send a victim straight to the Land o' Nod with a single touch to the forehead. Even Harrowed and other undead who still have something of their mortal soul inside are affected.

Such a power can make for a quick way to end a fight, and without much in the way of bloodshed. At least until the Harrowed gets around to having his way with the sleeping soon-to-be victim.

Taking a snooze while dealing with a manitou-infested corpse isn't the best way to reach retirement age. Sure, it's not exactly fair to blow away someone in their sleep, but manitous have never been known for their sterling sportsmanship. That's not likely to change real soon.

If the target resists being touched, the undead must make a called shot to the head with a *fightin': brawlin'* roll. This attack can do damage as normal, if the Harrowed wishes (talk about knocking someone out with a single blow), or she may decide to make the attack just a simple touch.

As the victim is touched, he and the Harrowed must make an opposed *Vigor* versus *Spirit* roll. The undead agent of slumber may add his power level to this roll.

If the target's *Vigor* result ties or is higher than the Harrowed's *Spirit* roll, the target resists and there is no effect.

If, on the other hand, the Harrowed's *Spirit* total is higher than the victim's *Vigor* roll, the victim falls to sleep immediately. He will not wake for hours unless he suffers some sort of physical pain (of the non-fatal kind—otherwise the issue of when the victim might wake up again is most likely academic) or is violently roused by means of shaking or slapping. Otherwise, the victim remains asleep for a total of 2d6 hours.

SOUL EATER

Speed: 1
Duration: Special
Dispositions: *Ailin', arcane background, aura o' death, greedy, grim servant o' death, hankerin', mark o' the devil, sand, self-righteous, unnatural appetite, yearnin'*

Soul eater is one of the undead's cruelest weapons. The Harrowed grasps her victim by the throat and squeezes as if trying to choke him. In a heartbeat, the victim's life force is drawn from his body and consumed by the Harrowed's hungry manitou.

A *soul eating* undead must first get at least one raise on an opposed *fightin': brawlin'* roll against the target. When she does, she has the victim by the throat and can begin to drain out his life force.

POWERS

Performing the actual draining is an opposed *Spirit* roll between the Harrowed and the victim. (If the manitou is in charge, use the manitou's *Spirit* in place of the Harrowed's.)

If the Harrowed is successful, the difference between the two *Spirit* rolls is the amount of Wind the Harrowed drains if successful. Otherwise, nothing happens.

The Harrowed can use the stolen life force to revitalize herself in some way. As her skill in the power grows, she has more options to choose from. The amount of Wind the power steals is determined by the level of the power the Harrowed is using.

The Harrowed can never hold more Wind that she normally has (she can't have more Wind than her Wind statistic). She can still steal Wind, though, even if she doesn't strictly speaking need it for herself at all.

Excess stolen Wind fades away immediately and cannot be stored for later use. The Harrowed can keep stealing Wind after a victim reaches negative Wind, right up until the hapless sodbuster dies.

Soul Eater

Level Power

1   **Restoration:** Stolen Wind restores the undead's missing Wind on a 1-for-1 basis.

2   **Enhanced Restoration:** Stolen Wind restores the undead's missing Wind on a 1-for-2 basis.

3   **Regeneration:** Every 5 points of stolen Wind regenerates a wound level in one area.

4   **Enhanced Regeneration:** Every 3 points of stolen Wind regenerates a wound level in one area.

5   **Bolster:** Every 5 points of stolen Wind raises the undead's *Strength* by one step. A step of the stolen *Strength* is lost every 10 minutes until it eventually returns to normal.

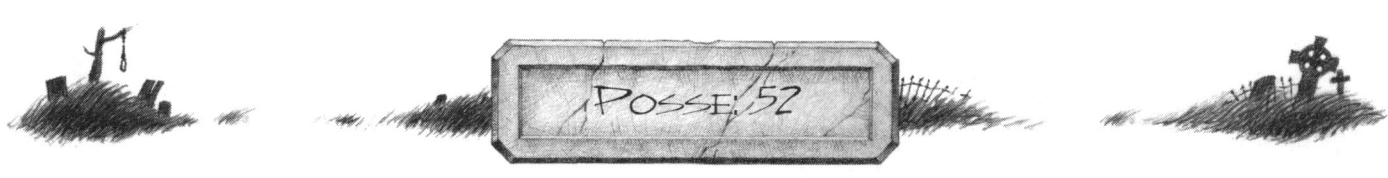

SOUL FLIGHT

Speed: 2
Duration: Concentration
Dispositions: *Ailin', angst, arcane background, geezer, haunted, heavy sleeper, keen, loco, night terrors, sense of direction*

Death has a way of detaching a person's spirit from her body—permanently. After a Harrowed manages to recover her spirit, she can sometimes let it loose again, but this time under some kind of control.

By means of this power, an undead can loose her spirit from her body and briefly travel the world as a spirit.

Soul flight is useful for scouting and spying, but for very little else. The soul of the Harrowed is completely invisible and intangible during this travel, and it cannot affect the real world in any way. It can pass through solids, however, and can hear and see just fine. With the exception of the *possession* power, other powers, spells, and abilities are lost while the undead is in this form.

Still, two Harrowed engaged in *soul flight* can see and speak with each other, although they can't affect each other in any other way. That makes the power potentially useful as a means of long-distance communication if a time and meeting place is coordinated ahead of time.

The danger of *soul flight* is that the body *and* mind of the Harrowed are unprotected while his soul is away. Others can destroy the body if they can find it, but worse, the manitou has a prime opportunity to take control while the human host is away.

If the manitou decides to take control of the Harrowed's body while he's gone, there's nothing he can do about it. Don't bother making a Dominion check, though the insidious varmint must still spend a chip as usual (the Marshal knows what we're talking about, partner).

The Pace of a detached soul is equal to the Harrowed's own *Spirit* die type. The level of the power determines how long the soul can stay apart from its normal resting place before it's drawn back.

Soul Flight

Level	Distance
1	1 minute
2	1 hour
3	1 day
4	1 week
5	Indefinite

Speakin' with the Dead

Speed: Variable (normally 1 hour)
Duration: Concentration
Dispositions: *Arcane background, aura o' death, big mouth, big ears, curious, death wish, gift of gab, superstitious, the voice*

Some Harrowed find it possible to speak even with the truly dead. They say that, after death, the memories a person has linger on inside his carcass, slowly decaying as the body's flesh rots away.

Questioning the dead, then, is more like browsing through a book than actually talking with a person. The information you seek may be in there somewhere, but who knows what page it's on. And considering that the book is rotting away as you read, who knows how much longer that page is going to be legible.

When a Harrowed questions the dead, no one else but another undead can hear the replies. To these damned souls, a dead voice sounds whispery and dry, sad and forgetful, as if every answer is an unimaginable effort.

To successfully question a corpse, a Harrowed must make an opposed test of his *Spirit* against the memories within that body. In game terms, this is handled just like an opposed *Spirit* test, with a random card drawn to represent the corpse's *Spirit* (unless the Marshal knows the corpse's Spirit). The Harrowed's power level determines just how old the corpse can be and still be questioned.

Success means the questioner can gain one piece of information or the answer to one specific question. Each raise garners one more piece of information.

Failure means the particular memories the Harrowed was after are already lost. He cannot ask questions pertaining to this subject again until he gains a new level in this power. He could ask other questions that get to the answer he's looking for, however.

The Marshal determines just what constitutes a piece of information, based upon the current circumstances. But keep in mind that the dead don't volunteer much of anything, and they don't really like to answer questions.

Using this power requires considerable concentration. While questioning a corpse, a Harrowed cannot do much of anything else. In order to hear the answer he seeks, the Harrowed needs silence in the area as well. (Unfortunately, this means that a body can't be questioned in a cemetery, because the rustling voices of the other dead make concentration impossible.) The inquisitor will have to dig the body up and cart it elsewhere.

The time required to do the questioning depends upon the Harrowed's power level and how long the body has been dead. Normally, a Harrowed must devote a full hour to the process for each piece of information to be gained. For each level of power the Harrowed has above that necessary for the condition of the corpse, the time is divided in half.

For example, a Harrowed with three levels of this power could gain one answer per hour from a body dead more than a week but less than a month.

A Harrowed may try to question dead beyond his normal ability, but it's difficult. First, the corpse's *Spirit* total is raised by +4. Second, and more importantly, the answer is even more vague and enigmatic than usual, being pieced together from mere fragments.

There are some problems inherent in possessing this power. For one thing, any Harrowed with this ability is constantly aware of the whispering voices of any dead in the vicinity. Passing a cemetery or crossing an old battlefield can be downright creepy. This makes it impossible for the Harrowed to rest in such a location.

There are also some serious dangers involved with questioning the dead. (But then again, the Harrowed are already walking on the dark side of existence.)

First, the living react really poorly to people digging up their friends and relatives for what they might view as some sort of supernatural ceremony. They tend to get violent about such things.

Second, nearby manitous sometimes enter a body when it's being questioned and pretend to be the memories of that person. Unless the questioner has some sort of way of seeing these manitous, he may be fooled into following false information. The Marshal will be especially prone to pull this little stunt if you go bust on your *Spirit* roll.

LOSTON-97

SPEAKN' WITH THE DEAD

Level	Time of Death
1	1 week
2	1 month
3	1 year
4	1 decade
5	1 century

SPIDER

Speed: 1
Duration: Concentration or 1 Wind/round
Dispositions: *Fleet footed, level-headed, mark o' the devil, scrawny, sense of direction, unnatural appetite, stubborn*

This eerie power allows a Harrowed to cling to walls and ceilings like a spider. The ability requires concentration, so while using it, the undead must spend Wind to maintain it and complete any complex actions. Still, it can be extremely useful when a rope or ladder isn't handy, or when the character wants to hide, and the only out-of-sight spot is on the ceiling.

A Harrowed high on a wall or ceiling should be careful not to start a fight. If she suffers a wound, her concentration is instantly broken, and then she's got to contend with falling (and landing) as well.

The level of the *spider* power determines how much weight the undead can bear without losing hold of the surface and falling. (See "Carrying a Load" in the *Deadlands* rulebook.) The Harrowed can always support his own weight, plus normal clothing and a personal weapon or two.

SPIDER

Level	Additional Weight
1	None. The character cannot cling to a ceiling, only to a wall.
2	None, but the hero can cling to a ceiling.
3	None on a ceiling; a light load on a wall.
4	A light load on a ceiling; a medium load on a wall.
5	A medium load on a ceiling: a heavy load on a wall.

SPOOK

Speed: 1
Duration: Instantaneous
Dispositions: *Angst, haunted, mean as a rattler, "the stare," veteran o' the Weird West, "the voice," ugly as sin*

This power gives a Harrowed's target a glimpse into the twisted corridors of the cadaver's dark soul.

It ain't a pretty sight.

The Harrowed draws upon the power of the manitou within to add a creepy element to her voice, appearance, and sheer presence when interacting with someone the Harrowed is trying to impress. This is an opposed test of wills between the Harrowed's *overawe* and the target's *guts* check.

Besides the normal test of wills results, a target who loses this contest must also roll on the Scart Table. The level of the Harrowed's power determines the number of dice the victim must roll on the Scart Table.

SPOOK

Level	Scart Dice
1	1d6
2	2d6
3	3d6
4	4d6
5	5d6

Stitchin'

Speed: Special
Duration: Permanent
Dispositions: *Bad luck, degeneration, heroic, nerves o' steel, overconfident, stubborn, thick-skinned, tough as nails*

Undead can heal themselves faster than ordinary folks. The manitous inside them draw supernatural energy from the air around them to stitch up their holes and keep them looking awful pretty. As pretty as a warmed-over, strutting corpse can get, anyway.

Stitchin' allows undead to regenerate their wounds even faster than the Harrowed normally can. The rate at which they do so depends on the level of the power. The time shown on the table below is how exactly often the undead with this power can attempt a healing roll.

This power can even be used to reattach severed limbs and other pieces of an hombre's body. The only trick is that the Harrowed has to be able to lay hands (so to speak) on the missing piece and hold it to his body until it heals on to his cadaver. Most Harrowed use stitches to hold themselves together until then.

Stitchin'

Level	Healing Roll Frequency
1	Every 12 hours
2	Every 6 hours
3	Every 3 hours
4	Every hour
5	Every 10 minutes

Supernatural Trait

Speed: Always on
Duration: Permanent
Dispositions: Any kind, especially already high Traits

A gunslinger with supernatural *Quickness* is deadlier than a Gatling gun. A mad scientist with paranormal *Smarts* can make an awful lot of Gatling guns, however.

This power raises any one Trait (chosen when the power is awarded or purchased) by one step per level. The power is tied to a particular Trait, though a character can have multiple supernatural Traits.

The Trait raised should somehow reflect the character's personality or past. A gunslinger might gain supernatural *Quickness*, for instance.

Trackin' Teeth

Speed: 1
Duration: Special
Dispositions: *big mouth, curious, degeneration, keen, sense of direction, stubborn, tough as nails*

The fact is that when you're dead, you sometimes have a tendency to lose body parts. Heck, some Harrowed would lose their heads if they weren't stitched to their necks with piano wire.

A character with this power can keep track of every one of his body parts, whether they're attached to the rest of his cadaver or not. This is particularly useful if he's been detached from a substantial part of himself and wants it back.

Clever Harrowed have found other uses for this power, from which comes the cryptic name. If the cadaver wishes, he can plant a substantial piece of himself in or on a thing or person and use this ability as a crude tracking device.

By "substantial," we mean a portion of your body that includes a chunk of bone, not something comparatively insubstantial like hair or a bit of rotting flesh. The most accessible pieces of bone available to any Harrowed are found framing his tongue, and this is what they usually use.

After all, you've got 32 teeth, and you're hardly going to miss one of them. With dental hygiene being what it is in the Weird West, few people are going to pay any attention to a cowpoke who's missing a few of his ivories. He'd be more rare if he had them all where they rightly belonged. With this in mind, of course, many Harrowed may not have 32 teeth to start with, having lost a few in their living days.

The level of the power determines how far away from the Harrowed the missing piece can be and still be tracked. If the piece ever moves out of range, the Harrowed loses track of it, but he can pick it up again if the piece returns within his range.

Once the piece is removed from the Harrowed, it immediately begins to rot. This is another reason bone must be used. Fleshy bits tend to fall apart a bit too quickly, and the smell of rotting meat can be a quick tip-off to anyone the piece is supposed to be hidden from.

The level also determines how many pieces the Harrowed can track at a time. If he likes, the Harrowed can abandon a piece at any time he wants. If it's within his range at this time, he cannot sense it.

However, the Harrowed can try to pick an abandoned piece up again later if he likes, he's under his total piece limit, and the piece is within range. To do so, he must make a Hard (9) *Spirit* test with a penalty of –1 to the roll for each level of the piece's range. Trying to pick up a lost piece that's 90 miles away, for instance, would result in a –3 penalty applied to the *Spirit* roll.

If the Harrowed fails, he can try to lock onto the same piece again only after 24 hours have passed. He can try to pick up as many pieces as he likes without additional penalties to each separate roll.

Even if the piece is out of range, the Marshal should let the Harrowed try to pick up a missing piece whenever he wants. The Marshal should make this roll secretly, though, so the player can't figure out whether or not the piece is actually in range.

When tracking a piece, the Harrowed knows the direction of the piece and its range. This doesn't tell him the quickest way to get to the piece, though. If it's on the other side of the Great Salt Lake from him, he's got some hiking or sailing to do, and if it's on the wrong side of a mountain, it's up to the Harrowed to find a pass.

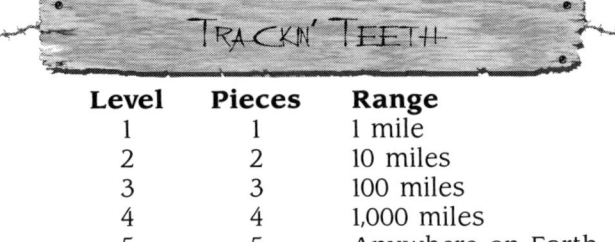

Trackin' Teeth

Level	Pieces	Range
1	1	1 mile
2	2	10 miles
3	3	100 miles
4	4	1,000 miles
5	5	Anywhere on Earth

Undead Contortion

Speed: 3
Duration: Permanent until reversed.
Dispositions: *Level-headed, sand, scrawny, tough as nails*

Some living folks are surprisingly flexible. Some are double-jointed. Some can even lay their legs across their necks, turn their feet around backwards, and contort their arms in all sorts of unnatural-looking positions that you would think would hurt like Hell. Sometimes it might seem like these folks got some kind of rubber frame inside of them in place of their skeletons. But none of these living folks can hold a candle to someone who can snap their bones together so small they can slide under a jail door.

Undead contortion allows a Harrowed to dislocate pretty much any and every bone in her body, including shoulder blades, ribs, pelvis, and even the separate plates of the skull. In a really tight spot, a Harrowed with this power can even break and crush her own skeleton.

Such contortions aren't without their price, however. In "normal" situations, the undead simply pops some bones out of their sockets. The damage this causes depends on the Harrowed's power level. Where any resulting wounds are assigned is up to the Marshal, or rolled randomly.

Damage caused in this way cannot be negated by Fate Chips.

The number of actions it takes to contort, as well as how long it takes to reassemble the body, also depends on the Harrowed's power level.

While using the power in this way, the undead suffers a –4 modifier to all rolls involving Corporeal Traits.

The above contortions should get undead through most tight spots, usually up to about the width of his own skull. That's the one bone a Harrowed doesn't want to mess with if he can help it.

But he can't always help it. If the Harrowed needs to get through a tighter spot, he's going to have to crack his own noggin. When this situation arises, the contortionist can fit through incredibly tight spaces, down to about 3" in diameter (small enough to ooze down drainpipes, by the way).

This is fairly dangerous, however, as the damage from using the power increases by an extra 2d6, and any resulting wounds are applied to the noggin. Again, Fate Chips cannot negate damage caused by one's self.

In this fractured state, the Harrowed must subtract –6 from any Corporeal rolls.

As a final note concerning *undead contortion*, the popping and snapping sounds made by the undead's joints while the power is being initiated or ended are fairly horrifying in themselves, but the end result is not at all pretty to look at either.

Most people are disturbed at the sight of a gal with her head all mushed flat and her shoulders and ribs folded down like the spines of an umbrella, sliding through an opening hardly big enough for a cat. This is at least an Onerous (7) *guts* check for anyone that happens to stumble upon a Harrowed in this state, depending on the circumstances.

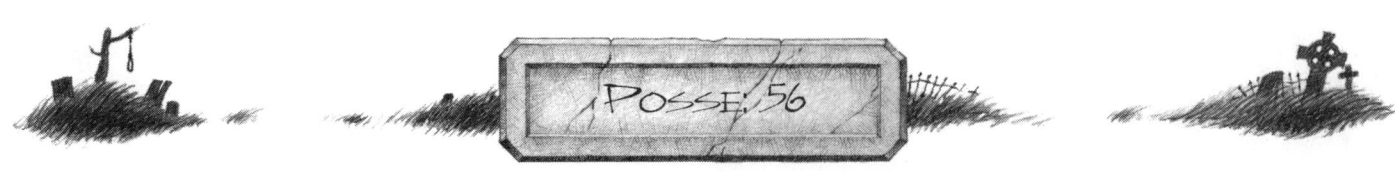

UNDEAD CONTORTION

Level	Damage	Time
1	3d10	5
2	3d8	4
3	3d6	3
4	2d6	2
5	1d6	1

UNHOLY HOST

Speed: 5 minutes
Duration: Permanent
Dispositions: *Friends in high places, grim servant o' death, law man, leadership, mark o' the devil, rank, renown*

You already know that sometimes folks come back from the dead. What you might not know is that a special few of them have been known to bring along a few of their old companions with them.

And these folks were once dead too.

The only problem is that the undead cohorts following the Harrowed about aren't Harrowed themselves. They're just plain old walkin' dead looking to make trouble in the world of mortals the best they can.

The walkin' dead are ruthless and unwavering allies, but they're also evil incarnate. They can cause a hero far more trouble than they're worth if he doesn't keep his glazed eyes on them every second. And they'll certainly do so given an ice cube's chance in Death Valley.

The hero doesn't have a mental link with his host, but when he gives them orders, they are bound to follow them. Walkin' dead are clever in their interpretations, however. Give them an inch, and they'll leave a slew of bloody corpses for a mile.

Think of them as devious children interpreting their orders in the most literal and harmful way possible.

Other than that, they're completely loyal, and won't let their champion die if they can help it. They might let him suffer and may get a good laugh out of it, but if the hero ever dies, they die too.

The level of the Harrowed's power determines how large his host can become. These zombies don't just appear, they have to be raised. Just how most Harrowed raise their host seems to vary. Some give them a kiss of life. Others simply open a coffin and say "get up." Regardless, it takes about 5 minutes to get the corpse up and moving.

UNHOLY HOST

Level	Number
1	1
2	2
3	3
4	4
5	5

UNHOLY REFLEXES

Speed: 1
Duration: Special
Dispositions: *Fleet-footed, Heroic, Level headed*

When lead starts flying, most people can't help but flinch. It takes a body a moment to react to trouble when it starts, even when you've seen it brewing. Adrenaline starts pumping through your veins, and your heart starts thumping loud enough to keep time with the piano player. Basically, you're just a palpitating wreck.

But the Harrowed don't have as much to lose as the living, so they don't hesitate as much. When you know you can survive just about everything that can be thrown at you, you can face danger a bit more calmly. That's especially true of Harrowed with the *unholy reflexes* power.

A Harrowed with this power can squeeze extra actions into a combat round. The level of the power determines how many extra Action cards the Harrowed can draw.

If the Harrowed goes bust on his *Quickness* total and gets no cards, however, *unholy reflexes* don't work either.

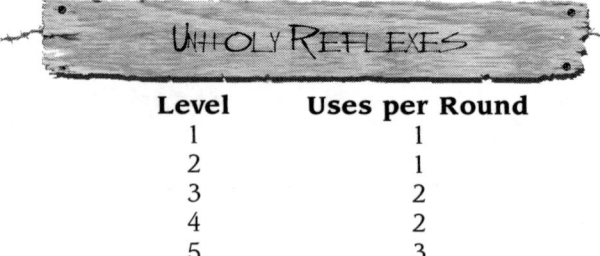

Level	Uses per Round
1	1
2	1
3	2
4	2
5	3

Voice o' the Damned

Speed: 1
Duration: Special
Dispositions: *The voice, a high ridicule*

A dead man's cackle is an eerie thing. Sometimes it sounds like wind rustling through dead leaves. Other times it is the inane babbling of a brook cold as the grave. In the end, it is always tainted with madness born of the manitou within.

This maddening power is a simple but powerful enhancement of any being's ability to taunt and intimidate their foes into cowering submission.

If the Harrowed beats his opponent in a simple contest of *Spirit*, the foe is automatically unnerved, distracted, or broken, depending on the Harrowed's power level. See the *Deadlands* rulebook for the specific effects of each condition.

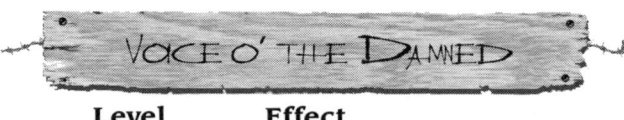

Level	Effect
1	Unnerved
2	Unnerved
3	Distracted
4	Distracted
5	Broken

Varmint Control

Speed: 1
Duration: Concentration
Dispositions: High *animal wranglin', horse ridin'* or *teamster,* shamanic powers

Normally, animals are instinctively spooked by the walking dead, but manitous come from the Hunting Grounds, where the animal spirits themselves dwell. In the course of their long existences, some manitous have learned a few tricks from the animal spirits and can control their flesh-and-blood kin on earth.

A Harrowed with this power is able to manipulate lower creatures by thought.

The animals must be within the Harrowed's sight for the command to be given and maintained. Only simple commands can be conveyed, things that could be expressed as a simple sentence, though the Harrowed need not actually speak. Examples might include: "Attack that person," or "Eat that person," or "Break that window." The varmints interpret the command as best they can and set to work.

The Harrowed can do nothing else while maintaining control, and as soon as his concentration is released, the control over the creature ends.

At lower levels, the power is limited to control of simple creatures like worms and insects, although it affects a mass of them rather than a single one. Of course, while being the target of a mass of worms commanded to eat you might be horrifying, it won't really do any damage—unless you're trapped or tied up and can't get away.

Higher levels allow the control of larger creatures, though usually only a single beast at a time. The exception is when an undead uses the power at a level below his maximum. For each level lower, he can control twice as many creatures. An undead with *varmint control* at level 5, for instance, could choose to control any of the following: one grizzly, two horses, up to four wolves, up to eight house cats, or up to 16 different swarms of bugs and worms. The same command must be given to all the creatures controlled at one time.

In any case, the power never affects creatures created by the Reckoners. Mojave rattlers and the like have no animal spirits roaming the Hunting Grounds from which the manitous could have learned their insidious tricks.

Level	Sample Creature
1	Insects, worms, and such
2	A squirrel, raccoon, or house cat
3	A wolf or dog
4	A horse or cougar
5	A buffalo or grizzly bear

WITHER

Speed: Special
Duration: Touch and concentration
Dispositions: *Ailin', geezer, lame, tuckered*

An undead with this power can accelerate the aging process by his mere touch, weakening or even wounding a victim. To initiate the power, the character must grasp the target's bare flesh (usually a hand or arm), which requires a successful *fightin': brawling* roll.

As his next action, the undead inflicts damage to the location being grasped. The Harrowed's *Spirit* rating is used as damage dice for the attack, and the target suffers Wind damage as well, as with any normal attack.

At higher levels of the power, the undead's damage rating with this power increases. Each level after the first raises the Harrowed's *Spirit* die type by one step for purposes of the *wither* power alone. Naturally, then, a Harrowed with five levels of this power can put some serious hurting on his victim.

This power can also be used on inanimate objects to make them age prematurely. Depending on the material being affected, the effects can range from rust to wither to rot or nothing really noticeable. To age something in this way requires 1 action.

It's up to the Marshal exactly how this power affects something it's applied to. It can easily be used to curdle milk or rot apples, but it likely only makes wood more brittle, rusts steel, or tarnishes silver.

Wither does not age living creatures directly. It can only affect an amount of material that can be enclosed in the Harrowed's hand. Because of this, it could never work on an entire human being.

The power could be used on tiny creatures like mice to *wither* them to death. While this might not do a lot to directly affect an opponent, it can sure go a long way toward putting a solid scare in him. Anyone witnessing something like this is probably in line for a *guts* check.

WITHER

Level	Damage	Aged
1	*Spirit*	1 day
2	*Spirit* + 1 step	1 week
3	*Spirit* + 2 steps	1 month
4	*Spirit* + 3 steps	1 year
5	*Spirit* + 4 steps	1 decade

CREATING NEW POWERS

The powers we've listed in this chapter are but a fraction of the manitous' power. Both players and Marshals should feel free to come up with new ones. Harrowed powers are meant to be closely tailored to individual characters. That's why we give you a list of dispositions with each power—to give you a guide as to what kinds of heroes are prone to particular abilities.

But we can only do so much without sneaking into your own living room and coming up with powers for *your* characters. So tailor the powers to your Harrowed heroes as you and the Marshal see fit. Consider the powers we list as guidelines or examples, not rules.

We know you've heard this before, especially if you've played other games, but it's doubly important when dealing with the Harrowed.

We're talking about the ultimate human experience here—death. Coming back ought to be pretty special. And any powers that come from that ought to be extensions of a character's personality, not just 20 new ways to kill bad guys picked out of a book. Anyone can do that.

BALANCE

When you do design your own powers, try not to just come up with new weapons. That's all fine, but anyone can say, "I shoot fireballs from my eyes that cause 10d20 points of damage."

Okay, maybe not just *anyone* would say that, but you get our point.

Instead of thinking in terms of power first, try working on it in terms of creepiness. If your new ability is truly unsettling, you're on the right path. Once you've got the other players in your group grinning and shivering, you can sit down and figure out exactly what it does for you.

THEME

All Harrowed powers draw on certain themes: death, the manitou, and the Hunting Grounds.

If you come up with a neat power, you need to try to tie it in with one of these themes. Don't just say your Harrowed can stick his arms in the air and fly. We tried that one ourselves, but in the end just couldn't see it. What does it have to do with the whole Harrowed experience? Not much. If it works for you however, go crazy.

We did work a type of flying into *Hell wind*, though. That's a good example of how you might try to retrofit an effect you're looking for to the kind of theme that fits well with *Deadlands*.

CHAPTER FOUR: DEALING WITH THE DEVIL

Harrowed Hindrances gave you the *bad* side of crawling out of your own grave. Harrowed powers are the *good* side. Now it's time to tell you all about the *ugly*.

We're talking about manitous. You can call them demons, devils, oni, or your Aunt Minnie. However you slice them, they're pure evil.

Manitous weren't put here to be the mice driving the wheel inside your hero's undead corpse so he could help his fellow folks. They have a single purpose in the Weird West—to raise Hell on earth.

Your hero must deal with the malicious little parasite every day. And here's how.

DOMINION

Dominion represents the constant struggle for control over the Harrowed's body and mind between the manitou and its host.

Harrowed characters have a number of Dominion points equal to their *Spirit*. Having more Dominion points than the other soul inside the rotting carcass doesn't guarantee control, but it helps. Each side gets to add its Dominion points to its *Spirit* roll during Dominion checks.

The details are hidden away in the Marshal's Handbook. What you need to know is you really don't want to let the thing inside your hero get out of your hero's control.

75

THE ETERNAL STRUGGLE

As we told you in Chapter Three, a Harrowed must "sleep" for 1d6 hours out of every 24. When he does, he suffers horrible nightmares and flashbacks of the troubles the manitou caused the last time it had Dominion.

Bad nights make for bad days. While the mind is still reeling from this horrible assault, the manitou takes the opportunity to try and steal Dominion at the start of every play session.

91

Both the manitou and the hero must make *Spirit* checks. The winner gains a point of Dominion for every success and raise gained over the opponent.

FEAR AND LOATHING

Some Harrowed think that once they haul their carcasses out of the dirt they can still go home. They want to be up front with their communities—or at least their loved ones—about what happened and be accepted. Unfortunately, that's just not the way it works.

The nature of the Reckoning means folks are jumping at every shadow. Even the nicest Harrowed is still a walking corpse. Mom might take you back, or your wife might run with you to Mexico, but there's no way the whole family is going to let you in through the door.

CHANGING THE RULES

We warned you in Chapter Two that we were going to change the rules on Dominion. Here's where we get down to that.

The posses of the Weird West told us the Dominion checks were too few and far between, so we all got together and came up with a new way of doing things that works even better.

Marshals, if you liked things just the way they were, then don't change them. Remember, it's your game and you can play it however you like.

Here's a quick synopsis of the changes we made. Full notes on most of these alterations can be found in this chapter, although some are in others. Anyhow, here they are in a nutshell:

It used to be you had to check for Dominion whenever a power went bust, was bought, or was raised to a new level. You don't have to worry about that anymore.

Marshals used to have to check for Dominion whenever the manitou was in control and was dealt a Red Joker. You players weren't supposed to know about that, but it doesn't matter now, since the Marshal doesn't have to worry about that anymore.

This is new: Check for Dominion every time you start a new gaming session. Each side adds its current Dominion points to its roll.

Manitous no longer have random *Spirit* values like they used to. The Marshal gets the lowdown on this in the Marshal's Handbook section. No players allowed!

Harrowed are cursed souls. Mortals cannot help but be repulsed and afraid of them. A few close friends might stick by an undead companion—for a while at least—but when word gets out to more than a few people, someone's going to start a bonfire. Only truly faithful trail companions who've seen their fair share of weirdness are going to stick by the side of someone everyone else wants to use as kindling.

A WALKING FEAR LEVEL

To reflect the loathing the living have for the undead, anyone who knows the Harrowed's awful secret must subtract -1 from any *guts* checks made while the undead is nearby. This is even true of friends who claim to have accepted their undead compatriot for what he has become.

"Nearby" usually means within sight, but even if the Harrowed is "about" the mansion the rest of the posse is investigating, the heroes are likely wondering if their cadaverous friend is lurking in the shadows, watching them with manitou-possessed eyes.

PINKERTONS, RANGERS, AND LYNCH MOBS, OH MY!

We've probably beaten this into your heads enough by now, but it bears repeating. Even if your hero somehow convinces a large group of people that he's really an all-right guy in a dead sort of way, there's still a danger in being so open about something so bizarre.

The first danger, of course, is the Pinkertons and the Rangers. If they can't recruit your character into working for them—and keeping her mouth shut—they'll spend every resource they've got to put her back in the ground. This time for good.

Similarly, any "normal" folks who find out an abomination lives in the same town as their wives and children will want to see the Harrowed burn. A couple of farmers with pitchforks might be easy pickings for an undead gunslinger, but a whole town full of angry folks with shotguns and torches can eventually send even the toughest hombres back to Hell.

Finally, the Reckoners thrive on fear. It does them little good if the undead become accepted or even commonplace, especially if they make themselves out to be something other than monsters. If your Harrowed gets too public, she might find all the powers of Hell turned loose upon her.

THE UNLIFE OF THE HARROWED

Now it's time to veer away from hard rules and talk a little about the soft, mushy side of being undead. Read on to understand a little more about how your hero might think, feel, and react to the strange new fate that's greeted him.

THE SCHOOL OF HARD KNOCKS

There's some things that can be taught, assuming a reasonable teacher and a willing student. Then there's others that can only be learned by experience. For those, Time is the teacher, and not always a very reasonable one. Worse, the student doesn't always even realize that school's in session.

Time isn't a careful instructor, by any means. It doesn't plan out how best to present information. It just throws stuff at a person till he finally learns how to duck.

That's certainly the way it is with the Harrowed. There's usually no one around when a body revives to teach the new undead the ropes. He's pretty much just got to figure it all out on his lonesome. Even those older Harrowed who could teach him a thing or two are either slaves of the manitou inside or are too busy keeping a low profile and learning their own lessons.

So what does a body learn after a few years out of the grave? Most undead go through "stages" of learning.

THE STAGES OF UNLIFE

Just like seasons in a year—or the stages of decay—a Harrowed goes through stages of development. Most go through pretty much the following stages, in the order they're given here. Still, Harrowed may go through these different stages at different speeds, some rushing right through one into another, while others may linger over a particular stage like they're never going to get past it.

STAGE ONE: DENIAL

Nobody wants to wake up in the tomb. Old, morose Poe had that pegged right, for certain. But even once a Harrowed is out of the grave, he can't even imagine that he actually *died and came back to life.*

It takes some time for the clues to assemble themselves enough that the stiff finally can't dispute it any more. It takes even more time before he starts to understand just what the situation really is and that there's a demon inside him fighting for control of his body and mind.

And even when they finally do admit they've died and come back—that their souls are bunkmates with some evil spirit—some Harrowed still seem determined to deny it in the way they act. They try to pretend that life can go on for them now the same as it did before they died. Though most can't return to their old family and friends (since those folks helped bury them!), they may try to start up again in a new locale, doing the same job they did before and trying to settle in like they're still alive.

It's as if these Harrowed think that by ignoring the problem, they can make it go away. Of course, that never works. Sooner or later, the manitou inside is going to have its way, or an old enemy is going to come looking for them, or the locals are going to catch on to their freaky, charnel stench. Somehow or another, fate is going to have its way.

At the end of this stage, many of the Harrowed look their worst. Fighting to repress the manitou, they refuse to sleep and therefore interfere with its ability to stop decay. Unconcerned with getting hurt, they take horrible chances and bear the resulting scars of damage. Drunk on power, they let their appearance go all to Hell, and they don't bother trying to hide their lack of life.

They don't care who knows they're dead and walking around, since they don't believe it themselves. At least until the local townsfolk, Pinkertons, or Texas Rangers come calling and put an emphatic point on that tip—usually right between the Harrowed's eyes.

STAGE TWO: REVELRY

Once Harrowed heroes finally work their way out of denying their doom, most start taking dark pleasure in their new superhuman abilities. For instance, it may be disturbing to get shot all to pieces—maybe even through the heart—and be right as rain again a few short hours or days later, but it's also damn comforting. Being able to come back from that kind of damage takes some of the iffyness out of mortality.

Add to this new powers like the ability to make animals do your bidding, walk across the ceiling like a spider, or draw down on some

gunfighter so fast he doesn't even see you move, and it can be downright intoxicating. Sure, it's all just another reminder that you don't belong among the living no more, but once that's been accepted, the raw power of being a Harrowed begins to sink in.

This can be a really dangerous time for an undead. It may seem to these Harrowed that all boundaries are off and they can do whatever they like. As the poet says, "Power, like a desolating pestilence, pollutes whate'er it touches."

Power corrupts. And compared to normal folk, the undead have incredible power. Worse, they gain more with the passage of time.

Often, Harrowed at this stage end up turning evil. They can't even blame it on the manitou inside. Nothing says the manitou and the undead himself can't both be monsters. And nothing says monsters can't fight each other for control. Lord help everyone when they learn to cooperate. Some people speculate that a lot of the world's legendary bogey men came about this way.

Harrowed at this stage tend to look their best. Most come into money through their adventures and buy themselves some new duds, perfumes, and enough whiskey to keep their flesh pickled. They're dead and loving it.

Stage Three: Resignation

Live long enough, and you begin to accept there are some things in life you just can't do a whole lot about. Like it or not, spring turns to summer, turns to fall, turns to winter, and back to spring. Try as you may, you can't keep the sun from setting at night just because you don't like the dark. All a person can do is decide how to cope. Life turns out to be mostly a matter of attitude.

That's pretty much the same for the undead as for anybody else. The Harrowed may be able to do some amazing things, far more so than the living, but they still have limitations, and the universe grinds on just as ignorant of them as of anybody else.

Harrowed who have survived long enough to reach this stage are past the point of reveling in their power, because they realize that in the end, it still comes down not to what their abilities are, but what to do with them. These undead are either firmly entrenched in their own evil, or they're set to do good no matter what.

In either case, they may lose control to the manitou temporarily, but they're sure to seize it

back quick. These Harrowed have either become the world's greatest heroes—unsung though they may be—or they're some of the worst villains on the face of the Earth.

With age comes subtlety, too. Unlike those undead who revel in their powers, these Harrowed use them only when necessary, and then with the precision of a watchmaker. That's the way to survive over the years.

Not many Harrowed live long enough to reach this stage, but those who do are certain to be around for a long, long time afterward. With experience comes wisdom.

Appearance-wise, the veteran undead tend to blend into the crowd. They don't want to be noticed, and they don't care much about impressions, just results. Most of the time, you won't even know they're around. But get in their way, and you might not even know what hit you. If you're lucky.

Stage Four?

It's possible there may be stages beyond those described above. A manitou's patience only lasts so long, and while the sort of manitou that creates a Harrowed may be more stubborn than most, sooner or later it's got to get tired of fighting for control, especially if it spends most of its time in the back seat of the buggy, just going along for the ride. Of course, by the same reasoning, even a human spirit has to get worn out after a while.

What happens to a Harrowed in such cases? If the manitou "gives up the ghost," does the undead's life end, or does that Harrowed find himself alive again, suddenly free of its evil influence? On the other hand, if the human spirit gives out before the manitou's, what kind of monster results?

If any Harrowed know the answers to these questions, they're not talking. But then, any undead old enough and experienced enough to know such secrets has to have been around since long before the Reckoning. There are a few, but thus far only one curious and secretive ancient undead has ventured into the American West.

Not much is known about this creature. He's known only as the Cackler. Most folks haven't even heard the rumors about this long-dead stalker of the High Plains, much less a full fragment of the legends surrounding him. As long as the Cackler's been around, it seems he's learned to cover his tracks well, even in his latest venture into the New World.

No Man's Land

Chapter Five:
Warnings from the Prospector

Howdy.

Yep, it's me again, your old pal Jenkins, the Prospector. Thought I'd drop by for a bit to see how things are going.

Well, actually, I know how things are going. I been listening, and from what I hear, you've been doin' me proud.

Congratulations. I don't have to blow your head off.

You know, though, if I'm hearing stories about you, that means others are too. So I thought I'd best take this opportunity to give you a warning of some things to watch out for.

The Texas Rangers

You're probably gettin' used to folks bein' pretty much clueless about the supernatural—when you first meet 'em, at least. Their ignorance helps you hide in plain sight, but not everyone's that naive.

The Texas Rangers, for one, is a group that's pretty danged well informed about what's goin' on in the world. They definitely know about your type, and they have a straightforward way of dealin' with the Harrowed. It's a little slogan that goes "Shoot it, or recruit it."

That means that if you run across the path of a Ranger, you'd best be prepared to do what he says or run. Don't even think about fightin' him.

First of all, Rangers are real hard-asses, and you're liable to find yourself even more dead. Second, if you do win, from that point on you've got the rest of the Rangers out gunnin' for you. 'Sides, they're just doin' their job. I don't want you shootin' no Rangers, comprende?

'Course, that don't mean I want you signing up with the Rangers. I got my own plans for the lot of you, and I don't want them spoilt by your bein' involved with those others. I 'specially don't want you spillin' the beans to the Rangers about your brother Harrowed and old Coot Jenkins.

So if you do meet up with a Ranger, I suggest runnin'. Just keep in mind the chances are he'll trail you. If you want to lose him, you need to give him something bigger to worry about. That means leadin' him to some other trouble that'll keep him occupied while you get away.

Maybe, just maybe, if you stick around to help him out of that trouble, he'll respect you enough to let you go your way. But I wouldn't count on it. Your best bet is to hightail it while he's busy and hope to put enough ground between the two of you that he gives up the chase.

THE PINKERTONS

If the Rangers are bad news for a Harrowed, the Pinkertons are worse. Their usual method o' dealin' with your sort is to shoot like Hell first, and don't ever bother getting around to asking questions.

They seem to know that some Harrowed are fightin' for good and all, but apparently they believe it ain't worth the risk to figure out whether you're one of those or not. Maybe it's just that they ain't got a Ranger's confidence in hisself to handle just about anything. Whatever the reason, you need to keep in mind that the Pinkertons are really dangerous.

If they do capture you somehow, rather than just killing you, there's some small chance that they may ship you out to this special place they got in Denver. They call it the "Star Chamber." I'm not certain what goes on there, but from what I gather, nine out of 10 Harrowed who go in come back out all crispy.

The other one in 10 comes out as a loyal agent of the Pinkertons. I've had to put down of few o' these turncoats myself after I found they were workin' as spies in my own camp.

I ain't got nothin' against the Pinkertons, y'understand, but I got somethin' cookin', and too many chefs spoil the pot.

The moral of the story is, don't let yourself be captured by the Pinkertons. Best bet is to avoid them. If you can't, take the same strategy as for dealing with the Rangers. And for God's sake, don't kill any of 'em unless you want the whole band on your tail. Just try to shake 'em if you can.

THE RECKONERS

You may have figured out by now that there are some real monsters in the world. Maybe you heard of the wendigos, for instance, or the hangin' judges?

Well, them stories are true. But there's even more to it than that. These critters ain't just workin' on their own. Pretty much every one of them serves something higher and darker, something that doesn't actually set foot on Earth itself, but that sucks up the fear these creatures harvest and puts it to even more evil uses. They're called the Reckoners, an' you definitely don't want to bring yourself to the attention of those bad 'uns. Their servants are bad enough for just 'bout anyone.

Most o' the monsters in the world don't know they serve a higher, darker power, but there seem to be a few that do. I've seen the Black Riders out Nevada way hunt down a Harrowed who got too big for his britches. And somebody got a hold of another near Lost Angels. I only found that gal's gnawed bones. An' I've heard more than one report about some kinda' "devil bulls" stompin' the Harrowed into li'l ol' greasy bits.

I can only guess that most of the monsters we've heard tell of are clueless abominations that serve the Reckoners just by goin' about their own business. But there are certain "favored" servants of the Reckoners down here on earth who know what's going on. An' these horrors see it as their duty to put a stop to anything that interferes with their master's plans.

Why? Well, you figure it out. Imagine here you are, this otherworldly badass, and you're just feastin' on the fear of the local populace when along comes this other supernatural thing, only it's "sold out" to Good.

Worse, this "Sunday School ghoul" is going around shootin' your young 'uns, and even stealin' some o' their power to use on the next monster to poke its head up.

Whaddaya expect the Reckoners to do, just sit there waiting for the "missionary monster" to ruin all their plans? 'Course not. They're probably gonna set up some sort of trap for you.

COUNTING COUP

Speaking of stealin' supernatural powers from these evil things, I've got somethin' to say about that. If you haven't figured it out by now, you can take something off the meanest varmints you put down. As they die, stand nearby and you'll find some part of their power is now yours. The folks I've been raisin' call this "countin' coup."

Be careful, though, 'cause there's always some sort of price to pay for countin' coup. That's part of why the original owner was as nasty as it was. A lot of them were involved in some sort of curse, which you're liable to pick up along with the power. So you'd best be careful about how much you go doin' this.

Now, I ain't tellin' you to ignore the monsters plaguing this Earth. And I'm not saying you don't wanna pick up something of their power when you kill them. What I am sayin' is be careful.

Take too much o' their taint an' you're liable to turn into something you don't want to be. And if you attract too much attention, you're liable to find a horde o' unholy Hell comin' after you.

FINAL WORDS

That brings me to my final warnin'. I've told you tonight 'bout a few types of people and things to be watchin' out for. Now I gotta remind you of the most dangerous.

That's me. If you thought the Rangers or the Pinkertons were bad news, they don't even compare to the trouble you'll be in for if I find out you've turned. No brag, just fact. I've got tricks up my sleeve you can't even imagine, and I've been studying your kind ever since you first appeared.

Remember, I've talked with one o' the Last Sons—the fellas that started this whole mess. I know where your power comes from and how to thwart it. I know exactly how much of a threat you Harrowed are, and I know how to destroy you if I have to.

Now, so far, you been doin' me right proud. I've got no reservations about you personally, understand. But I don't ever want you to forget just how things stand between us. I've got plans for you later on, something so difficult only a Harrowed can pull it off, and so heroic only someone who's cheated Death deserves to try.

But the time for that ain't come yet. And until that day comes, you just gotta keep what's left o' your nose clean. You understand?

All right, then. I'll be seein' you around.

THE BLESSED

There's one thing the Prospector didn't touch on that some Harrowed are going to want to know about. Or at least they're going to find out about it sooner or later, possibly (maybe even probably) the hard way.

The manitous swimming about inside of the Harrowed are evil, pure and simple. There's one class of people out there who's life's mission is to do battle with anything evil, no matter the cost. Call them priests, nuns, reverends, rabbis, or whatever you want. Collectively, we call them the blessed.

One of the greatest nemeses of Harrowed are the blessed. In general, these pious folk refuse (many would say wisely) to truck with folks that are literally vessels full of evil that might spill forth at any moment.

Some more educated blessed do manage to separate the sin from the sinner, though they're still careful around the Harrowed. After all, you never know when that manitou's going to take charge. Most folks don't like riding around with a loaded gun nestled up next to them like a snake in a bedroll on a cold night, and they're likely to want to take some preemptive action about it.

The best defense the blessed have against the Harrowed is the *protection* miracle. This works against the Harrowed even if the manitou inside is quiet as a church mouse. Even if the Harrowed is in charge, he's got a manitou squirming around somewhere inside of him, and the higher powers just aren't fooled because the evil bugger's not in the driver's seat for the moment.

Not to mention, of course, that a blessed with an *exorcism* miracle can always haul out the big guns and cast a manitou out of a Harrowed's body without so much as a goodbye kiss. If this happens, the Harrowed goes from undead straight to just plain dead with no chance to be Harrowed again.

Of course, for an *exorcism* to work, the Harrowed's got to sit still for 8 hours while the blessed works, and that's just not going to happen peacefully. Even if the Harrowed for some reason decided it was time to give up the ghost (so to speak), the manitou would do everything in its power to grab Dominion and break free.

Remember, whatever fate befalls the Harrowed strikes the manitou as well. No matter how its partner might feel, this is one mad dance the manitou is not eager to end.

NEW MIRACLE

Seeing as how the Harrowed got their own book and all, it seems only fair that we even it out a bit for those folks whose powers are granted by the countervailing forces for good.

Book o' the Dead tells you how to set the Harrowed up. This miracle shows you how to shoot them down. It's not a instant solution for undead infestations, but when facing up against them, every little bit certainly helps.

CONSECRATE ARMAMENT

TN: 7
Speed: 1 minute
Duration: Until the next sunset
Range: Touch

In their struggles against the forces of the unholy, the blessed sometimes encounter critters and people whose dark masters have granted them resistance to mundane damage (like the Harrowed, just to pick one out of the air). While certain relics may be able to harm these beings, not every preacher, monk or nun is in the habit of carrying around the sacred Sword of Joan of Arc. Fortunately, some of the blessed can invoke their patron deity's power to sanctify slightly more handy weapons when they need them.

To sanctify a weapon, the blessed character must spend a minute in quiet prayer, perhaps anointing the weapon to be blessed with holy water or the like. She must spend a chip and then make an Onerous (7) *faith* check. The chip spent determines the power of the consecration. It does not affect the *faith* check itself, although other chips can be spent in that way.

White Chip: The weapon is consecrated to work versus one specific individual, either a person or a creature. For example, "the hangin' judge haunting the trail between Houston and Amarillo" or "the Revenant." It has no supernormal effect on anyone but this particular person or creature.

Red Chip: The weapon is consecrated against one specific class of creature or individual in a specific location. For example, "the Mojave rattlers terrorizing the town of Hedricksburg" or "the vampires inside the crypt under the graveyard just down the road from the Santa Maria Cathedral."

Blue Chip: An entire class of creatures are affected if a blue chip is spent. For example "walkin' dead" or "members of the Cult of Worms."

If the blessed fails the *faith* check, the chip is still spent, so it is unwise to go about trying to cavalierly bless every weapon in sight. Prudent holy folks are not in the habit of invoking their patron's power lightly, just in case they might run into something a consecrated weapon would help against.

The consecration affects a single personal weapon, and the effects last until the next sunset after the weapon is blessed. Keep in mind that this means that if you're consecrating bullets all day long, they're not going to work that same night.

In the case of firearms, each individual bullet must be consecrated for the miracle to work. A blessed could consecrate a rifle, but it would only work against evil creatures if used like a club.

If the blessed likes, she can try to consecrate more than one weapon at a time, as long as every piece in the group is of a similar type (all knives, all bullets, all shells, and so on). In this case, simply add +2 to the target number for each piece after the first. Consecrating three weapons, for instance, would require a *faith* roll of 11 or more. If the roll is failed, none of the weapons are consecrated.

For the duration of this miracle, the blessed weapon or its ammunition (if any) can damage creatures of evil that are usually immune to normal damage. This includes walkin' dead, hangin' judges, werewolves, and Harrowed, amongst others.

Those with the *faith* Aptitude gain an additional bonus when using consecrated weapons or ammunition. When rolling damage for any hit the weapon scores on a target it's been consecrated against, the faithful may add the result of a *faith* check to the damage roll.

A blessed character can have consecrated a number of weapons or bullets equal to her *faith* active at any one time. So, Sister Cabrini (with *faith* 4) could bless up to four weapons or bullets. Blessed characters can consecrate their own weapons and can also add their *faith* dice to the damage roll as normal.

The Marshal should note that this miracle is not intended to create relics. True relics of faith are powerful objects and shouldn't be treated lightly. They certainly can't be created by heroes with something as simple as this kind of miracle. This effect is meant to give the blessed a bit of a quick fix for those situations in which they are confronted with the unholy and must deal with it directly.

THE
MARSHAL'S
HANDBOOK

Chapter Six:
Welcome to the Afterlife

Howdy, Marshal.

So your players have been reading the first section of this book, and now they're dying to play Harrowed heroes. But maybe you're just not feeling ready to kill off all their characters quite yet.

Maybe you've been thinking it over, and you're starting to wonder just how big a can of worms we've opened here. After all, Harrowed characters can do things other heroes only have nightmares about.

Sure, you say, the *Deadlands* book has rules for running undead heroes, but it starts out with the characters still alive. Under those rules, the players' characters aren't all that likely to become Harrowed. If fact, it's awfully damn rare. In each case, you as the Marshal have a lot to say about whether they die or not, and whether any of them come crawling back out of the grave—at least with those rules.

But now, with the *Book o' the Dead,* every player can start with a Harrowed character from the word "Go." You could end up with a whole posse of undead running loose across your campaign's countryside with apparently little to stop them.

No doubt about it, that's a big can of slimy worms to open. But as you'll soon discover, they're *grave* worms, perfect for horror and yours to command. You just have to remember who's the boss: you. The trick is to not let the players or their undead characters spook you.

We know that's a tall order. Especially if you have some pushy players in your group that *really* want to push the limits.

Sometimes this is a thankless job.

Somehow, week to week, you have to keep an entire posse entertained. You have to cook up just enough trouble to be challenging for them, and dish out just enough reward for the players to feel like their characters are getting somewhere, without letting them get too fat and sassy. We'd bet that so far you've been doing a fine job.

Harrowed characters just add more fuel to the fire, which means you have to keep things hopping if you don't want something to get burned. Being the Marshal's always been a juggling act. You've just got one more thing to keep in the air now.

Well, we're here to help you out. In the pages that follow, you'll find all sorts of tools and advice to help you make a Harrowed campaign the most fun your players ever had—and thoroughly enjoy yourself at the same time. Through it all, we're going to be frank with you about the dangers as well as the rewards. We're confident you can handle it all just fine.

In the end, we figure your players are going to gaze on you in awe. They'll think of you as the dark god of their tabletop, the bringer of chills and challenges, the giver of horror and hope. That's quite an image to live up to, so we're going to help you out.

AFTERLIFE

STARTING A HARROWED CAMPAIGN

Harrowed characters, more than any others in a *Deadlands* campaign, exist between the twin poles of heroism and horror. That's a tricky tightrope to walk, and sometimes it seems like it's greased from end to end.

Sure, other, living characters may have their dark sides. Outlaws may have a shadowy past that they can't seem to get away from no matter how fast or far they run. Inventors may hear evil voices and be plagued by gremlins in their strange devices. Hucksters play cards with the devils themselves for magical stakes, and sometimes they lose. Shamans walk in spirit through the deadly Hunting Grounds. And even the blessed make it their business to confront the forces of darkness wherever they may be found. All of these characters meet up with evil in one form or another.

But Harrowed characters carry that evil right inside their bellies. They wrestle with their manitous for control day in and day out. No one's fate is more tenuous than a Harrowed's, and they often have control of their destiny wrested from them, if only for a little while. But by the same token, on the flip side of that coin as it were, the Harrowed's potential for heroism is so much the better.

THE HARROWED HERO

Because the Harrowed don't just bargain with spirits, the way other characters do, but rather draw directly upon the power of the manitou inside them, their supernatural abilities are even darker and more dangerous to their own souls. A blessed preacher may call upon the power to *smite* an enemy, but a Harrowed can grow savage claws and rip that enemy to pieces directly. A huckster might call up a *Texas twister* to buffet her foes, but a Harrowed might eat their very souls.

Of course, it's that very darkness that makes a Harrowed's good deeds shine all the brighter. After all, nothing shows in the night like a light, dim as it might otherwise seem.

It's easy to do good when fortune smiles upon you, everything is going your way, and all the world's your friend. It's a lot tougher to walk the straight and narrow when you know the only thing keeping you breathing is a demon, when you figure you're doomed to wrestle with it for the rest of your days, and when you suspect your soul must already be damned, 'cause you know you're dead but you sure as Hell ain't in Heaven.

Some of your players may not recognize the importance of keeping their balance on that fine line they walk between power and perdition. They may come asking to play a Harrowed just because they think the special abilities are really cool.

As the Marshal, you may be worried that, as a result, your campaign might turn into a sort of dark superhero game with Harrowed characters showing off their powers in every town, terrorizing the living just because they can. You may be sorely tempted to just tell them "No."

But being a Marshal means being an entertainer. You have something of an obligation to making certain your players have fun. They're trusting you.

You'll find that, in terms of keeping your players happy, one good rule of thumb to follow is this: Why say "no" when you can say "yes" instead? If a player is excited about a particular character type, he puts all the more energy into playing it. It's better to have your players excited than grumbling.

So how do you deal with the problem of players focusing on the powers of the Harrowed and ignoring the problems? Well, depending on how you want to play it, there are two primary options you can choose from.

OPTION ONE: OVER THE TOP

It is important for a Marshal to recognize what her players are looking for. One way of judging this is by looking at what sorts of characters they've created or want to create for the game.

If most of them have concentrated on high mental Traits and lots of *sneak-* and *search*-type Aptitudes, your group probably wants a lot of mystery in their campaigns. They may not even consciously realize it themselves, but they have pretty much voted for that with their character choices.

On the other hand, if your players have pretty much focused on high corporeal Traits, with lots of combat Aptitudes, they're probably looking for every opportunity to blow things to Hell. Don't let them down.

Once you've determined what your players are looking for in the campaign, you're usually best off giving them just that. Why argue with them? You're all in this together, so you might as well have fun.

With that in mind, then, if a good proportion of your players have built some kick-butt Harrowed using the *Book o' the Dead* rules, if most of the powers they've chosen are dramatically supernatural, and if they've chosen the most blatantly supernatural Hindrances as well, the group is probably hoping to stomp around the Weird West like the Four Horsemen of the Apocalypse. So why fight it? Give them what they want, and save your subtler plots for later.

After all, real life can be hard, and sometimes people just need to blow off some steam. Roleplaying can be a great arena for doing just that.

As the campaign progresses, be sure to keep an eye peeled for any signs of encroaching jadedness on the part of your players. After a while, going from gunfight to gunfight can lose its appeal. If your players start to lose the thrill from "kicking butt and taking names," it's time to consider switching your train from one track to the other.

Deadlands is the kind of game you can play the way you like. "You," in this case, doesn't just refer to you the Marshal. It means you and all your players. The thing to keep in mind is that you want to build some sort of consensus and then go with it for as long as it works. Then just try something else.

OPTION TWO: EDUCATE YOUR PLAYERS

Another way to approach the problem of players who focus on the great powers in a Harrowed's hands—but seem to forget about the equally great problems—is to train them to your way of thinking. Talk to them individually about the character they want to play. Get them thinking about what human ties the character still has to the world. As they start to fill in details, the character comes alive in their imagination as a person, not just a collection of supernatural powers, and that means better roleplaying.

Ask about the character's home town. What was his childhood like? What were his parents like, and did he have siblings? Pretty much everyone makes friends during life; what sorts of friends did this character have?

The most important question out of all of this is: Who was there to mourn the character when he died? At least some of them should still be around for you to use as complications in the Harrowed's life. If you can, try to steer the player away from the idea that the character's whole family was massacred and this Harrowed hero came back to life only for vengeance. (All you have to say is, "Not that old shtick again," and most players jump at the chance to revise their character concept.)

While on the topic of the character's death, ask the player to come up with some details of how the character died. The character generation rules in this book provide general motivations for a Harrowed's death, but players should fill in their own details. Get them thinking about what loose ends remain dangling as a result.

As you go through this fleshing-out process, take every opportunity to point out the downsides to playing a Harrowed. Just as the questions above get the players thinking about deeper motivations and better-defined personalities for their characters, your purpose here is to plant the seeds of the Harrowed's tragic nature. Remember that when the hero died, he lost whatever it was he was fighting for as well.

It is especially important to go over the character's Hindrances with the player. As you do so, make certain that the player is willing to put up with the trouble each Hindrance can cause. As you discuss each Hindrance, mention how you can use it during play to complicate the character's life. Let the player know just how

much control each Hindrance is putting into your hands. Let your dark side show its gleeful anticipation of torturing the hero with each one. Then, if there are any Hindrances that the player seems hesitant to live with, suggest a change to something else.

While you're getting the player to think about how you plan on playing up his undead hero's Hindrances, don't forget to consider the details of the character's Dominion, as well. If the hero's a *veteran o' the weird west*, you have the opportunity to invent evils the cadaver did under the manitou's control, something he may not even have a hint about just yet.

Give the player a wicked smile, and let him know that you plan to come up with something really special for his hero later in the campaign. Such a seed of anxiety planted now can go a long way toward making the player consider the full consequences of the character's future actions.

Finally, if you really want to make certain your players perceive their characters as people and not just powers, you may want to suggest (or even insist) that they begin playing the characters while still alive. Tell them that you want to play through their heroes' deaths and "rebirths" for the drama of it all.

To do this, have the players design their Harrowed heroes as normal under the rules in this book, but ignore their Harrowed powers (and any related Hindrances) for the first few sessions of play. This can provide a fantastic opportunity for the players to connect to their characters from life to death to undeath.

How long you take to get to that death depends upon your own plans, the direction your campaign develops, and just how much fun everyone is having. In fact, some groups may never actually get to the grave! But knowing that you have guaranteed to bring these characters back from the great beyond if they do die adds an interesting twist to the campaign.

Keep in mind, though, that if your group includes more than one Harrowed character, and if you choose to start those Harrowed heroes out alive, you may need to do some fancy shuffling of events to make their deaths and resurrections fit both the unfolding campaign and the details of their character generation. The adventure at the back of this book provides one example of how that might be done. Chapter Eight gives a few more insights you might find handy in its discussion of merging several heroes' nightmare scenarios together.

Maintaining a Balance of Power

As the Marshal, you're the primary storyteller of your gaming group. You have a whole world full of characters to draw from to help ensure that things go the way you need them to. Of course, you should be a benevolent tyrant, steering events rather than dictating them, and confronting the heroes with decisions and consequences instead of enslaving them to your plot.

When it comes to the Harrowed, the cast of characters you can use to manipulate their actions is especially impressive. Let's look at a few examples.

The Posse Itself

First, there is the players' posse itself, assuming it includes any characters who are still alive. See, it isn't just the Harrowed who have to live with their condition. Any living heroes in the posse also have to cope with any backlash from the Harrowed's supernatural state.

Besides the threat of personal harm, there's also the problem of "guilt by association." Suppose, for instance, the posse has been traveling through the wilderness for weeks, hounded by whoever their current enemies are, and now, footsore, dirty, and tired, they come across the welcome sight of a town where they can rest up and resupply. Now suppose they get into town, and their Harrowed companion lets loose with a supernatural display to frighten off an annoying local. When the townsfolk get the courage to whip up a lynch mob, it isn't just the Harrowed character they're going to come looking for.

Face your players with that sort of situation once or twice and they'll soon join together to keep their undead pal in line.

Agents of Good

Not only that, but Harrowed who are flagrant with their use of the supernatural soon draw the unwelcome attention of groups like the Pinkertons or the Texas Rangers, depending on where they're traveling. Agents of those two organizations don't mess around. If they catch the rank wind of a Harrowed, they watch him. And if he can't be recruited, they put him down—for good.

AGENTS OF EVIL

Worse, Harrowed who are too open with their powers might actually draw the attention of the servants of the Reckoners. The result could go one of two ways, neither of them nice.

If the actions of the Harrowed are helping to boost the local Fear Level, any fearmonger in the area may take it as a kindness. In that case, any servants of that fearmonger might begin "helping" the Harrowed, mimicking his actions to further spread the fear. If the fearmonger is human or intelligent enough, it might actually come to meet with the Harrowed and offer a partnership of terror. If that isn't enough of a wake-up call to get your Harrowed players back on the straight and narrow, it's time for you to get some new players.

The other possibility is that the local fearmonger views the offending Harrowed as a challenge to its power. As explained in the *Deadlands* rulebook, maintaining the right balance of events to build the local Fear Level is a subtle thing. Blatant use of the supernatural can actually work against the Reckoners' minions. If Harrowed characters are mucking things up for a fearmonger, it won't be long before it comes looking for them with a vengeance.

But even if the Harrowed aren't causing a fearmonger that sort of trouble, evil creatures are often jealous beings, and they may feel challenged to show these upstarts who wears the scariest pants in the area.

THE ULTIMATE GOAL

Ultimately, your goal as Marshal is to make sure that everyone has a good time, including you.

Give your Harrowed characters as much free reign as possible, but don't let them overshadow everyone else in the campaign. Let them have chances to revel in their supernatural powers, then make them suffer the consequences, whether that be the reactions of other people or simply the Hindrances they've chosen for themselves.

In the end, they'll love you for it.

CHAPTER SEVEN: THE DEVIL INSIDE

Now it's time to look inside the dark hearts of the manitous. Tread carefully, 'cause they're nasty critters.

The main thing to remember about manitous is that they tend to be subtle in their methods. They're crafty spirits, always looking for ways to spread fear, but content to wait for the right moment to make their move. Most of all, they do not want to be caught. Tough as they are, they can be killed, and they'll do anything to stay alive.

DOMINION

When a Harrowed falls into torturous sleep, the manitou inside subjects him to horrible nightmares, images from the Hunting Grounds, and perhaps even memories of the grisly deeds it committed the last time it was in charge. On those occasions when the fiend feels its host's will begin to crumble, it attempts to steal Dominion.

To reflect those occasional nightmares where the mortal mind caves in to the manitou's torment, Dominion tests are made at the start of each play session.

To make the test, both the hero and the devil inside make opposed *Spirit* tests, adding their current Dominion to their rolls. The winner takes 1 point of Dominion for success and another for every raise. If neither opponent gets at least a 5 on this check, there is no change in Dominion.

TIME TO PLAY!

So when does the manitou come out to play? Basically, whenever it wants.

The Marshal should use the manitou as a plot device and a grueling Hindrance for the Harrowed *and* his companions. To that end, you should draw one extra Fate Chip at the beginning of each session for every Harrowed in your party.

Whenever you want a Harrowed's manitou to take over, you must first pay a Fate Chip. Then you make a *Spirit* roll for the manitou. The difficulty is Fair (5) plus 1 for every point of Dominion the Harrowed currently controls.

The Fate Chip is not applied toward the roll—it's simply the cost the manitou must pay to wrest control of the Harrowed's reigns for a while. You can spend additional Fate Chips on the roll if you want to, but you get no bonuses to the roll for the chip you spent to initiate the test.

While this extra Fate Chip you drew at the start of the game session is specifically meant for you to use to take control of the Harrowed hero, you don't have to use it that way if you don't wish to. You can use any of your Fate Chips that you've got, or you can opt to not take control of that player this session and use the extra chip for something else.

It's your game, and you're the boss, after all. It's entirely up to you.

Dominion Summary

As we told the players in Chapter Four, the rules for Dominion have changed more than a little bit. It might be confusing to keep the changes straight, so here's a quick look at how you should handle things with the new rules.

Don't worry. It's pretty darn simple, and you'll have the hang of it in absolutely no time at all.

Trust us.

- At the start of each play session, the Marshal gets to draw one extra Fate Chip for every Harrowed hero in the posse.

- The Harrowed and the manitou make a *Spirit* test at the start of every game session, each adding their Dominion.

- The winner of the Dominion test gets 1 Dominion point for success, and another for every raise over his opponent.

- When the Marshal wants the manitou to take over, he must first spend a Fate Chip.

- After spending a chip, the Marshal rolls the manitou's *Spirit* against a TN of 5 plus the number of Dominion points controlled by the Harrowed.

- If successful, the amount of time the manitou remains in charge depends on the color of chip spent.

- Additional chips can be spent to extend the duration of the manitou's control as long as you like (or your chips hold out).

Anyhow, the manitou is now in control up to an amount of time determined by the color of the chip spent, as shown on the table below:

Lost Control

Chip	Duration
White	1 minute
Red	10 minutes
Blue	1 hour

If you need the manitou to have a little more play time, you can simply pay additional chips for more time. You don't have to roll again or spend chips to initiate another takeover attempt. Unless, of course, you let control lapse at any time. Then you've got to start all over again from scratch.

Say a crafty manitou needs 4 hours to bury one of its hosts unfortunate and unconscious companions alive. The Marshal spends a blue chip to initiate the test, then gets the required *Spirit* total. He's got 1 hour, which is probably not enough to dig a six foot deep pit. He'll need to spend some more chips to get the whole job done.

On the other hand, if the manitou was interrupted in the middle of a job (say by the rest of the posse) and opted to give control back to the hero for a while, then it would have to make a whole new takeover attempt to be able to come back and finish what it started.

Total Dominion

If a manitou ever controls *all* a hero's Dominion points, it takes over for a good, long while. Exactly how long depends on the Marshal and what your plans may be, but the hero no longer gets to roll for Dominion points at the beginning of each game session.

Some Harrowed have been lost for years. When they finally do come around, they discover they have a lifetime's blood on their rotting hands.

The only time the mortal soul gets to fight back is when the manitou is affected by certain magic spells, relics, or arcane procedures. The Marshal might also give the hero a chance to fight back in particularly unusual circumstances.

If you want to keep the character in the game, the player is going to have to commit to playing a monstrous and conniving fiend. If the player isn't up to the task, you should take over the hero permanently and give the player a chance to start over with a whole new hero.

Breaking Away

Sometimes, a hero's will is so strong that it can overthrow a manitou's Dominion and keep it from doing something positively atrocious, at least for the moment.

These kinds of checks should be rare, because most everything the manitou does is downright despicable in one way or another. But even a subjugated hero might be able to fight back if his manitou is about to cause *direct* harm to a very close companion.

When the Marshal feels such an occasion is about to occur, he can let the Harrowed's player make an opposed *Spirit* test versus the manitou. It's entirely the Marshal's call as to if and when this should happen.

If the mortal loses, the manitou proceeds in its unholy task unmolested. The hero can do nothing but sit blindfolded in the back seat, unable to do anything while the horrible events unfold.

If the mortal beats the manitou by less than a raise, he hasn't won, but he can keep fighting. Reroll about every 5 seconds, or at the beginning of each round if in combat. While this is going on, the Harrowed's body hesitates in its activity while the internal struggle takes place. This alone may be enough time for the manitou's intended target to get away.

If the host wins by a raise or more, he regains control instantly. Any remaining time the manitou had coming to it is lost.

When a manitou loses its play time, it drops back down inside the Harrowed's psyche to sulk for a while. We won't say how long exactly, but the Marshal should wait at least a few hours to let the fiend regather its strength before trying its dastardly deeds again.

Letting a player character attempt to break Dominion should be a rare occurrence. When you think it might be appropriate, base your decision purely on the character, good roleplaying, and—most importantly—drama.

Most anyone would get to test if the manitou was about to kill his best friend, sidekick, wife, child, mama, or the like. A *heroic* character might get to test anytime the manitou was about to directly harm an innocent, or when an indirect action would cause amazing destruction (such as dynamiting a trestle as a train comes).

Oh yeah, one more thing. Manitous don't like being interrupted in their devious work. When they regain even temporary control, they'll pay their hosts back in spades.

The Evil from Before

Assuming a Harrowed isn't fresh out of the grave, most begin the game with a burden of guilt already on their souls. Any Harrowed that's been around for at least a year has lost control on numerous occasions. During that time, the manitou certainly committed sins that the character won't know about.

If you remember, we gave Harrowed characters 5 free points with which to buy powers during character creation. Here's where the hero has to pay them back.

All Harrowed have a 5-point Hindrance we call *blind spots*. These are times in his past when he lost total Dominion for a few days, weeks, or maybe even years to the manitou.

You don't need to figure out what happened now. And you don't need to confine yourself to a single event. As your campaign develops and you think adding a blast from the Harrowed's past would be fun, work it into the adventure. Take a few minutes and decide what mischief the undead did in his past that's got the locals all riled up by his presence.

If the Harrowed is entirely fresh, it may not even have committed the deeds that caused her *blind spots* yet. Don't worry too much about that. As the game goes on, there are going to be plenty of chances for the manitou to cause mischief. These moments then become the hero's *blind spots*.

What these evil deeds involved is entirely up to you. They needn't be quite so subtle or sneaky as the sorts of things this chapter has discussed so far, because prior to this, the Harrowed won't have been keeping company with heroes. Murder, rapine, pillaging, torture, wholesale slaughter, or any other dark deed might have been done by the Harrowed character in the time before the hero inside took control. Alternatively, the Harrowed can sneak off in between gaming sessions or adventures in a campaign and commit all sorts of heinous deeds that can come back to haunt the hero in the future.

This means you can invent any sort of crime you want and interject an event based upon it into your campaign whenever you like. If the posse is having a relaxing time in town somewhere, and you want to create a little havoc, you may decide to have some young gunslinger show up seeking vengeance for a murder one of the Harrowed committed in that pre-game time.

Or maybe an adventure leads the posse through Indian territory, and a tribe claims to recognize one of the Harrowed characters as the villain who destroyed its village or desecrated a holy site of its people. Now the Indians demand that the character pay restitution for his crimes. They may even want the rest of the posse members to undergo a ritual ordeal to prove their honor.

What's the Harrowed character going to do in any of these situations? He has to assume the crime was real. But he may not be able to give the victims the justice they deserve, especially if the party is hot on the trail of some greater evil at the moment. On the other hand, he can hardly feel justified in fighting his way out of the current situation. The only way out may be to run, and that certainly isn't going to help his reputation any.

Situations like these present the posse with a quandary with no good answer. It's a perfect way to torture the players of your Harrowed heroes. Don't feel at all bad about it. They knew the risks when they created their Harrowed characters, and they gained some pretty special abilities as a result. This is just another way in which they have to pay the piper.

What's more, these sorts of subplots and sidelines add a sense of depth to the campaign overall.

THE DEVIL'S ADVOCATE

If you've been following closely, you'll notice the way we handle manitous is subtly but dramatically different.

In *Deadlands*, a manitou who gained Dominion would rule its host for quite a while. Too long, in fact.

So we revamped the way they work. Manitous no longer take charge for long periods of time. They prefer to reside inside their hosts and take control only when they sense the opportunity to commit some dastardly deed.

The only time a manitou really takes over is when it gains complete Dominion. This helps you create plots in which a former hero has been taken over for good. If the posse wants to destroy the Harrowed ex-hero, they must kill the good guy trapped inside as well, putting them in the position of having to make a horrible decision about what serves the greater good.

So how often should you let the manitou take over? Whenever you want. Don't feel like you have to use the manitou every session. Once

you've used it a time or two, the hero and the rest of the posse should respect it enough to (rightfully) fear it. And that's the true nature of the manitou.

A PURPOSE IN UNLIFE

So what is the manitou's purpose exactly? Simple. To cause as much mischief, mayhem, confusion, and—above all—icy cold fear as possible. If the thing sees a chance to cause mischief and mayhem or has an opportunity to kill someone who's causing it problems, it tries to take over.

This doesn't mean a manitou struggles to wrest control every time its host draws a gun. If the fiend interferes too often, others are going to catch on and find a way to kill it. Those who already know but have to live with the manitou—such as a Harrowed's companions—usually put up with it as long as their friend does them more good than harm. But if the demon inside gets out of hand, they're going to be forced to put their partner down once and for all.

Manitous know this and so keep their existence and—most importantly—their *actions* secret from interfering mortals.

UNGRACIOUS HOSTS

Undead heroes make the perfect hosts for the manitou's evil deeds. Think about it. Most of the Harrowed wind up traveling the Weird West with their loyal companions (the posse) confronting horrors and fighting evil. You'd think this would be the last place an evil demon would want to show its ugly face. In truth, such heroes are the perfect vessels for the malignant manitou.

Here's why. Heroic posses head straight for trouble. What better place for the manitou to work its deviltry? When the demon gets to play with its host a bit, it can do any number of things to wreak havoc and turn a bad situation worse. Think about it.

RED HERRINGS

One of the most common tricks the manitous pull is to plant red herrings. A party convinced they're looking for a nosferatu is thrown for a loop when the latest victim was savaged by something that left fur in his dead hands.

What's the point of such a shenanigan? There are two. First, it confuses the party and causes doubt and fear among this small group. A good little appetizer for the manitou and its masters.

DEATH OF A FRIEND?

Here's a good example of how to use a manitou in a typical campaign.

Ronan Lynch (the gunslinger featured in the examples in the *Deadlands* rulebook) was slain in the *Deadlands* Dime Novel™ #1: *Perdition's Daughter.* Now he's returned from the dead and is wandering the Weird West, learning about his strange fate and dealing with the horrors that inevitably confront him. At his side are a sly huckster named Velvet and a hickory-toting Priest named Jebediah Smith.

Shortly after their adventures in Colorado, the posse heads northeast to Deadwood. There they wind up tangling with gunrunners selling firearms to rebellious Sioux braves who don't believe in the Old Ways.

After the party has had a few tense words with the bad guys, Ronan's manitou decides to make things worse.

One night, it takes control of Ronan and quietly slips off to find the gunrunners. The leader of the desperadoes, Boss Slade, lives in a large ranch house on the edge of town, while his gang sleeps in a bunkhouse out back. The manitou lights a match and burns the place to the ground, killing half the gunmen in their sleep.

The next day, Boss Slade and his boys come looking for the posse. They find the heroes in the No. 10 Saloon. Slade accuses the heroes of torching his boys.

Ronan has no idea what's going on, and Preacher Smith loyally (and predictably) stands up for him, but the jig is up when everyone notices the hairs on Ronan's arm are singed. One of Slade's gunmen goes for his hogleg.

Ronan drops the trigger-happy fool before he clears leather, but the Harrowed gunslinger is forced to get the Hell out of Deadwood to escape any repercussions from Slade's gang or the local law. The rest of the crew hastily packs their bags and vamooses with him.

Along the way, they're ambushed by what's left of the bad guys. It's night, and a storm breaks just as the fight starts.

Velvet, the huckster, starts dealing death while Ronan blazes away with his smokewagons.

Preacher Smith winds up getting separated from the other posse members in the darkness. His hickory stick smashes several of the assassins' skulls before he catches a slug in the hip.

Ronan hears Smith's cry and leaves Velvet to fend for himself. The gunslinger stumbles over the muddy hills until he finds Smith curled up under a tree.

The manitou worming about inside Ronan looks around, sees no witnesses, and takes control once again. Silently, it slips a rope off Ronan's mount, throws it over the tree and then loops it around the unconscious Preacher's neck.

Ronan senses the danger and fights back. A fierce struggle for Dominion rages inside the Harrowed's struggling corpse.

Preacher Smith wakes to see Ronan standing above him. The noose is in the gunslinger's hands and a wild look in his bloodshot eyes.

Smith, helpless from his wounds, starts praying that Ronan beat his demon. Otherwise, he's going to swing.

·LOSTON·'97

Second, it makes the posse look incompetent in front of the townspeople they're supposed to be protecting. Again, more doubt, uncertainty, and—best of all—fear.

DEATH

Though manitous often tend to work subtly, sometimes they just can't help sending a particularly annoying mortal straight to the Great Beyond.

Say the Harrowed comes upon a critically wounded companion. The manitou, having a little play time it hasn't used yet, and having no witnesses about, takes over. The wounded friend shivers with terror as the Harrowed grins evilly and drags her helpless form to Boot Hill to bury her alive.

When a manitou wants someone dead, it makes sure it's going to win. Playing fair is not a consideration. It never draws a gun on an opponent who can fight back. Nor does it reveal itself when there's a good chance someone could stop it.

As the Marshal, you need to be careful. The price of having a Harrowed in the party means these situations arise on occasion. When they do, you have another player dead to rights. If you and your group aren't willing to deal with this, you should come up with a good reason why the manitou passes up such a great opportunity.

SURVIVAL

A Harrowed who goes off on his own is dangerous for a manitou. Should the Texas Rangers, Pinkertons, or some other do-gooders come after her, she's more likely to get her head blown off. And then the manitou's otherwise eternal existence is over.

Having a posse of competent gunslingers, hucksters, or other heroes about is good protection. Even if these individuals are terrified of their friend, they know he's in there, and they usually do whatever they can to protect his dry husk from others.

The manitous delight in this paradox. And don't think they don't use it whenever they can.

CONTROL

Finally, traveling to the supernatural "hot spots" of the Weird West gives the manitou a chance to interfere with those who would tame them.

Planting red herrings, killing the heroes who fight evil, and generally sowing confusion and terror will protect the interests of the manitous' masters, and lead the creatures to greater power for themselves on earth.

THE NATURE OF THE BEAST

Now you know what the manitous are up to. But how do they do it?

You need to know what these demons can do, as well as what they can't. For though they are chaotic beings, even manitous must abide by a few rules.

POWER

The one that irks them most is that they can't use any power their host hasn't developed yet. They can use any the Harrowed has figured out, however, including coup powers stolen from their evil brothers.

They can also use the hexes and black magic skills of their hosts, but they can never access spiritual magic such as the blessed's miracles or shamanic favors. In the case of black magic, the manitou uses its own *faith*.

AWARENESS

Manitous can hear and see everything their host does when the Harrowed is in charge and they're riding shotgun. That's how they know when they might want to take over.

The opposite is not true. When the manitou is in charge, the host's consciousness is entirely repressed. The Harrowed hero doesn't have any idea what a manitou is up to when it has control.

The *subconscious* sees what's going on, and this is why the Harrowed can sometimes break the manitou's hold when it's about to do something incredibly evil.

And just in case you're wondering, a hex or miracle (and perhaps even hypnotism) that accesses the subconscious could find out what a manitou's been up to. The specifics depend on the method used, but don't think the manitou is going to sit back and let the hero reveal all its secrets without a fight.

KNOWLEDGE

Occasionally, a clever mortal has managed to trap a Harrowed who has lost Dominion. The famous Lacy O'Malley, reporter for the notorious *Tombstone Epitaph*, pulled this off once, as have the Pinkertons via their infamous Star Chamber (see *The Quick & the Dead*).

Both Mr. O'Malley and the Pinkertons thought they'd make the manitou spill the beans on this whole Reckoning business. Some of the manitous managed to avoid the questions by giving their host Dominion, at least for a while. When that didn't work and true death seemed imminent, the horrible creatures talked their forked tongues off.

Unfortunately, they just don't know much. Manitous know only that they serve distant masters concealed in the mists of the Hunting Grounds. They know they channel fear to these beings the mortals call the Reckoners, but they do not know why, nor do they know what is done with it.

ABOMINABLE ALLIES

By and large, manitous have no connection with the other servants of the Reckoners. A manitou with Dominion who stumbles across a wendigo is still in for a fight and may likely get gobbled up.

On rare occasions, a manitou has managed to convince an abomination to work with it, but these alliances were formed by persuasion and guile, not because of any shared purpose or mystical connection.

A MANITOU BY ANY OTHER NAME...

Not all evil spirits are created equal, but there's more to the issue than just strength of *Spirit*. Manitous have different personalities as well, just as people do.

What's more, different types of manitous are drawn to different types of player characters. Some are attracted to the incipient madness of inventors; others deal only with hucksters. But those manitous that are drawn to the Harrowed are truly a special bunch.

Think about it for a second. Most manitous aren't at any long-term risk in their haunting of the Earth. About the worst that can happen to them is to be defeated and banished back to the Hunting Grounds.

But when a manitou possesses a dead body, it's risking its very existence. If that Harrowed is ever destroyed, so is the manitou, completely and irrevocably. All it takes is one really nasty wound to the head or a forgotten stogie in bed and it's bye-bye manitou, forever.

Your players already know this means only the corpses with the best chance for survival are tempting enough to be made Harrowed. What they probably don't suspect, however, is that only the bravest, cockiest, most foolhardy, and/or lustiest manitous ever consider risking their immortal selves in such a joining. An evil spirit has to be particularly fascinated with the flesh—and particularly confident in itself—to make the switch from immaterial safety to the hazards of physicality.

There is a strange irony to this. Naturally, a manitou so bold isn't going to be drawn to a weakling. That's why Harrowed are so rare and the Weird West isn't overrun with pitiful, sniveling walking corpses. But the irony is that, on the other hand, the sort of person a manitou has the best chance for survival inside is exactly the type best able to wrestle control from that manitou.

These manitou, however, are nothing if not confident of themselves. They are, in every way, as big and bold as the people whose corpses they are drawn to. When they are in control of that body, they tend to be crafty in their wickedness, doing as much evil as they can get away with, but without risking themselves overmuch in the process. And even when they aren't in control, when their host has Dominion, they aren't just along for the ride. At those times, a Harrowed's manitou finds sneaky, subtle ways of working its mischief.

It often falls to you to play the part of the manitous inside your players' Harrowed characters. As if you didn't already have enough to do. But trust us, this isn't really any chore. Rather, it's a chance to have some real fun as you mess with the players' heads, adding new layers of mystery to the events around their characters and constantly giving them new things to worry about.

SECRETS OF THE MANITOUS

We generally frown on a lot of bookkeeping for the Marshal, but dealing with the Harrowed only comes up once in a while, and it's worth a few extra notes to give the dead their money's worth.

In the *Deadlands* rulebook, we told you to draw a card every time you needed to test the manitou's *Spirit*. We're going to amend that policy a bit by drawing a card once to determine its *Spirit* permanently. That same card is also going to tell you a little more about the manitou that's taken over the ex-hero.

Write the manitou's *Spirit* down wherever you keep other notes on your posse members. Note that if the hero's *spirit* changes in the future, the manitou's *Spirit* is unaffected.

MANITOU SPIRIT

Card	Spirit
2	Legion (see below)
3–8	Spirit is equal to the character's
9–Jack	Spirit is same die type but 1 higher Coordination
Queen–Ace	Spirit die type is one higher and Coordination is 2 higher
Joker	Greater manitou (see below)

LEGION

The hero is inhabited by a horde of lesser manitous. Whenever you need to know their collective *Spirit*, draw a card to randomly determine it, just like you would have with the original rules in the *Deadlands* rulebook.

Such legions are far more chaotic and destructive than their kindred spirits. Legions will make overt attacks on their friends, use their powers blatantly, and basically flaunt all the guidelines on subtlety we've been telling you about throughout this book.

Needless to say, Harrowed infested with legions of lesser manitous tend to have short unlife-spans.

GREATER MANITOU

The hero got hit with the unlucky stick. Hard. These ancient manitous are the biggest, baddest hombres in the Hunting Grounds. When they grab a mortal shell, it's for a good reason.

Greater manitous have a *Spirit* of 3d12+4. They're something like hunting dogs for the Reckoners. They're sent specifically to hunt down Harrowed and other servants of the Reckoners who have erred from the paths their distant masters set for them. Usually, these are Harrowed who manage to keep their manitous bottled up too easily and abominations that have become too blatant in their attacks.

Greater manitous have some influence with their hosts even when they don't take control. Through guile, trickery, or simple fate, their hosts always drift toward whatever threat the Reckoners want dealt with next. As the Marshal, you have to figure out just how to rope the unwitting hero into your nefarious plots.

THE DARK HEART OF THE MANITOU

That's it for the hard and fast rules on manitous. But before we leave you alone with these devils, we thought we'd give you a little more advice on how to integrate such a powerful and insidious force into your game.

CORRUPTION

When a Harrowed has Dominion over his manitou, your primary task should be to interject unsettling details into the Harrowed's presence and actions.

Think of the manitou as the Harrowed's dark subconscious mind, constantly tainting whatever the character sees and hears, perpetually casting a shadow over everything he says and does.

Your goal should be to unnerve any living characters in the Harrowed's vicinity, and that definitely includes the other heroes in the posse.

To begin with, never, ever let a Harrowed use a power without including some description of a disturbing detail or two. The descriptions of the powers themselves encourage this, but feel free to improvise beyond those descriptions, inventing new details to suit the current situation. After all, this is a storytelling session, not a board game. Drama is more important than mere adherence to printed text and numbers.

For example, imagine your characters are all spending the night locked up in the hoosegow, and one of your Harrowed characters decides to use the *ghost* power to walk through the bars to get the keys and free the others. You might take a moment to describe the way his body slowly fades to mistiness, then mention that the center of that cloud remains dark, especially black around his heart. That ought to give the rest of the posse a shiver of doubt about the condition of their Harrowed friend and make them wonder if he's really coming back for them.

But even if you're describing a cheery day to the posse, make a point to tell the Harrowed player how the light hurts his undead hero's eyes and the flies are biting, chewing little pieces of

him away. Use every opportunity that presents itself to torture the Harrowed with the thought that a demon dwells inside him and to remind the rest of the posse of that fact as well.

THE ROLE OF HINDRANCES

Hindrances play a central role in conveying the tragic nature of a Harrowed's existence. That's particularly true of the special Harrowed Hindrances described in this book. As much as possible, try to keep the heroes' Hindrances in mind as you work your posse through the campaign, and play upon them often. If your players start to wonder whether having taken on a Hindrance was worth the trouble it's causing them now, you can't be wrong.

Of course, keeping track of all the party's Hindrances can be a tall order, particularly if you have several Harrowed in the group, and especially when the action is running hot and heavy. One way of solving this problem is to liberally reward those players who remind you of their heroes' Hindrances, and who play them out on their own. This sort of encouragement goes a long way, and the tone of your campaign will benefit for it.

Then, after each game session is over, you may want to review *all* of the characters' Hindrances, to note any that the players ignored. Next session, you can make a point to dwell on those Hindrances, reminding those lax players

that their Fate Chips are low because their heroes aren't living up to their destinies. They might also get the idea that they need to portray those Hindrances themselves if they don't want something even worse coming of them later, at your hands.

GETTING OUT OF CONTROL

Players with incredible powers can often get out of control. But you're the Marshal, and you can reign them in when you need to. The really hard job is Marshaling yourself.

When a manitou has Dominion over its Harrowed host, it doesn't just go running wild across the countryside, creating all the havoc it can. Why not?

For one thing, that sort of blatant evil may be fine for short-term terror, but it doesn't serve the Reckoners' plans for long-term feeding on fear. For another, it's liable to draw enough attention to bring Pinkertons, Rangers, and a horde of other such hero types like a pack of wolves to a wounded doe.

Nor does a manitou-controlled Harrowed usually turn on the other members of its own party and begin a sudden bloodbath of gunfire and supernatural powers. For one thing, it knows it might lose that battle. One lucky shot to the head, and the manitou is gone, no matter how much carnage it caused in the meantime.

For another, it is much more fun for these malicious devils to toy with the rest of the posse, pretending to still be the friend they have come to depend upon, all the while surreptitiously causing them as much trouble and pain as possible.

A manitou has two primary goals. The first is survival; the second is mischief. It causes as much of the second as is possible without threatening the first.

As the Marshal, you get to concentrate mainly on the fun side of that equation. You get to think up all kinds of mischief the manitou can get into. The poor player of the Harrowed has to worry most about the other side—surviving the results of that mischief.

It's a tenuous position for the player. On the one hand, his Harrowed has become a monster, a servant of the Reckoners. As such, the character deserves to be destroyed. On the other hand, if the person inside can just hang on long enough to maintain control of himself, he can be a powerful force for good. Maybe then he can make up for all the evil the manitou has done—and then some.

TOTAL DOMINION

When a manitou gains total Dominion over a Harrowed, the Harrowed's fate becomes somewhat trickier. This is when you have to decide to let the hero become an extra under your control or let the player take the reigns and go on as the manitou.

Of course, the player needs to be able to keep a secret. If he can't or you don't think he can play a manitou without totally disrupting your campaign, then simply have the hero wander off somewhere. Maybe he'll return soon. Maybe he won't. That's up to you and the player.

If the player wants to try his hand at playing the manitou, he should act normally 90% of the time. But when he can, he must make life Hell for the rest of the posse. Even more so than usual. And that means the *player* has to keep real quiet about what's going on with his *character*.

He has to play out the evil of the manitou, following your direction, all the while trying to keep the character's condition secret. Maintaining that secrecy can be tough enough, but playing out that evil—when the player really wants to be acting heroically—can be even more of a challenge. Still, the player knew this would be a possibility when his hero passed from this life and into a new one.

Once again, the manitou's primary goal when in control is to heighten the atmosphere of fear in the area. If you are going to let the player continue running the character, this may be enough of a goal to give him. Just let him know that the manitou wants to keep the other members of the posse from discovering its dominance, and—without spoiling that secrecy—it wants to cause as much fear and tension as possible. Then let the player suggest ways this can be done.

Beyond these goals, the manitou's secondary objective is to consolidate its own power over the Harrowed. This means weakening the other heroes so that they aren't a threat, and then isolating the Harrowed from them. This way, even if he regains Dominion later, he'll have a hard time regaining their trust and companionship. This might mean abandoning the other posse members at a critical moment, selling them out to the opposition, or even turning on them at some point when their guard is down.

The manitou won't do this lightly, however, because it wants to be assured of victory before risking anything. Perhaps more importantly,

DEVIL INSIDE

treachery should happen at the most dramatic moment possible, because that makes the best story. If you're going to be ruining a character's life, you'd best make sure it creates a tragic and epic story in the process.

If your player is game for playing out this line of events himself, great. But be prepared to do it yourself should the job just prove to be too much for him.

HOW NEW HARROWED POWERS MANIFEST

Just as players should be encouraged to justify any new levels of Aptitudes and Traits they purchase for their characters, the same is true for Harrowed powers. That's why the power descriptions list Dispositions, to give some indication of why a certain power would show up in a particular Harrowed hero. But the unfolding story of your campaign should also have some effect on what powers develop in a Harrowed hero and when—as well as what—new Hindrances he picks up.

Those new powers are liable to have a considerable effect on your campaign. More so than any new Aptitude might. That's more than enough reason for you to put your two cents worth in when a player is choosing new Harrowed powers.

You may even want to *assign* powers as a result of play. After all, the Harrowed have no choice over what coup they gain from an Abomination; that's completely in your hands. So why not do the same with Harrowed powers, at least on occasion? But it helps if you can justify that to the player in terms of story.

The rationale behind the Marshal assigning Harrowed powers and revealing them with a hint here or there is that these abilities aren't conceived of by the Harrowed hero. Rather, they spring from the manitou inside.

With these things in mind, you can influence, strongly suggest, or even outright dictate what powers and Hindrances the Harrowed character can develop. At the same time, you're reinforcing the importance of the unfolding campaign story over mere game mechanics.

NIGHTMARES

-LOSTON-

MARSHAL 90

CHAPTER EIGHT: THE NIGHTMARE SCENARIO

Running the nightmare scenario for a brand-new Harrowed can be one of the trickiest jobs a Marshal must do. That's why the *Deadlands* rules provide a quick mechanic as an option. But it can also be one of the most enjoyable tasks. There's nothing quite like seeing the look on a the face of a player as she walks through the nightmare that she herself gave you, and learns what special touches you've added just for her.

See, there's something very significant about the description players write down for their characters' nightmares. Without even realizing it, they're giving you an insight into exactly what spooks their character more than anything else in the world. What's more, because it's something they wrote themselves, they can picture it all the more vividly. Part of your job is already done for you, before you even open your mouth.

In this chapter, we're going to talk about some general direction and specific details to help you in setting up and running a nightmare scenario. So get ready to have some fun. We'll even cover the possibility of melding characters' nightmares so that Harrowed who died together can play out their quest for Dominion together.

And don't think that just because the rules in this book let players build Harrowed heroes who have been around for a while that there's no longer any reason for using their nightmare descriptions. We've got a couple of ways you can incorporate those nightmares into play over and over.

Through all of this, though, keep in mind that the point is for everyone to have fun. *Deadlands* is about creepiness, campiness, and weirdness, not about making your players feel overly uncomfortable. (Well, that's okay for a bit, but you shouldn't overdo it.)

Your players have put themselves in your hands, especially in providing you with their heroes' personal nightmare descriptions. It may be your job to torture them, but do it with a kind hand.

It's fun to scare people and fun for them to be scared in the safety of your living room, but you always have to know where to draw the line.

YOUR FIRST NIGHTMARE

When you sit down to devise a nightmare scenario, the first thing to realize is that it doesn't have to follow the rules of a regular adventure any more than a dream follows the rules of waking life.

Now, to a certain extent, that's just obvious. A dream doesn't bother justifying why you find yourself where you are; you just are. Nor does it have to explain how other people and things show up or why they have the powers they have. They just do.

But these rules for nightmare scenarios go even further than that. They also affect the way you should lay out the plot. To understand how, let's consider the topic of adventure plots overall.

NIGHTMARISH PLOTS

The simplest adventure plot is like a train. The players' heroes start at one end, let's say the caboose, and work their way to the other end, in this case the engine. Along the way, they pass through the scenes like those were the cars of the train, moving from one to the next in the order you hooked them up.

This is called a "linear" plot because the characters walk straight from one end to the other. The heroes don't really have any means to get off the train, and if they do, they derail the entire plot and may have difficulty getting back on track. Of course, in a nightmare scenario, they don't even have that choice.

What most players write up for their nightmare is actually a climactic event. It's a foregone conclusion that the hero is going to end up at that spot. So what you need to decide is what's going to happen along the way?

Don't be afraid to contrive the events between the nightmare's beginning and its ending. Remember, this scenario is supposed to convey a dream. Nobody expects to be in control of every detail in their dreams. They just have to react and hope for the best.

And therein lies the biggest secret to devising a successful nightmare scenario. People expect the dream to happen to them, and their job is to react to it.

In terms of the *Deadlands* nightmare scenario, their reactions determines who comes out on top—the hero or the manitou. Their expectation that the dream will follow its course, however, is what gives you the power to build a fun and effective game event.

FLESHING OUT THE NIGHTMARE

As you sit down with a player's nightmare description and begin building it into a scenario, it may help to think of the final product as nearly ritual in nature. Your job is to devise the events that occur to test the hero, and to line them up in some sort of order. Unlike most linear adventures, however, whether the hero succeeds or fails at an event, he'll have to keep on going to the very end. There's no getting off this train.

That's just fine. The hero isn't supposed to have control in a nightmare, and that convention works in your favor here.

As you might recall from the *Deadlands* rulebook, you need to set up several milestones as events in the nightmare scenario. The events you choose to portray can be either monumental or minor or even a mix of both, depending on how many the nightmare contains and what plans you might have.

Remember, that's a function of the hero's *Spirit*. A character with a *Spirit* of 12 requires 12 events to test her Dominion, while a hero with a *Spirit* Trait of 4 requires four. There is nothing that says the 12 events in the first character's scenario must all be as significant as the four in the second character's. All that's important is that each is a test.

Every test the hero passes is a point of Dominion for him. The manitou picks up a point for every test that's failed.

CREATING THE MILESTONES

When you're deciding upon events, think in terms of exactly what it is that each event is testing. Because the point of the nightmare scenario is to determine Dominion points, most of them should test the hero's doggedness and self-control.

Ethical questions are a good bet, making the hero wrestle with whether anger or violence is okay in a particular situation, for instance. Some of the events can even be tricky, suggesting that the character act one way but then punishing him for it. Remember, this is a dream, and dreams frequently pull the old bait-and-switch on the dreamer.

One good way to look at some of these tests is to ask "how do you feel?" as often as you ask "what do you do?"

Finally, we suggest that—during the running of the scenario—you not tell the player how the hero is doing. Let him worry that he's making all the wrong decisions and taking all the wrong actions. That actually helps convey the panicky atmosphere of the nightmare that much more effectively. Just make sure the player understands it's nothing personal; it's just the nature of a nightmare.

THE RECURRING NIGHTMARE

One of the most frightening things about nightmares is that they so often seem to repeat themselves as often as they like. Once a nasty one has got its hooks into your soul, it has a tendency to come back to haunt you over and over again.

RONAN'S NIGHTMARE

Every hero's nightmare scenario is different, but it's useful to look at one as an example. Ronan Lynch's time in his own personal Hell is a good place to start.

Ronan Lynch has a *Spirit* of 6, requiring six testing points during his nightmare.

The description Ronan's creator has given for "Your Worst Nightmare" involves working for a railroad company to protect it from rival gangs. A gunman from another gang calls Ronan out, and Ronan shoots him, only to discover his own face under the hat.

Ronan's story hints that he's scared of becoming a cold-blooded killer. We decide to frame his dilemma with a nightmarish train ride, ending in a little whistle-stop town and culminating with the gunfight.

Test One: Our first event opens with Lynch standing tensely in the cab of a train engine. It's a nightmare way to start, right in the middle of things. We tell the player that Ronan knows the railroad has been threatened, and he has the strongest feeling that an attack is going to come any second now.

The test here is to determine whether Ronan just blankly accepts that attitude or questions it. If Ronan's player goes along with the feeling, we give him a Fate Chip as a reward for good roleplaying, but we give the manitou 1 point of Dominion for making the character unquestioningly suspicious.

Test Two: Now it's time to throw a tricky one at Ronan. In fact, we're going to cheat. We tell the player the train is coming around a curve toward a trestle bridge and that Ronan can see what appear to be children—little boys—playing among the supports of the bridge. But the train engineer pulls out a rifle and begins shooting the kids. Ronan's choices are to fight the engineer or let him alone. The man won't stop long enough to discuss the matter.

If Ronan stops the engineer from shooting, he winds up in a gunfight with the man. Just as the fight ends, the train reaches the bridge, which collapses, pitching the train into the ravine and killing everyone aboard except Ronan. It turns out that the "kids" were actually gremlins ruining the bridge.

If, on the other hand, Ronan lets the engineer alone as the train passes over the bridge, Ronan can see the bloodied bodies of the little boys scattered across the ravine below. They were just harmless little boys. The engineer grins with a mouthful of pointed teeth, then vanishes.

Either way, Ronan loses a Dominion point to the manitou, although we certainly won't let Ronan's player know this. The only way for Ronan to gain the Dominion point is for him to insist that this test just wasn't fair. That isn't likely to happen, but if it does, it demonstrates the kind of insistence a Harrowed is going to need in order to survive.

Test Three: For this scene to work, the train has to be wrecked. If the gremlins didn't destroy the bridge in the preceding test, then we have a landslide do it for us now.

One way or the other, Ronan finds himself lying among the wreckage with the mangled bodies of the rest of the crew around him. Suddenly, a bright tunnel opens in the sky above, and the spirits of the dead begin floating up toward it. Ronan feels it tugging at his own soul as well.

RONAN'S NIGHTMARE, CONT.

If Ronan gives into that tugging, the manitou gains a Dominion point because this is only a dream. Despite what Ronan might believe, the bright tunnel has nothing to do with anything outside of his own rotting head. Even so, Ronan rises out of his dream body until only one foot of his ghost remains attached, and that foot refuses to come loose. A few minutes later, the tunnel closes, and Ronan finds his spirit sinking back into his body. A sense of despair washes over him.

If, on the other hand, Ronan refuses to leave his body behind, for whatever reason, he gains a Dominion point for his determination, something that's going to serve him well in his second chance to walk the Earth.

Test Four: In this test, we decide to pretty much give Ronan a freebie Dominion point, to make up for the cheating we did in test two. The local townspeople come out to the wreckage and haul Ronan back to town. As a nightmarish note, we tell the player that every roof in the whole town is on fire, but nobody seems to notice or care. They walk blithely in and out of buildings, ignoring the continual blaze above their heads. Still, it lights the dark sky garishly.

Ronan finds that he heals immediately upon reaching the town, and the people pin him with a Sheriff's star, though they never actually speak. Immediately afterward, the rival gang's gunfighter shows up for a shoot-out. If he goes out to fight the gunman, Ronan gains a Dominion point for bravely facing up to his fate. Otherwise, the manitou gets the point.

This shouldn't be much of a decision for Ronan. After all, he's a gunslinger, and this is what he does.

Regardless, Ronan finds himself on the street, facing off with the gunman. It would really mess things up for the nightmare if the other gunfighter were to win, so we won't allow for that possibility. Rather, we just tell the player that Ronan is faster and he shoots the other man down.

Tests Five and Six: What we plan to do next counts as two tests, focusing a lot of attention on the climactic scene.

In the player's nightmare description, Ronan looks down on the dying man, and sees his own face. That's pretty tragic, but we figure we can do the player one better.

We tell him that perception shifts suddenly, and he finds himself on the ground, bleeding and looking up into the demonic face of his killer—himself. The question is, of course, which is the real Ronan Lynch?

If Ronan accepts that he's now lying on the ground, bleeding to death, the manitou has succeeded in tricking him and gains a Dominion point. If, on the other hand, Ronan denies the perspective switch, insisting that he's the one who did the shooting, he's showing appropriate stubbornness necessary for a Harrowed, and he gains a Dominion point.

In either case, dying on the ground or standing over the dying man, if Ronan attacks the other figure, he gains a Dominion point for standing up to the manitou. If he just watches and waits, however, the manitou gets the Dominion point.

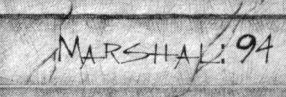

The same can be true of a Harrowed's nightmare scenario. Your use of that scenario doesn't have to end once the nightmare has been run once. You can continue updating that nightmare and use it again some other time when the Harrowed hero has failed a Dominion test against the manitou.

Rather than just giving the manitou a number of Dominion points based on how many raises it gained on the *Spirit* versus *Spirit* test, you can give the character a chance to play out a struggle for double the number of points the hero lost when he next sleeps. This way, the character has a chance of preventing the manitou from gaining any points at all, but he is risking more points for that privilege.

The fact that the character has already been through the events of the nightmare before can make them all the more nerve-wracking. Every change to the scenario hints at some dark purpose. Every test that stays the same suggests a trick, with the manitou ready to change the outcome as soon as the character repeats the previous decision. The player should be just as nervous the second, third, or fourth time through the scenario.

The Shared Nightmare

Following the guidelines in this chapter, you can actually combine the elements of several characters' nightmare descriptions into one joint nightmare. That assumes, of course, that all of these characters died and became Harrowed at roughly the same time—or at least that they're facing another battle for Dominion at the same time.

If you decide to do this, keep in mind the various *Spirit* Traits of your characters. A character can only risk as many *Spirit* points as he possesses. Any events he faces beyond that do him no further good nor harm, but they can help or hurt the other heroes involved in the joint nightmare.

Some of the events you put into the nightmare can serve multiple duty, facing each character with exactly the same test. Others should be intended for a specific individual. If one of the other heroes faces that test instead, the character for whom it was intended should automatically lose that Dominion point for not stepping forward when he should have. In the Ronan Lynch nightmare, for instance, every hero involved in the nightmare would face the tunnel of light, but only Ronan should face the rival gunfighter.

Given that the players originally wrote their own nightmare descriptions, it should be fairly evident which events are intended for individual heroes. You don't have to feel compelled to remind them of those facts, though. They should be able to figure this out themselves.

The Delayed Nightmare

Nothing says you have to have a Harrowed's nightmare scenario prepared the minute that character is ready to return from the grave. You can take your time crafting the scenario until you deem it ready.

In the meantime, feel free to let the player run the character with an undetermined number of Dominion points, just keeping track of any gained or lost during the course of play. Later, after you have found the time to run the nightmare scenario, the player can use that record to adjust the number of points the character acquired during the nightmare. If the result puts the manitou with total Dominion, you can rationalize to the player that the spirit only let the hero think he was in the driver's seat to torture him by seizing control when he least expects it. Now it's time to pay the piper.

Exceptions to the Rules

This chapter has presented the recommended way for running nightmare scenarios, but certainly not the only way. As Marshal, you may decide to build the scenario more like a full-fledged adventure, especially if the whole posse is somehow involved.

The more concretely you prepare the adventure, the less dreamlike it may seem to the players, of course. But then, if the players have come to expect surrealistic nightmare scenarios, a more concrete dream sequence may be just the ticket for putting them off their guard once again.

It should be mentioned too that, on occasion, a player may write up a nightmare that is more a setting and situation than a climax. If that happens, feel free to set the events of the nightmare as the first few tests of the scenario and then build from there.

For that matter, even the Ronan Lynch scenario could have started with the gunfight, and then proceeded in a much different direction, with Ronan facing off against several other people and discovering that he was shooting his own family members or best friends. The possibilities really are endless.

NIGHT WALKERS

Just in case you didn't think being a Harrowed was tough enough, there's something else you should know about, something that's guaranteed to keep even the most imperturbable Harrowed more than a few sleepless nights.

Sometimes even the mind of a cowpoke who's cheated death can't handle the terror it's subjected to in the course of its nightmares, those nocturnal excursions to the Hunting Grounds. When this happens, the line between the two worlds gets blurred, and some of the nightmare may just follow the poor soul back to the physical world.

Night walkers are dream creatures that occasionally slip out of the stuff of a Harrowed's nightmare and into the real world. The undead host's unusually close link to the spirit world makes such occurrences easier for the night walkers, though they have occasionally managed to make their way out of the nightmares of mortals as well.

BIRTH OF A NIGHT WALKER

When a Harrowed shuts down for the night after contesting with his manitou for Dominion (basically the first time he beds down after the start of any game session), he is subjected to horrible nightmares straight from the dark heart of the Hunting Grounds This is especially true if the Harrowed's player opts to have you run him through a recurring nightmare after losing a Dominion check.

Sometimes, these nightmares prove to be too much for even these living dead to grapple with. That's when all Hell really breaks loose.

Whenever a Harrowed must actually make the Dominion check against his manitou and goes bust on his *spirit* roll, two things happen. First, he's likely going to lose some Dominion to his manitou (although this isn't definite—the manitou could fail its roll too).

Second, and by far the worse, the Harrowed has given the spark of life to a horrid creature born of his own nightmare.

Just because the dream-tortured Harrowed's soul flies screaming from the Hunting Grounds doesn't mean the horrors the manitou created to scare him with are ready to dissolve back into the mists. Sometimes, these shades are able to follow the fleeing soul and "leak" out into the real world, refusing to go gently into that good night.

These leftover horrors of nightmare are called "night walkers". They fade into the world soon after the Harrowed hits the hay after his busted *Spirit* check, and they exist until sunup of the next morning.

Night walkers always fade into life in some dark, secluded place far away from bystanders. They are themselves fashioned from the stuff of dreams, and so they are ethereal and without form while in the Hunting Grounds. When they reach our world, though, they assume a solid shape.

The form they take is called their "guise." If a night walker appeared as a tumblebleed in a Harrowed's nightmare, then it's enters reality in a tumblebleed's guise.

From the moment of its dark birth, the nightmare demon's purpose (as well as its form) is drawn from its guise. If it's an old enemy of the hero who summoned the fiend, the foe comes hunting for him. On the other hand, the nightmare version of Dracula might leave the dreamer and his companions alone to find easier prey the next town over.

It all just depends on the guise the night walker takes on and whatever plans you might have for it. If the night walker decides to leave the posse alone, its entirely possible that neither the Harrowed nor any of his companions will ever learn of the night walker's existence, except by the ramifications of its deeds.

It's possible, for instance, for a Harrowed to dream of an evil version of himself, much like Ronan Lynch did in the example in this chapter. If so, that doppelganger might commit crimes using the Harrowed's face. Given the nature of Harrowed, the hero might seriously doubt whether or not he actually was the perpetrator. This is a fantastic way to help the hero (and player) doubt himself more than ever.

POWERS

The monster's particular appearance, powers, weaknesses and other abilities come from the creature it represents, but the fiends have a few other powers and limitations regardless of their current form.

DAMAGE

A night walker has whatever attack form is appropriate to its guise. If it appears as a demonic gunslinger, it might have a pistol that fires blazing bullets. If it looks like a giant squid, it has crushing tentacles.

Regardless of what the thing's attacks look like, the damage its attacks cause is equal to the *Spirit* of the character who summoned it.

Unlike a *Strength*-based damage roll, however, the summoner's *Spirit* is rolled and added. So if a dreamer's *Spirit* is 3d6, the creature then does 3d6 damage whenever one of its attacks hits, and it rerolls Aces just as if it were a pistol.

Since a night walker's attack is spiritual, armor offers no protection, and Harrowed and other undead are not immune to it. This means a killing "blow" to the guts from a night walker will kill him just as dead as a shot to the guts.

Killing a Night Walker

Night walkers are tough to kill. First, if its guise is invulnerable to certain types of attacks, then the night walker is as well. This way, even a posse who somehow learns the nature of night walkers still has to figure out how to kill each one separately.

An attack form that would harm the guise harms a night walker just fine, but there are some catches. The damage of an attack that can actually harm the creature doesn't use the attack's normal damage. The attacker's damage is his *faith* score instead.

The first time you use a night walker in your campaign, you might want to let the players roll both damage and *faith* so they don't know *exactly* what's going on.

When the night walker is slain, it collapses into a small pile of crusty dust—something like that which forms on the lids of a sleeper's eyes.

A mortal who has this dust sprinkled on them falls asleep instantly if she doesn't make an Incredible (11) *Vigor* roll.

Coup

A Harrowed who absorbs the essence of a night walker gains insight into the illusionary world of nightmares.

The essence of a night walker adds +1 to any of a Harrowed's Dominion checks. After three such creatures have succumbed to a Harrowed, she may no longer count coup on night walkers and receives no further bonuses from their demise.

ABOMINATIONS

-LOSTON-

Avoiding Coup

Of course, since there is a downside to counting coup, you may find that there are some heroes who don't want it. That's fine, as long as they back off from the fearmonger's remains as it shuffles off this mortal coil. A few yards is far enough.

Many Harrowed may not realize this, though, or they just might not be able to get away from the creature as it expires. Those death grips can be awfully hard to break out of, even for the Harrowed.

If a Harrowed can't get away, it must take the power. That's assuming, of course, there are no other Harrowed nearby to steal the coup instead.

Stealing Coup

When a fearmonger gives up the ghost once and for all, there may be a mad rush by all the nearby Harrowed trying to get close enough to count coup on the beast. The trick of the matter is that only one Harrowed can count coup on a fearmonger as it dies.

The coup powers are derived from the fearmonger's powers. Since there's (presumably) only one fearmonger that's been killed, there's only one coup to be counted.

If more than one Harrowed tries to count coup at the same time, then they must each battle for it. Every Harrowed involved in the struggle must make a *Spirit* roll. The Harrowed with the highest result wins the coup, stealing it from the others' grasps.

Harrowed struggling over coup can spend chips on their *Spirit* rolls, and this can often clean them out. Fortunately, now that the fearmonger's dead, they may not need any chips for a while.

Of course, it's never that easy, right?

A Dark Reflection

Some of the monsters loose in the world of *Deadlands* originated as Harrowed characters. They were once mortal, and they enjoyed the fruits of life as much as any other. Despite the fact that their breathing days are long since behind them, they still recall what it was like to walk among the living as one of them.

Whenever your Harrowed heroes encounter such a monstrosity, it ought to give them pause to wonder if this is what the future holds for them, as well. If they're not careful—and lucky with their Dominion checks—it very well may.

As the Marshal, it's your job to play up that sobering thought all the way to the hilt. You might start by confronting the posse with normal Harrowed who are simply under the control of their manitou, at least for part of the time during which the heroes encounter them. The evils these things commit should haunt the Harrowed heroes, because they are indications of what these heroes may do if they lose control of their own manitous.

When you decide to introduce a new fearmonger into the campaign, you can have some evil Harrowed working in league with the thing, again reminding your undead heroes of the darkness that lurks within themselves. This also hints at the thought that the evil Harrowed seek to become more like the fearmonger they serve, raising the same possibility in the minds of your undead heroes. Maybe their manitou could tempt them with such powers in the future (or at least your players might believe so, whether or not it's actually true). The line between human and monster blurs that much further.

Finally, when your heroes encounter the fearmonger itself, you owe it to the players to let their characters find bits and pieces of legend that identify the monster as having originally been human, even if it was many centuries ago. Only the most obtuse of Harrowed heroes could walk away from that knowledge without wondering if the same might happen to him some day.

Now the stage is fully set for the aftermath of the fearmonger's defeat. Conscious of the appeal that this abomination has shown for other Harrowed—and aware of its own human origins—the posse's undead heroes find themselves absorbing the evil thing's very power, along with its dark price. They cannot help but wonder if, given time, this coup power might not subvert them as well.

If you really want to torture your Harrowed heroes, have the fearmonger revert to human form as it dies (if this seems at all in the monster's vein, so to speak), and have it thank the coup-counting hero for lifting its burden and freeing its soul. Faced with that experience, the Harrowed virtually has to believe that he has just taken a snake to his own bosom. From all the evidence, the power he just absorbed from the villain led to the doom of the nemesis he just defeated. How can he expect that it might do any less with him?

This kind of torture ain't subtle, but it's definitely fun.

ON UNDEAD AND MANITOUS

There's a big difference between the Harrowed and zombies or some other loathsome undead. All sorts of undead might look something alike on the outside, but it's what's inside their decaying sacks of skins that count. And no matter what kind of corpses they happen to be, what's rattling around in their decaying carcasses is rotten in more ways than you can shake an ugly stick at.

Before you start breaking down undead into their various shades of green and gray, you should realize that there are two basic types: independent and possessed.

INDEPENDENT UNDEAD

Independent undead are beings who retain at least some part of their original mortal soul. At some point in their existence, most independent undead were mortals. Being "undead," after all, means that the being must have once been alive.

These beings were not created by the Reckoners, but they may have been given their power by them. Liches, vampires, and Harrowed are all good examples of independent undead.

Of course, Harrowed are something of an anomaly, since their corpses contain both the host's soul *and* a manitou. But hey, we're talking about the undead here. They're not particularly inclined to follow all the rules.

POSSESSED UNDEAD

Possessed undead are abominations such as walkin' dead, zombies, nosferatu, wights, and most anything you might classify as "lesser" undead.

These are undead corpses without the creamy filling we call the mortal soul. They may *act* like the mortal they've replaced, and they might even be able to draw on residual memories left inside the corpse. But if Aunt Minnie rises from the ground as a walkin' dead, don't feel guilty when your posse blows her head off, because Minnie isn't home.

Possessed undead are inhabited by damned souls. These souls are the tortured spirits of evil mortals who have died and are now serving their penance in Perdition, Hell, or—as we like to call it—the Hunting Grounds. They're doing time concurrently on planet Earth.

The soul inside a zombie made from the corpse of Aunt Minnie isn't the soul of Aunt Minnie herself. In fact, the "soul" no longer knows "who" it is.

This soul can draw on some of the lingering memories of its shell—in this case, poor old Aunt Minnie—and it usually thinks that's who it is. But in truth, the spirit might once have been a murderer put to death over a thousand years ago. Or a horse thief hanged last Wednesday.

In any case, the spirit is a little mad and a whole lot evil. That's why possessed undead are relatively mindless when compared to a vampire or a Harrowed. It's also why they're invariably meaner than rattlers.

Possessed undead don't really have the capacity to do good. A vampire can show mercy if he or she wanted, and a Harrowed is in charge of his actions almost all of the time. But a walkin' dead is nothing but pure evil wrapped in a decaying human carcass. Kind of like a big, spoiled burrito.

CREATION

Possessed undead are created in many ways. Maybe a voodoo shaman pours some magical elixir in a cemetery, or an evil cultist says a dark prayer over a graveyard. The Reckoners hear the request, and if they feel it suits their purposes, send a number of damned souls down to inhabit the corpses.

There doesn't *have* to be a summoner involved. Sometimes the Reckoners just create a horde of walkin' dead for their own reasons.

DEATH AND THE UNDEAD

So what happens when an undead dies *again*? Well, it depends.

When a zombie or other possessed undead is killed, the damned soul goes back to the Hunting Grounds. That's why these creatures relish their time on Earth so much. As long as they survive, they avoid returning to the torturous whims of the Reckoners and the manitous.

Vampires, liches, and the like are just like mortals. When they die, their soul goes to the Hunting Grounds if they were evil, or to Heaven, Nirvana, or the Happy part of the Hunting Grounds if they were good. No, it doesn't happen often, but it is possible.

The Harrowed's soul does the same. But the manitou is in big trouble. It's dragged kicking and screaming from the mortal world straight to that dark part of the Hunting Grounds where the Reckoners dwell. What happens there is anyone's guess, but the manitou does not return.

UNDEAD AND QUICK HITS

If your posse is fighting hordes of undead (and what self-respecting posse isn't?), you probably don't want to keep up with all their wounds. But how can you use the quick hits system (Chapter Fourteen in your trusty Deadlands book) with a passel of wailing zombies?

Easy. As long as the posse takes into account the penalty for shooting at the walkin' dead's noggins, subtract full damage from the zombies' hits. The heroes should *not* roll bonus dice for shots to the head, by the way. There's just not much left inside their skulls but that one important but tiny brain.

If the posse does not aim for the head, subtract only 1/4 of their total damage.

MANITOUS

You now know more about the undead of *Deadlands* than Van Helsing himself. But what about manitous without human carcasses?

Manitous are like the shattered shards of the Reckoners themselves. In an insane manner, they mirror the Reckoners' parasitic need for pain, fear, or other dark human emotions. But the small amount they need to survive on pales when compared to the incredible needs of their unknowable masters.

Unfortunately for them, manitous cannot directly affect the mortal world without a vessel. Whether this is a cultist or huckster who opens a channel to the Hunting Grounds, or a Harrowed with a taste of Hell in her gizzard, the manitou can use the link to create mischief on Earth.

Chapter Ten: The Prospector's Plan

By this point, it should certainly be obvious that Harrowed heroes are tough hombres. The supernatural powers and abilities available to them make them some of the toughest hombres *Deadlands* players can run. In fact, if a Marshal isn't careful, they could easily end up hogging the spotlight, overshadowing the group's other characters, and running roughshod over all of your carefully designed plots.

But there are certainly disadvantages to playing Harrowed, as well, as we've talked about elsewhere. It's your job, as Marshal, to make those detriments plague these undead characters to help balance things out and to discourage players from running nothing but Harrowed heroes in your campaigns. After all, every *Deadlands* character has the potential to be really exciting and fun given just half a chance, and the best games have more than a bit of variety in them, even in their selection of protagonists.

One of the best tools at your disposal for keeping the Harrowed in line is the Prospector, Coot Jenkins. Old Coot can serve in as many different roles as you care to cast him: commentator, provider of assignments, parole officer, rescuer, revealer of secrets, external conscience, and even (Heaven forbid) executioner, depending on your current need. But in order to use him, you have to know something about him. That's where the information in this chapter comes in handy.

The Prospector's Origins

As Coot himself explains, in the opening chapter of the *Deadlands* rulebook, he met up with a dying Last Son one day, entirely by accident. That Indian, a fellow by the name of Running Wolf, apparently felt guilty about the part he had played in Raven's Reckoning because he spilled the beans about the whole thing to Jenkins. Coot didn't really understand it all, but he knew that something terrible had been released upon the world.

That much, your players know.

The *Deadlands* rulebook later goes on to explain to the Marshal alone all about the secrets of the Great Spirit War and Raven's plan to release the evil the Old Ones kept bottled up in the Hunting Grounds.

When old Coot heard Wolf's story, it set him to some serious thinking. Another man might have ignored the dying Last Son, or leastwise refused to believe, but Jenkins was already something of a philosopher of a style that only a self-educated, lone-wolf sort of individual can be.

The Prospector took Wolf's tale to heart, and as horrific changes started taking place across North America, his faith in its truth was confirmed. He decided to do something about the situation.

To safeguard himself somewhat and to protect his friends and family, Coot took to calling himself the "Prospector." For day-to-day business like buying beans and chaw, he still goes by Coot or Jenkins with the live folks he meets. But he prefers his grisly agents call him the Prospector, just in case prying eyes are on them.

Somewhere along the line, the Prospector learned about the nature of the Harrowed. He's never revealed where he got the information, but you can assume the Prospector knows nearly everything there is to know about these undead characters. He certainly knows everything covered in the book you're now holding.

What's more, the Prospector has an elixir that can bring back even those Harrowed who have succumbed to total Dominion. Now, Coot wanders around the Weird West, tracking down Harrowed, pouring the elixir down their gullets, and then either impressing them into his secret army or destroying them.

THE PROSPECTOR'S MISSION

The Prospector is ruthless in his treatment of the Harrowed. On the face of things, he talks a lot about how much he respects them for their courage against the manitou inside. But truth is, he doesn't really trust any of them. Worse, he believes the Harrowed no longer have a true soul..

Jenkins figures that once a person dies, his God-given soul goes right on to its final reward, and all that remains is the shell. When a manitou invades a corpse, it becomes a surrogate soul for that person, able to access all the memories of the original inhabitant.

To the Prospector's mind, these memories aren't really the person, they're just a leftover from the person's life. There's enough Egyptian mythology dealing with different parts of the soul leaving, while other parts hang around to give Jenkins "evidence" to support his viewpoint, and the ancient Greek stories of Hades as a land of forgetfulness seem to match up right nicely for him too. As we've said, Jenkins is a self-educated, opinionated old cuss.

Now comes the really interesting part, as far as the Prospector is concerned. He knows the Old Ones invaded the Hunting Grounds to block up the passages back to Earth, thereby imprisoning the evil manitous within that spiritual realm. He knows that the Last Sons went in and slaughtered those Old Ones,

releasing the Reckoners' minions again. The Prospector figures that somebody else needs to go back and take the Old Ones' place, if the danger is ever to be ended. This is where the Harrowed figure into his plan.

Who better? By taking on this role, the Harrowed carry their own internal manitous back to the Hunting Grounds where they belong, and seal things up nicely. Because they have no human souls (at least in his opinion), the Harrowed aren't even making the same sacrifice that the Old Ones (who were fully human) had to make. It is just the sort of fortuitous convergence of events that bears the signature of fate.

One day, then, the Prospector plans to lead his army of Harrowed back to the Hunting Grounds. He's even plotted out a place to do it: the geysers of Yellowstone. Jenkins knows that one of them opens into that otherworldly realm.

First, though, the Prospector has to find out more about what's going on and get his army into shape to do the job. Once the latter's been accomplished, he plans to fill them in on his "glorious" plan.

In the meantime, though, Coot keeps his grand ideas to himself. Not even his most trusted companions know what he's got in store for them. After all, nearly every member of his army's got a spy of the Reckoners nestled against its lifeless heart. It wouldn't do to have them reporting the Prospector's scheme back to their distant masters.

Eventually, of course, Coot's going to have to spill the beans, but he's putting that off as long as he can. By the time he starts jawing about what's on his mind, he hopes it'll be too late for anyone—even the Reckoners—to do anything about it.

THE PROSPECTOR'S PROGRAM

To build his Harrowed army, Jenkins has to keep traveling about, following rumors of zombies and ghouls until he finds new inductees. Then he starts his training program.

STAGE ONE

Once the Prospector has found a likely subject, the first step of his program is to make certain the manitou doesn't have total Dominion. The Prospector's elixir helps by giving the humanity inside a chance to come screaming

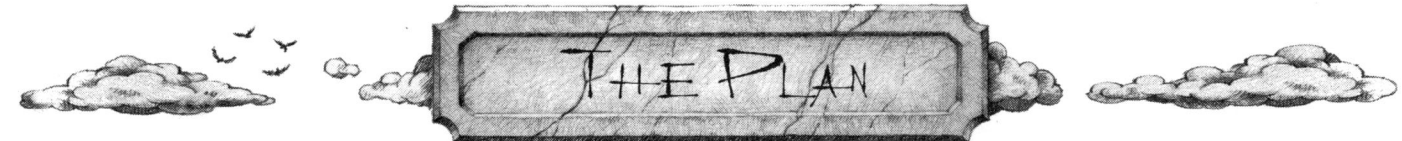

The Plan

back to the surface of its tortured consciousness, but it's no guarantee. If the manitou retains control and isn't able to fool the Prospector, Coot destroys the Harrowed immediately.

Assuming the human mind takes control, however, the Prospector gives the Harrowed his patented "you owe me" speech, laying it on however thick he needs to in order to make the person a willing servant. If the undead refuses to bow to this pressure, Jenkins is inclined to destroy him as often as not. Sometimes, though, he relents, seeing a latent heroism in the Harrowed that he figures he can play on later.

Stage Two

Assuming he is satisfied with the state of affairs, the Prospector usually gives the newly rescued Harrowed a minor mission of some sort to accomplish. It may be to gather some specific information, to defeat some threat the Prospector has learned about, or just to wander in a particular direction to learn what the Harrowed can. These jobs are not usually very difficult. The point is as much to establish the Harrowed's obedience to orders as for any other reason. While going about this mission, the new undead agent may not see the Prospector again for months or even years.

Stage Three

Harrowed who have proven their loyalty and their ability to control their manitou are given progressively more difficult tasks. Sometimes, Jenkins himself shows up unexpectedly to deliver his new orders in person. Other times, another Harrowed delivers it in his stead.

If the mission is general enough to be delivered without great detail ("Scout North," for instance) and the intended recipient has been hanging around a particular locale, the Harrowed may even receive his orders through the mail or by telegram. However they're delivered, the Harrowed is pretty much left alone to carry out these orders on his own.

Stage Four

Eventually, when the Prospector figures he has enough Harrowed to accomplish the task, it will be time to launch the final stage of his plan, the assault on the Hunting Grounds. When that might happen is uncertain, but it will probably be several years.

For one thing, Jenkins isn't certain yet just how many Harrowed he's going to need for the job. For another, if the truth be told, he knows the mission is a mighty tall order, and deep inside he's still somewhat afraid to give it a try. For now, he stalls off the day, waiting for some sort of sign that the "stars are right."

As long as the Prospector has Harrowed to hunt down and train, however, he can justify keeping his own "Reckoning" on hold.

The Prospector in Your Campaign

When it comes to dealing with the Harrowed heroes in your game group, Coot Jenkins is your devoted servant. Pretty much whatever you need to have done, the Prospector can serve to do it. All it takes is a little bit of imagination on your part to justify using him. Then, not only can he take care of your current problem, but your players should feel really luck that he has visited their little corner of the *Deadlands* world and they've gotten to meet him.

Prospector as Patron

How a Marshal presents the first few details of an adventure to players has a marked effect on how they feel about that adventure. You might remember that we mentioned back in Chapter

Eight the concept of linear adventures, and how players can feel that their characters have no choice but to follow your predetermined plot line.

Normally, then, you want to just drop a few events in front of them to make them want to pursue things further. A lot of times, those sorts of events are called "hooks" because they hook a character the same way a fish gets caught on a line. Once the heroes are on the trail, you can string them along from event to event. They don't know they're following your linear plot, and what they don't know won't hurt them.

If you'd like a little more control over whether they bite in the first place, however, you may want to use the Prospector to put them on the adventure's trail. If the characters care about what the Prospector has to say (and they'd better, or he'll make them wish they had), they're certain to follow up on his assignments without squabbling.

Coot as Communicator of Secrets

When you use Jenkins in this way, have him show up mysteriously and tell the posse about a concern he has. The Prospector usually doesn't just give assignments. Rather he lets his agents know there's a mystery afoot, and their own natural curiosity and eagerness to please him gets them going.

Sometimes, he might quiz the heroes about a particular event until they begin to realize that they don't know much and would like to know more. Other times, he presents them with some clues and asks if they can make sense of those things. Naturally, this tends to get them curious to know more.

Once in a while, he might even show up with special equipment and mysteriously say, "I think you're going to be needing this before long." When the adventure starts happening around them and they find that gear critically helpful, the legend of the Prospector grows, and the heroes are even more prone to follow his lead in the future. It's just all in how the Marshal presents things.

Prospector as Parole Officer

On a different note, if your players are starting to get out of hand and their characters are wreaking havoc through the Weird West, with no regard for the normal (and often innocent) people who have to live there, the Prospector can serve to bring them back into line. This is especially true with the Harrowed, of course, who are also more prone to such excesses. On occasion, the temptation to spook some townsfolk right out of their wits is just too great. The Prospector can help set the heroes back on the straight and narrow.

Sometimes, all it takes is a reminder from the Prospector that he has his eye on the group. Whether he shows up for a personal visit or sends a telegram, either way the players are confronted with the fact that the Prospector knows what their characters are doing, he doesn't like it, and he might just have to do something about it. Usually, the very thought that the Prospector disapproves of their actions is enough to make the heroes reconsider.

Coot as Conscience

When possible, and when the misdeeds aren't terribly out of hand, the Marshal can use the Prospector to question the heroes' actions. He asks them to explain what they've been doing. Then he points out all the ways in which innocents have suffered as a result, the trouble the heroes are inviting on themselves by risking bad reputations among the general populace, and the danger into which this puts his eventual plans for the Harrowed.

Of course, Jenkins doesn't reveal any particulars of those plans. He just tries to convey to the heroes how important they are going to be to him when the time is right, and the Earth is going to need heroes of their stature. In other words, when possible, the Prospector appeals to the heroes' good side, hoping they respond.

Prospector as Punisher

When subtlety and an appeal to conscience isn't enough, Jenkins certainly has the wherewithal to make his displeasure stick. He isn't above hunting down a renegade Harrowed himself and blasting that fool to kingdom come if need be. For tougher problems, he just sends an older Harrowed or two to punish the offending undead.

Among the Harrowed who follow the Prospector, stories have become legendary of the lengths to which he has gone to punish those who have gone astray. As a result, no one in his right mind wants to get the old guy peeved.

Consider the rest of the Prospector's undead horde. They won't take kindly to some half-wit hero stirring up trouble and drawing attention to them. Now imagine your Harrowed wakes up to find three other grisly gunfighters staring at him.

The undead rarely warn their enemies more than once.

Coot as Cavalry

On the other hand, the Prospector can serve as an excellent means of rescuing your heroes when everything is going against them. It happens to the best of Marshals sometimes. Just when you think you have an adventure all planned out, with hair-raising dangers but plentiful means of escape, your players roll nothing but busts throughout the session or they find a way to get their characters into trouble so deep it seems there is no way out.

That's when it can be a great thing to have someone like the Prospector waiting in the wings. While you don't want to have to rely on this too often, having Jenkins show up with a couple of his unliving retinue can send the toughest foes fleeing with their tails between their legs. Your posse will thank him for a much-needed breather without your having to pretend that their terrible rolls would have been enough to overcome their competition.

Used in moderation, this can be a campaign saver. Use it too much, however, and you may overshadow the player's own heroics.

The Prospector's Elixir

No one is sure just where the Prospector got his recipe for making the glowing green elixir he uses on the Harrowed. What is certain, however, is he never has much of it at a time. It would seem, then, that the stuff must be difficult to brew up. Indications are that he can make about one application's worth per week.

To use the elixir, Jenkins has to pour it down the throat of a Harrowed. Obviously, this usually requires that the undead is currently unconscious. In the case of more degenerated Harrowed, where the flesh has decayed too much for the elixir to be swallowed, it need merely be poured over the appropriate part of the corpse. Even a skeletal Harrowed can benefit from it, then, as long as the elixir is poured along the front surface of the bones of the neck.

Obviously, a manitou doesn't take kindly to the use of the elixir on its host. Consequently, for the Prospector to apply it, the Harrowed must be unconscious. All too often, that ends up meaning the undead was just freshly dug up out of the graveyard.

The Prospector's elixir is a relic. For more about relics and how to use them in your game, check out *The Quick & the Dead*.

Power: When the elixir is applied, the human mind within the Harrowed gains an immediate chance of a Dominion test. The Harrowed character also gains a Blue Fate Chip to be used exclusively for the purpose of improving her roll on this test. This chip cannot be used for anything else, but it can be a great help in besting the manitou and seizing multiple Dominion points. Harrowed heroes are free to spend their own Fate Chips on the roll as well. There may never be a better time to regain control, and they'd better take advantage of it.

Control can be regained even if the manitou has total Dominion.

Taint: None.

THE DARK CANYON
A HARROWING ADVENTURE

Things are heatin' up along the Ghost Trail in Arizona (events I mean, not the weather, that's already hot enough to fry eggs on a dead man's skull). Seems a number of wagon trains headed for the promised land in California have disappeared along the stretch of trail between Tombstone and Yuma.

Now, what happened is—Hey! I don't see no Marshal badge on your chest. Unless you're lookin' for trouble, I suggest you trot your sorry carcass on out of here. If not, you've been warned.

THE STORY SO FAR

Our story begins, strangely enough, in a peaceful village of Apache Indians in southern Arizona. The inhabitants of this village scratch what food they can from the dry soil and generally try to keep clear of any trouble as best they can.

Until recently, that is. Their village is located along the Ghost Trail. In the trail's early days, this actually helped the struggling community. The Indians were able to trade for supplies with passing ghost-rock caravans.

Now, increasing traffic along the trail threatens to destroy the tiny village. Passing travelers use the Apache wells, take what they need from their fields, and occasionally steal their livestock—leaving little for the rightful owners.

The village's leader, an Apache named Atsidi, has decided to strike back at those who are endangering his people. He knows the villagers are not a fierce warrior tribe like the Apaches—the few weapons they possess are used only to defend the village from raiders—and they would be quickly wiped out if they took to the warpath. Instead, he has recruited some of the older boys of the tribe into an army of thieves.

These young braves use their knowledge of the area to sneak into the camps of unsuspecting travelers at night. They take whatever they can get their hands on and then disappear into the darkness. The boys only prey on small groups and are under strict instructions to take no unnecessary risks—Atsidi would rather see them come back empty-handed than risk being captured.

Their latest heist, however, was a wagon-load of dynamite owned by none other than Coot Jenkins, the Prospector. Worse, without the dynamite, the entire region is doomed.

THE SETUP

This adventure has been designed with the idea of introducing Harrowed characters into your campaign. It works especially well for players who already have a favorite character which they'd like to play as a Harrowed. They'll get their wish. But as the old saying goes, your players should be careful what they wish for!

DARK CANYON

It also works great as a campaign opener, an initial story to get all your heroes together for the first time and give them a motive to work as a team. No need to have the players all invent rationales for how each hero knows the others and why they all hang together. Just dump the heroes into the adventure, and they'll come to know and rely on one another soon enough.

HARROWED CHARACTERS

This adventure works best if your heroes don't know they're dead right away. Let them make normal characters or choose from the standard archetypes you have available. If they want to play an archetype from this book, that's fine, but tell them their character isn't dead yet. In fact, lie and say you'll get to it in the *next* adventure. They'll find out the truth soon enough, but it's best if they're as confused as anyone else at the beginning of this tale.

Also, don't worry about Dominion, taking over as the manitou, or staging a nightmare. All those things are taken care of for you in the story you're about to read.

A FINAL WORD OF WARNING

The opening scene leads your players to believe their heroes have all been killed. Well, the truth sometimes hurts.

Truth is, they're deader than doornails. Hey, you're the one who bought the *Book o' the Dead*. What did you expect?

If this doesn't really suit your tastes, or if you'd like to use this adventure in your regular campaign without killing anyone off, or if you just think some of your players would rather be alive, it's not a problem. Certain actions will be out of the player's control. Normally, this would be on account of those rotten manitous, but we've got a way for you to buffalo living heroes as well. We'll tell you all about it soon enough.

Promise.

When you're ready to begin this twisted tale, move straight on to Chapter One. You won't need a Setup to get the posse started this time.

CHAPTER ONE: DIA DE LOS MUERTOS

As the story opens, the heroes awaken on the floor of a simple log cabin. It's night, but the embers of a dead fire cast the room in an eerie, Hellish glow.

None of them remember how they got here. Their last memories are of traveling along one of the local trails. (If it makes sense in your game, you can say they were all part of the same caravan heading for the Maze. The story in the newspaper at the end can fit into place nicely if you choose this option.)

At any rate, the last hours of their lives are forgotten, wiped clean for the moment by the creatures living inside of them.

For the moment, however, there's no reason for the posse members to suspect they're dead unless you're holding this book up in front of your face. (In fact, why don't you put the book down and try to look innocent, Marshal. Let 'em wonder if they're dead or not for a while.)

Since the characters probably didn't pay much attention to each other when they were alive, give them a few minutes to tell everyone else who they're waking up next to. Given the unusual circumstances of their meeting, they may be suspicious of one another. After talking, however, they probably come to accept that they're all in this fix together.

THE CABIN

Searching the cabin, the posse learns a few interesting bits of information. For one thing, it used to belong to a trapper. (There are a number of rusty or broken traps stored in a corner). For another, it hasn't been used in some time. (Cobwebs are thick in the corners, window frames, and rafters.)

Someone else has been here recently, however. The fireplace contains the ashes of a recent fire, and near it there is a bushel basket with a dozen or so empty glass bottles. Anyone who smells of the bottles notices a strange odor to them. These flasks once held doses of the Prospector's mysterious elixir.

One of these bottles sits on a small table near the fireplace. A note is stuffed inside it. It reads:

> *Howdy. I bet you're wondering what the Sam Hill you're doing here. Don't worry. I'll explain everything to you soon enough.*
>
> *I've gone to Hilliardston to gather some supplies. If I ain't back by the time the moon is full, you had best start looking for me.*
>
> *—a friend*

A look outside the cabin reveals that it stands on a hillside surrounded by dry scrub and cacti, far from any signs of civilization. There is a dry creekbed nearby, and its edges are clear enough to serve as a convenient path downhill through the scrub. Other than that, there are a few meandering game trails that don't lead anywhere in particular.

A Fair (5) *trackin'* roll notices the dust outside the cabin bears the imprint of wagon wheels, as does the edge of the creek bed. A closer look and an Incredible (11) *trackin'* roll reveals that the hoofprints of the mules drawing the wagon are deeper pointing toward the cabin than going away from it. This suggests the friend's wagon was loaded the last time it came to the cabin, and empty when it left. Yet there are no heavy supplies or other cargo nearby.

The moon hangs full in the desert sky. A lone coyote howls mournfully in the distance.

Bounty

Give the heroes 2 bounty points once they decide to go after their mysterious benefactor.

Chapter Two: The Slaughter

Following the creek bed down the hill eventually brings the posse to the Ghost Trail. Characters with the appropriate background or a Hard (9) *area knowledge* roll can recognize this after traveling upon it for a mile or so. The wagon tracks turn onto the main trail and head west.

After a few hours travel, the group comes upon a grisly scene. A number of bodies and horse carcasses lie strewn across the road. The men and women, were experienced riders in trail-worn clothes. Their faces are frozen in horror, and most have been picked over by buzzards. Any hero who investigates the scene should make a Fair (5) *guts* check. Increase the difficulty to Onerous (7) at night.

Most of the bodies are riddled with bullets. A few have been hacked to pieces, and still others were beaten mercilessly.

A Fair (5) *trackin'* roll—Hard (9) if it's night—reveals the riders were likely guards escorting a wagon. Due to the purpose of the Ghost Trail, the wagon was likely loaded with ghost rock.

Chapter Two: Ghost Town

Hilliardston, AZ—Fear Level 3

As twilight breaks the next morning, the posse comes in view of a small town. Its name is Hilliardston—as a sign proclaims—population: 96. Someone has crossed out that number and written "0" in its place. It was a small trading town which provided water, food, and liquor to the hard-bitten riders of the Ghost Trail.

As they approach, the heroes hear the ghost-like sounds of a dead town. A sign sways somewhere in the breeze, making an eerie creaking sound that never ends. A buzzard flaps its wings. Flies buzz hungrily in the distance.

Several of the buildings in town seem to have been burned some time ago. The twilight makes them little more than jagged silhouettes, however, so the heroes must venture closer to learn more.

WELCOME TO HELL

Between the population sign and the town are three wooden poles jammed into the hard Arizona soil. The poles are blackened, and scorched bones lie amid the ashes at their base.

Once in town, the posse can examine several sites of horror and debauchery detailed below. The town is full of dead bodies. They lie in the street, they hang from balconies and windows, and they sit crumpled against walls. Many of them have guns in their hand and lie amid scores of shells. Whoever or whatever killed this town gave their victims time to fire back.

Several horse carcasses lie festering in the morning sun as well. None of this makes for a pleasant smell, especially in the stagnant Arizona morn. The entire town smells rotten.

This might be a good time to let some of the flies begin picking at your Harrowed's flesh. You don't have to be blatant about it, but you want at least some of your players to realize their new condition as this chapter develops.

Let the party explore this abattoir for a while. Once you feel they've found all the clues they're going to, move on to the climax of this chapter, "The Three Amigos."

THE BONFIRE

A large bonfire lies at the center of town. Within are several human skeletons. An Incredible (11) *search* roll or a Fair (5) *medicine* roll reveals many of these unfortunate folks were likely tossed into the bonfire alive.

THE LOCAL RAG

Hilliardston was home to a telegraph office. As such, the owner and operator ran a small printing press to relay "world news" to the men and women who passed through.

A sign on the outside of the building reads "The Hilliardston Relay." Telegraph wires lead in through the roof and vanish out into the desert.

When the posse first enters the building, they notice that red ink drips from the printing press. A number of messy, hard-to-read single page issues of the Relay lie scattered about the floor.

On closer inspection, the "ink" turns out to be mostly blood. The owner of the Relay has been run through his printing press, his smashed corpse trapped between its now-broken rollers. This calls for an Onerous (7) *guts* check, and don't forget that nasty Fear Level, Marshal.

THE HIGHWAYMAN'S SALOON

The town's only saloon is another scene of carnage. A young woman hangs from the picture window, impaled on glass that didn't shatter like in all the dime novels.

Beyond the busted swinging doors, more horror and death await. A piano player lies at the feet of a broken piano, the bloody stumps of his fingers caught in the closed key cover.

The bartender lies sprawled upon his countertop. The broken bottles jammed into his flesh make him look like a human pincushion.

Several saloon gals lie dead upstairs. Some of them have been savaged beyond description.

If the heroes feel they need a drink, there's plenty left. In fact, one of the heroes' favorite brand of rotgut sits half-empty on the bar.

Whiskey burns as it slides down the posse's dusty gullets, but somehow it just doesn't seem to take the edge off the horror that surrounds them. This might be another chance to hint at your Harroweds' new nature.

THE GENERAL STORE

Outside the store is a clue that even an inexperienced tracker should catch. On a Foolproof (3) *trackin'* roll, the "friend's" wagon

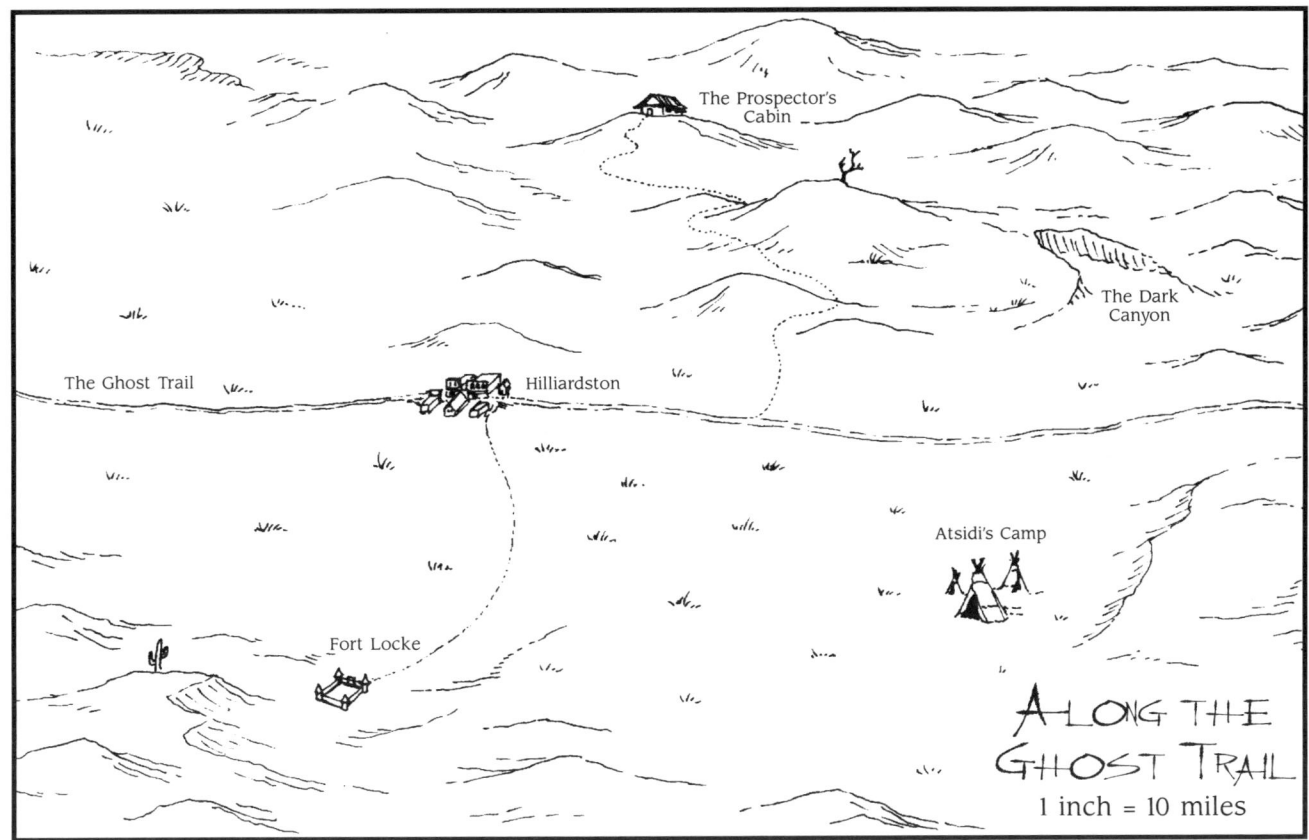

The Prospector's Cabin

The Dark Canyon

The Ghost Trail

Hilliardston

Atsidi's Camp

Fort Locke

ALONG THE GHOST TRAIL

1 inch = 10 miles

wheels are detected. They are fresher than any other tracks in town, and they lead from its edge straight to the general store. They leave much heavier than they arrived, and they head due south, along a well-used trail. You need to make sure the posse finds this clue eventually to move on to Chapter Three.

Inside, Hilliardston's only dry goods store has been ransacked. It never had a solid selection of stores to begin with, but the posse can likely find critically needed items if they look hard enough. Ammo, however, seems to be in short supply.

In the back is a storeroom with a busted door. Someone has shot the lock out with a shotgun. An inventory list on the wall reveals that dynamite is usually kept inside, but the store sold out a few weeks ago.

THE TOWN JAIL

The front of the town jail is a grisly scene. Two lawmen—a town marshal and a deputy—are lashed to the porch posts with barbed wire. They've been beaten, cut, shot, and later picked over by buzzards.

Inside, the jail is a single-room building with an iron cage set in one corner, a desk and a gun rack occupying another, an army cot in the third, and a simple coat rack in the last, near the only door to the outside. There are two small windows opposite each other in the side walls, but none in the front or back. A sign above the door proclaims this is the office of the town marshal.

In the cells are two men, apparently criminals arrested before Hilliardston's demise and trapped in their cells as the raiders (which the *Relay* calls the Dust Devils) ran amuck through the town. Both have been shot like fish in a barrel.

THE CHURCH

Like several other buildings in town, the church has been burned to the ground. Disturbingly, there are scorched timbers nailed across the windows and doors. A number of blackened arms reach eternally from the openings.

The residents who weren't shot in the streets rallied here. Then the fiends who destroyed this town nailed them in and set the church on fire.

And All the Rest

The other buildings of Hilliardston are pretty much what might be expected of a frontier-style town of this size. Most are homes, but there is also an inn with six sparse rooms upstairs.

A search of the town indicates that if anyone got out alive, they didn't take much with them.

The Three Amigos

These three desperadoes (Carlos, Enrique, and a Moroccan French Foreign Legion deserter named Ahmed) have taken up residence in Hilliardston—at least for a few days. While they're not crazy about the creepiness of the town itself, the free food, booze, and loot eventually persuaded them to stick around.

The trio are sneaky and murderous bastards. They try to isolate the heroes one at a time, then kill them for their loot. The Moroccan is especially good at throwing silent, deadly knives.

Unfortunately for the amigos, their attacks won't likely kill any hero they're after (unless they get lucky with a head shot.) That means that after one botched murder attempt, the scene is likely going to turn into a running gun battle.

That's fine. These murdering swine are here as red herrings for the massacre, and it's time for some of your Harrowed to start learning about their powers.

If you haven't picked powers for your heroes, do so now. By this time, you should have an idea for how your friends are playing their characters, so choosing powers shouldn't be too difficult. Don't worry about extra Hindrances right now. You can start adding these in your next adventure. We're giving them the shaft on a couple of things in this adventure anyway.

Profile

Corporeal: D:3d8, N:2d6, S:3d6, Q:3d8, V:3d8
Dodge 3d6, fannin' 3d8, fightin': brawlin' 4d6, horse ridin' 4d6, quick draw 3d8, shootin': pistol 3d8, shootin': rifle 4d8, shootin': shotgun 4d8, sneak 3d6, throwin': knives 2d8 (5d8 for Ahmed)
Mental: C:3d8, K:2d6, M:3d6, Sm:3d6, Sp: 2d6
Area knowledge: Ghost Trail 3d6, guts 3d6, overawe 3d6, search: 3d8, survival: desert 3d6, trackin' 5d8
Gear:
  Carlos: Single-action Colt Peacemaker, Winchester '73.
  Enrique: Two Colt Thunderers, single-barrel shotgun.
  Ahmed: Colt Dragoon, 4 balanced throwing knives (subtract -1 from range penalty).

Vengeance

As the Harrowed near the climax of their battle with the three amigos, the last of the bandits to go stares up in horror at the heroes.

In Spanish or French, the man screams over and over again that the heroes are dead and that he and his friends killed them.

In fact, they did. The three villains were the ones who ambushed the caravan and dumped it into the canyon, which is what started this whole sordid mess.

There's a lot of opportunity for roleplaying here. Your heroes might decide to deal out a little justice the Old West style—at the end of a rope. Or they may decide that to forgive is to be divine. Whatever their choice, it's likely going to cause a few heated arguments among the group. That's good. A little Harrowed head-butting lets your posse interact and grow, and you can reward your players for excellent roleplaying.

Bounty

Give the posse 2 points if they defeat the Three Amigos, and another 2 once they discover the wagon trail south.

CHAPTER THREE: DOMINION OF FEAR

Somewhere in Arizona—Fear Level 1

The trail to Fort Locke is a long one, and the heroes have no horses. Somewhere along the way, night falls and the group likely sets up camp. If the posse are all Harrowed, they shut down for the night to regenerate their decaying tissue. If some of the heroes are alive and wish to stay awake, they fall asleep as well (you'll see why in the last chapter—just trust us for now.) In short, the whole group falls asleep, even if they try to fight it.

The group won't even know they're about to share a horrible nightmare if you're careful. Since the bad dream takes place in the same surroundings they've set up camp in, the posse should have no reason for thinking this scene is a nightmare.

THE RESTLESS DEAD

Sometime after the group beds down, one of the characters (preferably one who believes he is still on watch), hears something out in the brush.

Make swishing sounds as if something were moving through tall grass, and see if the first hero "wakes" the others. The noise is headed directly toward camp.

After a few moments of suspense, the posse sees a number of folks walking slowly toward them. The man in the lead looks like a preacher, by his black garb and his white collar glistening in the moonlight.

As the preacher gets nearer, however, the group can see his face and hands are blistered and blackened as if by fire. His dead white eyes glare impossibly from lidless sockets as he raises clutching hands and emits a baleful wale.

It's time for some old-fashioned Hard (9) *guts* checks all the way around, Marshal.

GHOSTS

The preacher and the others behind him are the ghosts of the people of Hilliardston. They stalk slowly but unwaveringly toward the posse in the darkness.

Bullets don't harm the ghosts, nor do magical spells. In fact, nothing can harm them. But their chilling touch causes 1d6 Wind loss every round. You can roll some fake attack scores if you want, but every player essentially takes 1d6 Wind per round from the numerous spirits that

surround them. Those who try to run find other ghosts moving in on the camp from other directions.

The truth is, the posse can't really win. They're supposed to "die" in the nightmare.

This is their overdue test for Dominion.

DETERMINING DOMINION

Now is the time to determine your characters' Dominion.

If they're all dead and looking depressed, give them half their Dominion points minus 1. That's just how the manitous like their undead: complacent.

On the other hand, if the heroes are dead and complaining, give them half their Dominion points plus 1. As we've said before, dogged determination is what keeps the Harrowed in charge of their demon.

Finally, if they fought really hard to stay alive, whether through clever actions or just gunning down spooks till death came, give the characters one more point of Dominion over their manitous.

AFTERMATH

Once you've killed everyone, wait a bit. Let everyone go refresh their sodas and calm down a bit. Then, when everyone's picking at fresh nachos, tell them they wake up in the field where they fell. They're not in their bedrolls anymore, but they aren't wounded either (restore all their Wind).

BOUNTY

Award the posse 2 bounty points just for getting through this scene. Then give out an additional point to each player who came out ahead on Dominion points.

CHAPTER FOUR FORT LOCKE

Fort Locke, AZ—Fear Level: 3

Eventually, the group gets going along the Ghost Trail and moves into progressively clearer terrain covered in tall grass. From about 2 miles out, they start to see the remains of a Confederate Army outpost: Fort Locke. As they get closer, they see that portions of the wall around the post have burned, the gate is wide open, and the buildings inside have all been put to the torch as well. A Fair (5) *Smarts* roll reveals that the fire burned out about four days ago.

  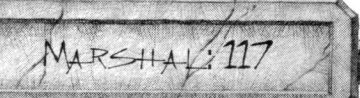

Further investigation of the site reveals a few dead soldiers lying in the open in the middle of the compound, shot, stabbed, or worse. There are also several incinerated human bodies inside the burned hulk of the barracks and the various officers' quarters. Some have bullet holes in their skulls, as if they were shot while sleeping.

The bodies in the officers' quarters are mainly women and children (the officers' wives and families), apparently massacred in the middle of the night. One large pile of embers was obviously a stable, because it contains half a dozen or so charred horse carcasses.

The bulk of the men assigned to this post are currently out riding around in the Arizona wilderness, chasing the fiends that razed Hilliardston. They are completely unaware their fort has been sacked in their absence, and their friends and families slaughtered.

Evidence of their passing can be found outside the fort. A Fair (5) *trackin'* roll reveals that a large column of cavalry left the fort a few days ago, heading east. This is the unit which headed out in pursuit of the Dust Devils.

POKING AROUND

If the heroes poke around in the ruins, they find a scene shockingly similar to that of Hilliardston.

The ever-reliable wagon tracks lead directly to the fort's central stores, then circle around and head back out again. A close inspection of the ruined supply house reveals an inventory sheet. Missing are several barrels of black powder.

DEVILS AND ENGELS

One woman survived the attack—Mrs. Sarah Engel. Sarah is the wife of the fort's young company commander, Lieutenant Anthony Engel. She was out painting the Arizona sky when the attack occurred. She hid in the brush nearby, watching the carnage, and then went completely, stark-raving mad. In fact, she has lost the capacity to speak. From now on, she can communicate only through her paintings.

Engel can't bring herself to stay in the fort, so she has camped out nearby. During the day, she

awaits the return of her husband and paints the scenes burned into her ruined mind

Sarah's husband always made her carry a rifle with her when she went out painting, and she still has it. When she spies the heroes poking around the fort, she assumes they are the Dust Devils returned, and she opens fire from cover.

It's nearly impossible to see or stop Sarah from a distance. Her vantage point on a small grassy knoll gives her the perfect sniping position. The posse must sneak up on her, wait until she runs out of ammo (she has 15 shots), or talk her into stopping.

At any rate, you should work it so that Sarah isn't killed by the heroes. If she's shot, make it a nasty arm wound. That makes her quit firing and gives the characters a chance to talk to her.

When they do finally find her, they see a young girl covered in dirt and blood. Actually, the "blood" is paint, but they probably won't guess this at first. Sarah is 21 years old, has blond hair, a trim figure, and Hell in her blue eyes.

Prairie Pictures

Once Sarah has been stopped, it takes a calming voice and an Incredible (11) *persuasion* roll to convince her the party is not responsible for the massacre.

If the group is able to calm her down, they discover Sarah is mute. They probably won't have any idea her trauma caused the defect, but it doesn't really matter. Assuming they are kind to her, Sarah eventually takes them to her paintings.

Sarah paints something like an impressionist, so her images are blurry. Still, there are important clues hidden inside.

Three canvas paintings lie on the other side of the knoll from which Sarah fired on the posse. On one is a picture of the fort.. It is smoldering, and the souls of the dead are winging their way toward Heaven. Strangely, a figure in a buckboard wagon is driving away from the fort. The figure is on the heavy side, with a white beard and a floppy "prospector's" hat. In the back of the wagon are several barrels (actually, kegs of gunpowder, but Sarah doesn't know that). She watched the party's "friend" come here two days after the fort was burned, and she added him to her painting.

On the second canvas is a gory display of carnage. Several figures are attacking the innocent women and children left behind in the fort in the absence of the soldiers. Some are firing guns; others are engaged in other savagery. Seeing such a disturbing painting come from

FORT LOCKE

1 inch = 50 feet

such a beautiful young woman is cause for a Foolproof (3) *guts* check.

The attackers in the picture are wearing some of the same colors as the posse, so it is easy to see why Sarah mistook the party for the Dust Devils, but of course there are no details to the figures so it is impossible to tell much more about them.

The last painting is of an Arizona skyline. Or at least it was. Sarah has painted a picture of her husband overtop it. His face is green and decayed, as she is afraid he is now dead at the hands of the Dust Devils. The party will likely mistake this for a picture of the leader of the murderous band. Red herrings swim in the deserts of Arizona, too.

SARAH'S FATE

The posse must decide what to do with Sarah once they've learned all they can from her. Leaving her out here alone shouldn't be an option for most heroes. On the other hand, taking her with them may be even more dangerous, especially since they figure they'll run across the Dust Devils at some point.

We can't give you a right or wrong answer on this one, Marshal. Your players have to figure this one out on their own.

BOUNTY

The posse persuades Sarah to show them her paintings:: 5 points.

CHAPTER FIVE: HIJACKED!

Once the posse has been to Fort Locke, they should have some leads to investigate. They can either set out after the cavalry or try to pick up the wagon's trail once again.

The cavalry trail leads east to the Apache village shown on the map. Though the cavalry patrol doesn't believe the Apache are responsible for the Hilliardston massacre, they had to check—or at least ask if the Apaches knew who was.

The wagon tracks lead off into the grass a short ways from the fort. There the posse can find a two-day-old campfire and an empty can labeled "BEANS."

From here, the wagon tracks continue in a northeasterly direction. An Incredible (11) *trackin'* roll notices several new prints as well—those of small moccasined feet.

SPILLING THE BEANS

The party's mysterious friend was caught here by the young Apache thieves. They don't usually take prisoners, but they had already started leading the wagon away when the sole occupant emerged from under the tarp in the back (where he'd been napping out of the Arizona sun). They managed to capture this person and took him back to camp to figure out what to do with him.

ATSIDI'S CAMP

AZ—Fear Level:1

The Apache village lies in a long, low plain alongside the Ghost Trail. The depression gathers more moisture than most other areas, which allows them to scratch a few meager vegetables out of the ground.

What the band can't grow, they steal. And what they can't steal, they buy with money from other things they steal.

There are seven rough-shod adobe buildings in the village. Atsidi is the chief. There are seven Apache warriors, fourteen women, and eight children. Four of the children are teenage boys and girls who do the village's thieving.

At the center of the village is a campfire. Chained a few feet away to a large wagon is a grizzled old prospector. In fact, it is *the* Prospector, Coot Jenkins.

The Apaches captured the Prospector and his load of gunpowder yesterday, and they've been debating what to do with him ever since. Fortunately, Atsidi and his people are not violent sorts; otherwise they would raid instead of steal.

THE RESCUE

There are two ways the heroes can play this. They can rush in with guns waving, or they can try and talk to the Apaches.

Either approach works just fine. Unless the posse shoots someone, the Apaches simply back off and let them have what they came for.

Should the characters get unnecessarily violent, the Apaches fight back with everything they've got. Atsidi, by the way, realizes the heroes are Harrowed after the first of them shirks off a wound. He warns his fellows, and after that, all the Apache attacks are head shots.

BOUNTY

The posse frees the Prospector without killing any Apaches: 3 points.

POSSESSION

The truth is the living posse members, if any, are in the unusual position of playing living host to an evil spirit: they're possessed. See the next page for more about this, but here's what you need to know in a nutshell.

Like Harrowed characters, possessed heroes have Dominion points equal to their *Spirit*. The same rules apply as to when the manitou can attempt to take control, except a living character, whose soul is more tightly bound to his body than a Harrowed's, gets +4 on all Dominion tests.

If the hero should ever gain total Dominion, the manitou has been evicted. An exorcism also does the trick.

Possessed characters can ignore Wind and pain modifiers just like the Harrowed. The manitou grants them this ability for one simple reason, it wants the hero to die—a fatal wound to the guts or noggin kills a manitou host as dead as any other character.

If a possessed hombre dies, he automatically returns as a Harrowed, but this time the shoe is on the other foot. Because the manitou was present at the moment of death it can assume control of the body before the deceased's soul has a chance to object.

This means a possessed character who is killed always returns with the manitou in total control.

CHAPTER SIX: THE CHASE

Once the Prospector is freed (no matter how), he wastes no time hooking his mules up to his wagon. As he does so, he tells the heroes the following:

"Thanks for the rescue, friends. Now if you'll excuse me, I'm in a hurry. Get in if you want to find out what's goin' on around here."

POSSESSION

The nature of the canyon's dark past makes it possible for the manitous to possess *anyone* buried in the canyon—living or dead.

This means as the Marshal, you can allow living characters to play this adventure as well. You can even let them believe for a while they've been killed and have returned.

Living characters possessed in this canyon have Dominion points and can be controlled just like a Harrowed. Even better, they get all the powers of a Harrowed.

At the end of the adventure, when the source of this power is blown to smithereens, you can take back all the freebies the living guys and gals got. Easy come, easy go. This way you don't have to worry about messing your campaign up even worse than having a ton of Harrowed crawling around your carefully carved world.

We don't recommend letting this kind of thing happen often in your campaign (giving the living Harrowed powers, that is), but the Dark Canyon is a pretty special place, and we want you to be able to use this adventure even if you're not ready for a whole party of undead.

It doesn't even matter when you decide if certain heroes are Harrowed or not. You can watch your players for a while and decide their characters' final fates based on their reactions to the situation.

If you have any players who seem particularly distressed or disappointed by the thought that their heroes are now undead, you can choose to reveal those heroes as living at the end of the adventure. On the other hand, if any players bug you to know what powers their heroes have now, that's an indication that their heroes should be confirmed as Harrowed by adventure's end.

At that, the Prospector whips the mules along. He only waits a moment or two for the party to climb aboard before taking off.

REVELATIONS

As the Prospector drives south towards Dark Canyon, he'll tell the heroes a little more about what's going on. But only a little.

"This gunpowder'll put an end to the shenanigans. But we don't have much time. We've got to get to a place called el Cañón Oscuro quicker n' flies on sugar.

"There's somethin' there, somethin' that's made...um, made the raiders that destroyed Hilliardston and Fort Locke do what they did."

HERE COMES THE CAVALRY

About this time, have everyone make *Cognition* rolls. The highest sees a dust cloud in the distance.

As the cloud draws closer, the heroes will begin to see the gray uniforms of the Confederate cavalry riding towards them, Hell bent for leather.

When someone points this out to Coot, he drives his mules all the harder.

"Damnation, if that ain't bad timin'! We gotta outrun 'em, boys. Just trust me on this. Now lay those kegs flat afore they start shootin'! And don't kill none of 'em, they're after the same thing we are!

"Now one of you take over these reins and let me get to work on the powder!"

With that, the Prospector jumps in the back and starts twisting together fuses he draws from a tattered satchel.

A HARROWING RIDE

It's time for some high action. You have to make sure the wagon gets to the Dark Canyon intact, but don't let the players know that ahead of time.

First, have the driver make *teamster* rolls every round. When he gets a low total, have the others suffer -2 to anything else they're doing, and then describe how the pursuing cavalry is getting

closer. If he goes bust, make up something fun, like describing how the wheels are falling apart, or bumping one of the other characters over the side, grabbing onto the buckboard at the last moment. That character can then make *Strength* rolls to pull himself back in.

In the back, take 4 shots a round at the passengers. The cavalry's penalties for being mounted and running should keep them from hitting much. Even if they do, those who are lying flat in the back get a point of armor from the buckboard's back panel.

Finally, have a shot or two strike the powder kegs.. They don't go off, fortunately, but you can roll some dice and pretend there's a chance they will.

The point is to scare the heroes a bit and keep them honest without really killing them.

If Sarah is in the wagon, you can make things really difficult on your friends. When she sees the cavalry, she finally gets her voice back and starts yelling for her husband: "Anthony! Anthony!" The rest of the soldiers get even more determined once they see Sarah in danger. There's no real effect from this; just tell the group the cavalry is closing faster now.

INTO THE CANYON

After six rounds of this frantic chase, the wagon careens into Dark Canyon. At the entrance, the group sees poles adorned with the skulls of men, a warning for others not to enter this evil place.

A clever character might think of sticking a fuse in a keg and then lighting it and dropping it off behind them as they careen along. This causes a rockslide and blocks the cavalry's pursuit. If a hero doesn't think of this, the Prospector suggests it to them anyhow.

By now, the buckboard is full of holes, the wheels should be just about gone, and the posse should be sweating bullets. For two more rounds, make the driver sweat by describing the deep ruts and rubble piles he must swerve around. Then the wagon reaches the end of the deep ravine.

With nowhere else to go, Coot tells the driver to stop, then yells for the others to help him get the rest of the powder kegs out.

BOUNTY

Give the posse 2 free points just for the joyride, but take them away if any of the cavalrymen are killed.

CHAPTER SEVEN: LAST STAND IN DARK CANYON

While the Prospector readies the fuses for the kegs and the cavalry struggles to negotiate the blockade, the posse has a few moments to look around.

The shape of the canyon is that of a spoon. Its walls are over 60' high, with deep shadows covering the rubble-strewn bowl. The blockade caused by the powder keg is roughly 50 yards from the back wall up the neck of the spoon.

An overturned stage and several horse carcasses lies to one side of the spoon. They are broken and shattered, as if pushed into the canyon from the cliff above. Any heroes who look at the wagon or the horses may recognize their own animals, for this is where they were "unborn." Those who do this feel a chill, as if someone just walked over their grave.

At the center of the bowl is a cenote (sen-OH-tay), or deep pool, 30' wide. This particular cenote is dark green and murky and bubbles occasionally. When it does, the bubbles break with a low rumble like that of distant—perhaps even otherworldly—thunder.

THE BIG BANG

After you've given the posse a few minutes to look around, Coot ties off the last fuse and pulls out a match. Before he lights it, read the following:

> **"You savin' my skin back in the Apache camp makes us even.**
>
> **"That's right. I said even. Y'see, I already saved your carcasses once.**
>
> **"You do know you're dead, don't you? Sorry if it's a shock. Most o' the folks like you take weeks to get over it, if they ever do. But you ain't got time to feel sorry for yourselves right now. We got business.**
>
> **"In case you ain't figured it out yet, you died right here in this canyon. Or at least that's where your killers threw your corpses after you were buzzard bait. I suspect a trio of banditos I saw the other day, but you'll have to chase 'em down later.**
>
> **"Anyway, you got dumped in a bad place. An' I mean bad. See that pool? It's got demons in it. That's right, I said demons. An' ever one o' you's got one**

crawlin' around inside you. That's why you're able to walk around without no heart.

"The demons'll make you do things. Bad things. Fortunately, I know how to take the likes o' you down easy. An' once I did, I fed you some o' my special brew to force the demon down.

"You should be okay for a while longer, but there's no tellin' how long my potion'll last. Those Apaches that took my wagon told me that those raised by the pool always come back mean, so I reckon my elixir is only a temporary remedy for your case o' the evils.

"I see on your faces you're realizing what you've probably suspected all along. What your mind told you when you saw the dead at Hilliardston and Fort Locke. When you gazed into the dead's eyes and saw reflections of your ugly mugs burned into their Hell-singed eyes.

"That's right. *You* folks are the killers that destroyed Hilliardston and Fort Locke and every living thing in either one of them. Or the demons inside you at least. And you've got some makin' up to do to the world.

"Now get in the wagon so's I can light this fuse.

OH YEAH?

Coot lights the fuse and climbs up into the driver's seat of the wagon. Just as he's about to tell the others to get on, the demons still inside the tainted pool decide to fight back.

There's a sudden rumbling from the cenote's depths, and then, after a suitably dramatic pause, it erupts! The Prospector's mules bolt before any of the hero's can jump on board. The buckboard goes racing back down the neck of the spoon toward what's left of the blockade.

The dark water from the pool shoots 30 feet into the air, launching a shower of human bones and green slime.

The fuse is put out and ruined instantly. The heroes are also soaked and hit by a rain of bones and bone shards for 2d6 damage.

Moments later, some of the bones pull themselves from the muck to form slime-covered, groaning skeletons.

During the chaos that follows, the group may see the Prospector bottom-out on the blockade. He jumps out and starts unhitching his mules when he sees the slimy skeletons come to life.

There are far too many slimy skeletons to fight. In fact, there are so many that we're not even going to tell you how many there are. Just keep pulling them together from the slime until the heroes get the idea they'd better figure out a way to seal the pool forever and run for it.

Guardians of the Pool

These are the animated corpses of hundreds who were sacrificed to this tainted cenote in ages past. The slime that covers them is something of a poison to the Harrowed (or the living who were possessed here). When a hero is touched by one of the slimy guardians, she must make an opposed *Spirit* roll. If the character's roll is less than the guardian's, the manitou inside gains total Dominion, and the hero turns on his fellows.

Profile

Corporeal: D: 2d6, N:1d6, S:3d6, Q:2d6, V:2d8
Climbin' 1d6, dodge 2d6, fightin': brawlin' 3d6, sneak 3d6
Mental: C2d10, K:1d4, M:1d4, Sm:1d4, Sp:2d6
Size: 6
Terror: 9
Special Abilities:
  Bony Claws: STR + 1d6
  Undead: Can only be destroyed by maiming the noggin.
  Poison (to Harrowed): Those Harrowed or living that were possessed in this canyon must beat the guardian in a *Spirit* test or lose total Dominion.

The Big Boom

Conveniently, the powder kegs are still sitting near the evil cenote. It's only the fuses that are wet and ruined.

If the heroes try to run away and fire at the kegs from a distance, the guardians of the pool stand about the kegs and block the incoming shots with their bodies. The manitous were listening to the heroes' plan after all.

Even if someone does manage a shot, the wet wood blocks any possible sparks and keeps the powder from igniting. This one's going to come down to a sacrifice. One of the heroes is going to have to get right up to a keg and jam his pistol down in through the top. The flash of the pistol is more than enough to set the powder off.

If the players don't think of this themselves, you can have Coot yell the idea at them as he tries to lead his mules up the blockade.

Only a Harrowed can possibly survive such a feat. And he's attacked by numerous guardians as he fights his way to the keg.

If someone manages, however, they're going to get the big bang of a lifetime. The damage of the first keg is 6d20. The second detonates immediately after for another 6d20, and the third after that for 5d20 (it was a little empty). Assign the wounds randomly and cross your fingers they don't blow the Harrowed hero's noggin off.

It's time to atone for the Dust Devils' sins.

Anyone else in the canyon when the powder goes off takes damage appropriately (damage dice are halved every 10 yards past the kegs).

Aftermath

The cavalry patrol saw the end of the battle with the cenote's guardians, and fortunately Coot is a friend of the commander. They let the Harrowed pass unmolested (after getting Sarah back if she's around), but they want the "Dust Devils" the Hell out of Arizona, pronto.

Coot travels north with the heroes to a town where they can buy horses. Then he gives them his standard opening speech and is on his way.

Should the heroes be persistent in trying to follow Coot afterwards, he lets them tag along for a while until he meets a lone man walking through the night. Then the two are suddenly swept up into the night on a *Hell wind* and disappear into the darkness.

Coot leaves the posse with these words.

"I've got business to take care of elsewhere, but you'll be hearing from me soon enough. Till then, keep yer heads on yer shoulders."

Bounty

The posse destroys the cenote: 5 points
Sarah Engel makes it into the canyon but doesn't come out alive: -2 points
A hero sacrificed himself for everyone else: 2 extra points for this character alone.

The Hilliardston Relay

Only 2¢   **Weather:** Same as always, hotter than Hades.   August 8th, 1876

"Bandits Strike Again!"

Word continues on the trail that the band of highwaymen kno[w] only as the "Dust Devils" are stalking the Ghost Trail. As [if] banditos, deserters, and Y[an]k[ee] saboteurs weren't enough!

As you all know, it was [o]nly a few days ago that a group of passengers traveling from the east went missing. Though their wagon [w]as found looted, their bodies, as [we]ll as their horses, have thus far [re]mained at large.

Now it seems the bandits have struck again. According to the last express that ran through our little town, the wreckage of another wagon was found along the roadside two days west of our location.

This time there were plenty o[f] bodies to attest to the savagery o[f] the highwaymen.

One of the guards on the express that brought this news, a Mr. Knowles from Alabama, claimed that he'd fought in s[eve]ral Indian campaigns and in the [ ] offensives against the Union in the East, and he had never witnesse[d] such a scene of utter horror.

Knowles says th[e] [b]odies near the looted wagon were a shambles. Some had been shot, others had been stabbed, and some had been mutilated so badly we cannot print it in the Relay.

"Witness Found!"

A single person has thus far witnessed the riders. M[ ] Hildebrandt claims an [ ] gi[rl] living in the village eas[t] [o]u[r] location saw the entire incide[nt] mentioned ab[ove.]

The girl call[ ] [th]e [ban]dits the "D[ust] [De]v[ils]." [She] saw them e[me]rg[e] [from the] cr[ee]k [k]icked up [by the] wa[gon]'s wheels.

Th[ere] were betw[een] [one] of the vi[llage]s. The ri[ders wer]e [ ]ore "the kin[d of] clothe[s you might] find on a [ga]mbling [da]ndy," sa[id] Hildebrand[t. W]alter [K]etchum of [the] Texas Ra[nger]s [says] his [ ] [men] group [will s]o[on be] deta[iling a]ddi[tio]nal patrol[s to the] trail around [H]illiardston. [ ] from our g[ood] friends a[t] Locke has [already comb]e[d the] [ ] [ ]a[n tow]n[, but] th[ey have failed to] [ ] [ ]r[a]

BOOT HILL

AHMED

Attack:
Pistol 3d8/3d6
Fanning 3d8/3d6
Thrown Knife (4) 5d8/3d6
   (take -1 from any range penalties)
Defense:
Dodge 3d6
Brawling 4
Hits: 30

CARLOS

Attack:
Pistol 3d8/3d6
Fanning 3d8/3d6
Rifle 4d8/4d8
Defense:
Dodge 3d6
Brawling 4
Hits: 30

ENRIQUE

Attack:
Pistol 3d8/2d6
Single-barrel shotgun 4d8/2d6+4d6
Defense:
Dodge 3d6
Brawling 4
Hits: 30

SARAH ENGELS

Attack:
Pistol 3d8/3d6
Rifle 4d8/4d8
Defense:
Dodge 2d6
Brawling 3
Hits: 30

ATSIDI

Attack:
Pistol 4d8/3d6
Rifle 4d8/4d8
Knife 4d8/3d6+1d6
Defense:
Dodge 3d8
Brawling 3
Hits: 30

APACHE BRAVES

Attack:
Pistol 4d8/3d6
Rifle 4d8/4d8
Knife 4d8/3d6+1d6
Defense:
Dodge 3d8
Fightin' 4
Hits: 30

CAVALRYMEN

Attack:
Pistol 3d6/3d6
Rifle 5d6/4d8
Defense:
Dodge 3d8
Fightin' 3
Hits: 30

GUARDIANS OF THE POOL

Attack:
Bite 3d6/3d6
Claws 3d6/3d6+1d6
Defense:
Dodge 2d6
Brawlin' 3
Hits: 30
Special Abilities:
  Undead: Can only be destroyed by maiming the noggin.
  Poison (to Harrowed): Those Harrowed or living that were possessed in this canyon must beat the guardian in a Spirit test or lose total Dominion.

TM

Hey You! Get Lost...

...in the Great Maze!

In 1868, California dropped into the sea, leaving behind a shattered landscape of water-filled channels and canyons. Soon after, the stunned survivors discovered a fortune in gold and ghost rock in the fractured cliffs.

Now everyone wants a piece of the Maze—the Union, the Confederates, the Mexicans, the French, even the Chinese. Visit one of the roughest places in the Weird West™, where life isn't worth a plugged nickel.—but a cowpoke'll pay a king's ransom for a decent meal.

The Great Maze is a $30 boxed set for the *Deadlands*™ roleplaying game. In it, there's everything you need to know about the Maze, its occupants, and it's deadly secrets, revealed by the renowned Robin D. Laws. The Set includes a 128-page sourcebook (which gives posses and marshals the lowdown on the Maze, the City of Lost Angels, the Triads, and more), a 32-page half-sized book explaining the ancient secrets of Kung Fu, a full-color, poster-sized map of the Great Maze, and two full-scale color vehicle cards for use with your *Deadlands* miniatures.

If you're not careful, your hero just might get lost in *The Great Maze*—permanently!

 PINNACLE ENTERTAINMENT GROUP, Inc.